Terror in the Cherokee Strip!

A sharp, flat crack of a rifle rolled over the plains. Startled, Jessie turned, heard a man cry out, and saw one of the men she was riding with spill from his saddle. She grabbed for her Colt and wrenched it free as a second shot followed on the heels of the first. Her mount shuddered beneath her, dropped on its forelegs, and sent her sprawling. She hit hard and rolled, then raised herself on her hands and saw the horsemen atop the low hill to the west...

◆◆ **WESLEY ELLIS** ◆◆

LONE STAR

IN THE CHEROKEE STRIP

A JOVE BOOK

LONE STAR IN THE CHEROKEE STRIP

A Jove Book/published by arrangement with
the author

PRINTING HISTORY
Jove edition / April 1986

ISBN: 0-515-08515-4

Jove Books are published by the Berkley Publishing Group,
200 Madison Avenue, New York, N.Y. 10016. The words
"A JOVE BOOK" and the "J" with sunburst are trademarks
belonging to Jove Publications, Inc.

PRINTED IN THE UNITED STATES OF AMERICA

★

Chapter 1

Jessica Starbuck urged the sorrel mare up the rise, reined the mount to a halt, and stretched wearily in the saddle. Below, over the shallow muddy river, the longhorns milled restlessly. The last of the stragglers had crossed an hour before, but the sticky summer air was still thick with their dust. Jessie could see the near side of the herd—red dirt and the slanting, evening sun turning their hides the color of brick. The bulk of the cattle, however, were lost, hidden in a heavy, golden haze. It was a big herd, nearly 2500 head. They'd started from a ranch southwest of San Antonio, following the trail north. Now, five hundred miles and a long sixty days were behind them.

The herd had made good time since it crossed the Red River at Doan's Store. Some fifty miles in under five days. In the morning, they'd leave the north fork of the Red and head to Dodge City. Two hundred more dusty miles would finish the job. Jessie imagined the men had already spent the hundred dollars they'd get for the trip. A new pair of boots and a fancy shirt. They'd see how much bad whiskey they could drink, how many pretty ladies they could bed. In the morning, perhaps there'd be enough left for breakfast—or, knowing cowhands, maybe not.

Two men paused by the river and glanced up at Jessie. She was a tall, graceful woman, and both of the hands noted she sat in her saddle as easily as any man. The faded cotton shirt and tight-fitting denims graced the soft curves of her figure and the slender lines of her legs. Strawberry hair tumbled freely over her shoulders from under the brim of a black Stetson. The late evening sun streaked her hair with bands of copper and turned her creamy skin to burnished gold. Her eyes were a startling shade of green, the color of deep water. To the men down below she seemed cool, distant, and unattainable. Yet, there was a subtle hint of mischief in her eyes and in the lines at the corners of her mouth.

Jessie sensed the men watching and smiled politely in their direction. The pair nodded soberly and looked away, embarrassed at getting caught. Jessie flicked her reins and guided the mare down to the water, avoiding the wide stretch where the longhorns had turned the sandy bottom into a mire. She could see the top of the chuck wagon, set in a sparse grove of oaks at a bend in the river. The grove was the only shade on the flat and nearly featureless prairie. The men who weren't bedding down the herd had already gathered in the trees, making smokes and waiting for beef and beans. Jessie could smell the aroma of coffee, drifting across the river. The river was wide, but only half a foot deep at the crossing. It was nearly midsummer, and the rains had likely quit until the fall. Another month and the bottom might crack and go hard.

Jessie saw him coming before she was halfway across. He pushed his mount hard, sending sprays of bright water into the air. He rode from behind her and to her left, which meant he'd been watching, waiting for her to cross, knowing she'd find it awkward to ride anywhere but straight across the river.

Jessie swallowed her irritation, determined not to let him get to her. He rode right past her, then turned in a narrow semicircle, jerking the mount smartly to a halt and doffing his hat. It was a fine, graceful maneuver, but Captain Heywood Street simply made it look foolish.

"Evening, Miss Starbuck," he grinned, "end of a long day, is it not?"

"Yes, it is. A very long day."

Street eased his horse up beside her, pacing the mount to hers. He was a big, heavyset man on a sturdy black gelding. He rode as close as he could, making Jessie's mount skittish.

"I'd be pleased to guide you across," he said sternly. "These shallow rivers can be deceiving. Most deceiving. I have encountered quicksand more than once. Saw a horse disappear like *that*. Very treacherous waters."

"Thank you," Jessie said coolly, "I expect I can manage. I crossed a river once before. All by myself."

"Heh?" Street blinked and then laughed aloud, Jessie's words going past him. "Why, yes, I expect you have at that." He beamed, showing rows of white teeth under a carefully tended mustache. His face was florid and had thick features. His hair was as pale as wheat and his eyes were a watery blue. His uniform was stained with sweat and red dirt.

"I will say one thing," Street told her, leaning toward her

2

out of the saddle, "I do not mind traveling with the herd. No, ma'am, I do not. It's slow as blazes, but the food is first rate. Better than army field rations, I assure you. A man doesn't tire of good beef."

"Trail food isn't always this good," Jessie said. "Just because there's plenty of cattle doesn't mean the men get to eat it. You can thank the owner and Mr. Morgan as well. He seems to take an interest in his men."

"Ah, yes—well, I suppose that's so." Street turned sour at the mention of the boss. Jessie repressed a grin. She had deliberately mentioned Morgan, knowing there was no love lost between Street and the herd's top hand. Jessie had joined the drive where the trail crossed the Brazos, traveling west from Fort Worth with Street and his troopers. Morgan and Street had locked horns the moment they met. The captain figured his escort duties automatically put him in charge of Charlie Morgan and his men. Morgan set him straight at once and Street didn't like it.

"I hope you will take this in the proper spirit, Miss Starbuck," Street began. "I must say I greatly admire your courage. Yes, indeed. I truly do."

"Oh? And why is that?" Jessie asked warily.

"Why, traveling alone and all, of course. The savages are not entirely tame, you know. In spite of what you might have heard. No, ma'am, I assure you they are not."

"Savages. You are referring to the Indians, I suppose."

"Yes, yes, whatever you wish to call them," Street said impatiently. "What I am saying is there is a danger, a great risk in this country. Especially for a woman."

"I feel very safe, Captain Street."

"And you are, dear lady," Street said emphatically, raising a hand to make his point. "You are under the full protection of the United States Army. The full protection."

"That's most reassuring," said Jessie.

"A privilege and a pleasure. An honor, Miss Starbuck." Street paused and appeared to study the darkening sky. "Miss Starbuck," he said finally, his voice dropping to an earnest, confiding tone, "if I may, I would like to mention that I have a very fine bottle of brandy in my gear. Not the common fare you find in saloons and such places, mind you. This is, I don't mind saying, the finest offering of France. I would, uh, consider it most gracious of you if you would agree to join me for a touch of the spirits after supper. Perhaps by the river. They

3

say brandy is an excellent aid to the digestion."

Nearly ten days on the trail and you finally got up the nerve, Jessie thought darkly. She hid her disgust and showed him a generous smile. "Why, I would be pleased," she told him. "That's very kind of you."

"You—you would? Well, now..." Street puffed out his chest and grinned with delight, stripping her naked with his eyes. "That's marvelous. Yes. I look forward to our little get-together with great anticipation."

"And I as well," said Jessie. "By the river, you say?"

"I think that would be prudent, don't you?" He gave her a broad and knowing wink.

"Oh, I do," Jessie agreed. "And what time would be convenient for you and Mrs. Street?"

"What? Uh, what's that?" Street colored, his face showing anger and confusion and dismay. "Miss Starbuck, really now."

"Yes?"

"I hope you don't think—"

"Think what? That you intended to meet me *alone* by the river? Without Sarah? Why, I would never imagine such a thing."

"No, certainly not." Street brought himself up stiffly and cleared his throat. "It appears to be getting dark rather quickly, Miss Starbuck. If you will excuse me, I think I'd best see to my men."

Without waiting for an answer, he nodded curtly and kicked his mount harshly into a trot, leaving Jessie to face quicksand and whatever other perils might be about.

Jessie grinned and watched him go. Not very subtle, she thought, but subtlety was useless with a man like Street. She'd been avoiding him since Fort Worth and nothing seemed to work. He would never forgive her for wounding his pride, but at least he'd gotten the message.

Jessie crossed the rest of the river, left her mount at the rope corral, and walked to the chuck wagon. It was nearly eight in the evening. The eastern sky was purpling fast. Cowhands sat about the grove, tin plates piled with thick biscuits, hot beef, and beans. They were tired from the day, too weary to talk but not too tired to eat.

Captain Street was nowhere in sight. Jessie figured he'd had an attack of conscience and decided to eat with his wife. His troopers had taken their plates to their own camp, somewhere back in the trees. They ate from the chuck wagon, the

same as everyone else, but had little to do with the hands—
Street's idea, Jessie knew, and not theirs. Soldiers and civilians
don't mix, he'd informed her. You can't keep discipline that
way. Of course, civilian women were different, Jessie noticed.
It was all right for officers to mix with them.

The men from Camp Supply were all black, except for Street
and Lieutenant Banes. At first, Jessie had thought the business
of separate camps had something to do with Street's feelings
about race. Street, though, treated Banes with the same disdain
he used on his men and the hands who worked the cattle, she
discovered. Apparently, his real prejudice was that he didn't
like anyone at all.

Jessie got coffee and a plate of food. Charlie Morgan waved
her over and Jessie joined him on a dead log.

"You've got a good cook," Jessie told him. "I've seldom
seen better on a drive."

"Been my experience," drawled Morgan, "that the longer
the drive, the better your cook's got to be. Anything you don't
need for four months in the saddle is bad food."

Jessie grinned and piled thick slices of beef on top of a
biscuit. The trail boss was lean and spare, a grizzled man in
his forties who wore every year on his face. He always seemed
tired, slow, and ready to drop in his tracks. Still, Jessie knew
there wasn't a man in his crew who could match his pace.
Long, broiling summers and a greasy, brown Stetson had baked
half the hair off his head; his eyes had a permanent squint from
the sun.

"You like some more coffee?" Morgan asked. "I'm thinkin'
on getting up."

"I'm fine, thank you," said Jessie.

Morgan shook his head. "I swear to God ever' time it's over
I'm not going to do it again. I could lose less money playing
poker somewhere—a hell of a lot quicker, and in considerable
better surroundings."

"Then why don't you?" Jessie asked.

"You answer that and you get the prize," Morgan said wryly.
He caught the beginning of a smile on Jessie's face and raised
a brow. "Ma'am, if you're trying to get me to say somethin'
downright ignorant like I just plain couldn't do without this
outdoor living, don't bother."

"Now why would I try to do that?" Jessie grinned.

"It's lacking the sense to figure out how to stop," Morgan
growled. "I been up many different trails many times. One

5

time a couple of years back I figured how many miles that'd be. Scared me so bad I quit counting." He paused and looked thoughtfully at Jessie. "Don't know why I'm telling you all this. You aren't any greenhorn when it comes to trailing."

"I haven't seen as many as you have, Mr. Morgan."

"Lord help us, I hope you aren't tryin' for my record." The trail boss made a face. "It's nothing any person in their right mind'd care to do."

Jessie set down her plate and looked at the fire. Night had suddenly closed in on the camp. "You said you know Bill Haggerty, Mr. Morgan. When we talked the other day—"

"Said I *knew* him—'bout, oh, three years back up on the Cimarron. I was working for the Figure-4 outfit during fall roundup and Mr. Haggerty's Crescent-H bunch was close by." Morgan shook his head. "That was 'fore the trouble started up—the raids and all the killings." He looked glumly at Jessie. "You'll find him changed, if that's what you're asking. They say he isn't the same. Don't guess a man could be, watching his home burn down and his wife and family with it. You know 'bout that, of course."

"Yes, yes, I know about that. It must have been terrible for him."

"Him and everyone else up there," said Morgan. "Near every outfit's got a grave or two on their spread and can't anyone do nothing about it." He ground the worn heel of his boot in the dirt and Jessie could read the anger in his eyes. "Damn army couldn't find a snake in a bottle. Excuse the language, Miss Jessie, but it's so. That captain from Camp Supply's a plain fool and so are the officers he's got with him."

Jessie didn't need to ask who he might have in mind. Morgan's eyes had shifted unconsciously toward the trees where Captain Street had set up his tent.

Jessie could understand his frustration, his hatred of Street and the army in general. Still, it was hard to place all the blame on the troops at Camp Supply and the commands at Fort Reno and Fort Sill. The cattlemen in No Man's Land and the Cherokee Strip were a powerful group with hundreds of men at their disposal. Yet, like the army, they had been unable to stop the raiders. In spite of their efforts, the rustling, burning, and killing continued unabated. The raiders struck fast and disappeared, seemingly melting into the barren landscape.

"Might be this is none of my business," Morgan said suddenly, "but I'll say it just the same. I've seen that bluebelly followin' you around. He gives you any trouble . . ."

"Thank you," Jessie said warmly. "It's nothing I can't handle, Mr. Morgan."

Morgan grinned broadly. "I didn't figure it was. Not with Street. He ain't much of a—now what the hell's *that* all about?"

Loud and angry voices came from the trees; Morgan stood at once, tossed his cup aside, and stalked irritably in the direction of the noise. Jessie followed. A crowd of troopers and men from Morgan's outfit were gathered in a gully past the grove. Morgan pushed his way through. Two Indians on horseback were the center of attention. One, lean and barechested, was only a boy. He sat on his horse straight as a rod. His face betrayed no expression at all, but Jessie could see he was frightened.

The other Indian was a different case altogether. Captain Street stood two feet away, a rifle raised to his shoulder and aimed directly at the Indian's head. The Indian stared at Street with stone-black eyes, a faint trace of amusement touching the corners of his mouth.

Morgan stopped, nodded at the Indian, and spoke to Street without looking in his direction. "Lower your weapon," he said soberly. "There's no cause for it."

"Keep out of this!" Street blurted. "These savages are my prisoners. Damned horse thieves is what they are!"

A black trooper next to Street shook his head. "Beggin' the captain's pardon, I didn't say they was stealin' horses, sir."

"If I want your advice, sergeant, I'll ask for it!" snapped Street. He reluctantly lowered the rifle and glared at Morgan. "Do I have to remind you that this is precisely why the army is here? To prevent this sort of incident."

"I don't figure there's going to be any incident," Morgan said quietly. He turned to the Indian. "How are you, White Bull? World treatin' you all right?"

"A-oh-a-wo-haw. Moh-gan," White Bull spoke from deep within his chest. "A-oh-a-wo-haw."

"Ten good steers you got," Morgan said agreeably, "as per usual. And talk plain English, if you don't mind. You just run through 'bout all the Kiowa I know."

White Bull almost smiled. Jessie marveled at the man's manner, his complete disdain of the armed troopers around him. He sat his horse proud and easy, as if he might pronounce judgment on the men on foot at any moment. He was a strong, thick-bodied man dressed in a buckskin vest and trousers. The vest spread open to reveal the broad expanse of his chest. His hair was crow's-wing black, parted in the center of his head, and tied with red cloths on either side of his shoulders. His features slanted downward toward the sides of his face—a stern slash of a mouth, prominent nose, and deep-set brows. In contrast, the sharply planed bones of his cheeks rose almost to the base of his eyes. His horse seemed to suit him, a spirited white horse with a dark mane and eyes the color of bullets.

"Come on back around sunup," Morgan said. "You can cut out the animals you want. I'll meet you west of the herd by the river."

"Yes, Moh-gan." White Bull nodded. His eyes darted quickly in Street's direction; then he kicked his mount and jerked the animal about. Street had to back off fast to keep from getting butted aside. The young boy followed White Bull up the gully and into the dark. The troopers and cowhands drifted off toward the trees.

Street glared after the Indians in disgust. "Christ, Morgan, why didn't you ask 'em to stay for supper!"

"He didn't want supper. Just some cows to feed his people. It's the custom."

"Extortion's more like it," Street flared. "Extortion pure and simple."

Morgan gave Street a weary look. His expression reminded Jessie of the Indian's a moment before—tired of explaining what he thought a man already ought to know.

"Might be White Bull figures since it's his land we're crossing, the cows he's getting are his due," said Morgan. "I'm inclined to think he's right."

"The land's his as long as we say it's his," Street said flatly. "It might be well if he remembered that."

"Captain, I reckon he knows that better'n you," Morgan said solemnly.

★

Chapter 2

Jessie usually had no trouble falling asleep after a long and weary day following the herd. Still, well after midnight she found herself tossing restlessly in her blankets, staring up at the stars. Charlie Morgan's words kept playing at the edge of her thoughts: "You'll find him changed . . . They say he isn't the same."

She had seen no reason to tell Morgan more than he needed to know, that she hadn't seen Big Bill Haggerty since she was a child. Then he'd been a frequent visitor at the Circle Star ranch, a close friend of her father for many years. She remembered him as a big, blustery giant of a man with a large belly and a great booming laugh to go with it. He was a legend even then, one of the first of the true cattle barons, a man who had seen opportunity on the hoof after the Civil War and carved himself an empire on the plains.

While growing up, Jessie read about his exploits now and again. Then, soon after the murder of her father, Haggerty wrote her a long letter, telling her of his sorrow and recounting the good times when he and Alex Starbuck were young. Jessie didn't learn until later that tragedy had struck Haggerty as well; raiders attacked his ranch, burning his home and killing his wife and two sons. Haggerty never mentioned this at all. Jessie learned what had happened from mutual friends.

She wrote to thank him for his letter and didn't expect to hear from him again. To her surprise and pleasure, he promptly wrote back, this time inviting her to come up and be his guest at the Crescent-H. And, ever the businessman, he didn't neglect to mention the opportunities for expanding the Starbuck cattle interests. Jessie strongly considered his words. Now, the once heavily-grazed plains near his ranch offered the finest spread of grassland in the West. Cattlemen were taking advantage of the lush grazing land so close to northern markets.

Finally, Bill Haggerty began to hint at the trouble plaguing the precious feeding grounds in No Man's Land and the Cher-

9

okee Strip—raiders determined to drive the cattlemen off the prairie. Jessie questioned him about this and Haggerty began to tell of his suspicions that outside, foreign business interests might be behind the raiders. Jessie came instantly alert at this news. She wrote Haggerty, couching her questions in careful terms. Meanwhile, she made inquiries of her own.

Eventually she was convinced Haggerty was right. More than that, she was sure the cartel itself was involved—the powerful group of Prussians she had faced more than once since they had brutally murdered her father. She accepted Haggerty's invitation, left the Circle Star, and journeyed north. At Fort Worth, she looked up friends in the U.S. Marshal's office and made arrangements to ride with two deputies crossing the Red River the next day. The pair worked for Judge Isaac Charles Parker, who wielded the only law in the Indian Nation from his offices in Fort Smith, Arkansas. Jessie felt lucky to be traveling with these two—they would move fast and get her where she was going without delay.

At the last moment, the marshals received word of outlaw trouble north of Cooke County, Texas, which bordered the Indian Nation. Jessie had to make other arrangements. She learned of the cavalry platoon in town that was to escort freight wagons back to Camp Supply. On the way they would travel with a herd moving up the Western Trail. It was much slower going than Jessie liked, but traveling alone in the Indian Nation was out of the question.

Jessie turned over restlessly and looked at the dying fire. She thought about Captain Heywood Street and White Bull, the proud Kiowa brave. One, a good man fighting for a cause already lost. The other, a lesser man in every way, who had the power to bring the Kiowas to their knees. It was not a just world, Jessie reflected, but then no one had ever told her that it would be.

At sunup, Jessie ate a quick breakfast and rode out with Morgan to watch White Bull and five of his men cut ten good steers out of the herd. Morgan's crew already had the cattle moving out, flowing away from the river toward the north. She was sitting her horse on a bluff watching the sight when Morgan pointed to a rider coming straight at them over the prairie, pushing his mount hard. In a moment Lieutenant Banes and a sergeant rode out to meet him. The rider slid out of his saddle, clearly exhausted, and walked the lathered mount back to camp.

"Whoever he is, he rode all night to get here," Jessie mused.

"Come on, we better go and see what's the trouble. Never seen the army bring good news yet." Morgan guided his horse down the bluff and Jessie followed.

Captain Street was waiting in the grove. A sergeant was bawling orders; troopers scurried about, clearly excited over something.

"We've got trouble," Street told Morgan and Jessie. "Raiders hit a freighting outfit on their way to Fort Reno. Maybe fifty miles north. Boy who rode in's from Fox Troop out of Reno. They're at the site now or on the way. We're going up to join them." He squinted at Morgan. "I've got an understrength platoon here, twelve troopers. I'm taking eight and moving out. Lieutenant Banes will stay behind to escort our wagons. Mrs. Street will stay, of course. I am sorry to leave you without more protection."

"Don't see how we'll manage," Morgan said dryly. "Can't ever recall driving cattle without the army close by."

Street flushed but held his anger. "At any rate, you've been duly informed of our plans. We will ride out at once. Miss Starbuck..." He nodded curtly and touched his hat.

"I'm going with you," Jessie said suddenly.

"What?" Street looked puzzled and then frowned and shook his head. "I am afraid that's out of the question. This is army business, a forced march."

"That's why I'm going. I need to get to Camp Supply. That's maybe a hundred more miles. If I stay with the herd, it could be another eight days on the trail. I can't afford the time."

"Miss Starbuck," said Street with a patronizing smile, "perhaps you didn't hear. We are riding into a possibly hostile situation. I cannot allow civilian personnel to tag along."

"Then don't," Jessie told him. "Just ignore me. I'll ride along behind. I promise I won't be a part of your platoon."

"No," Street said sharply, "you will stay here with the others. That is final, lady."

Jessie showed him her best smile. "Maybe you didn't notice that I don't have any stripes on my sleeve. And I don't take orders real well."

"Damn it, woman!" Street's features went taut. "I will not be responsible for your foolish actions!" Clenching his fists at his sides, he jerked around and stalked back to his men.

Charlie Morgan stroked his chin. "You sure this is a good idea?"

"No. I'm almost certain it isn't. But I need to get up to Camp Supply."

"Uh-huh. Well, I'll cut you a good horse. You'll need it."

Morgan didn't question her motives. He led his mount off into the trees and called out to one of his men.

Jessie knew she wasn't being entirely fair to Heywood Street. Whether he sanctioned her presence or not, if anything happened she was his responsibility. And that's all right too, she thought coolly. He's so eager for my company, and now he's got it.

It took only moments for Jessie to roll her few belongings in her pack. She hesitated before strapping the pack behind her saddle, hefting a small ivory-handled derringer in her palm. Finally, she wedged the pistol snugly in the top of her right boot, lifted a larger weapon from the pack, and eased it under her belt below her jacket. It was a double-action .38 on a .44 frame, a finely balanced weapon with a slate-gray finish and peachwood grips. A gift from her father, the revolver had been crafted to fit her hand.

If they were riding into trouble, she would take care of herself as best she could and not depend on Captain Street. Calling on the man for help was out of the question. If it ever came to that, she'd simply turn and ride off in the other direction.

The canvas-covered wagon sat in sparse shade at the end of the grove, near the far bend of the river. The sturdy freighters were waiting nearby, hitched and ready. Jessie found Sarah Street loading the last of her belongings aboard her wagon, checking boxes and lashing them down for the ride.

"Sarah," Jessie called out, "any way I can help?"

Street's wife turned too quickly, clearly startled by Jessie's approach. "Oh, look, I'm sorry," Jessie said. "Didn't mean to sneak up on you."

"Don't think anything about it," Sarah told her. "Guess my mind was wanderin' off somewhere." She showed Jessie a shy, nervous smile, drawing her head into the shadow of her bonnet. She was a gaunt, raw-boned woman with no flesh to spare. Jessie had never seen her without the drab, earth-colored dress and the bonnet that hid her features. She had once been a most attractive woman, Jessie knew; the ghost of a former beauty was still there, somewhere behind full lips now pressed tightly together, lost in the large and haunted eyes. She and Sarah were near the same age—the difference couldn't be more than two or three years. Sarah, though, had been married ten years to Heywood Street.

"I wanted to drop over and say good-bye," Jessie said. "I don't know whether you heard, but I'm going on ahead. I need to get to Camp Supply as soon as I can."

"Yes, I heard," said Sarah. Her hands busied themselves at her waist. "You have a safe trip now, you hear!"

"I'll do that. And maybe we'll see each other when you get settled in. The ranch where I'm staying isn't all that far from Camp Supply."

"That would be most enjoyable," Sarah said thoughtfully. "Yes, I will look forward to that."

Jessie waited. Sarah stretched slightly forward, poised as if she had more to say.

"Well, then . . ." Jessie spoke to fill the awkward silence. "It's been a pleasure traveling with you. I hope you find good fortune in your new home."

Sarah didn't reply. She seemed to fix Jessie and hold her from the shadow of her bonnet. "I know you had nothin' to do with him," she blurted suddenly. "I know that for a fact, Jessie. You've been a friend to me and I'm grateful."

"Uh, Sarah—"

"No, I mean that," Sarah rushed on. Her hands clasped tightly together, holding herself so stiffly the motion bowed her shoulders. "He didn't want me coming out here you know. It was my idea, not his. I just wrote and said I was coming and got on the train to Fort Worth. He's got no use for me at all, but I've got a right. I'm his wife an' he can't just toss me away at his will. I can't stop what he does with other women. But he cannot put me aside!"

Jessie let out a breath, not sure at all what to say. She wanted to tell this woman that hanging on to a man like Street would do nothing but bring her more misery. But that, of course, was something she already knew.

"I'm sorry, Sarah. Really I am. I wish there was some way I could help."

"There's nothing I can do," Sarah went on, as if she hadn't heard Jessie at all. "I can't do a thing but make him look me in the eye every day. Make him know I'm alive. I don't guess that makes any sense to you, does it?"

"I hate to see you doing this to yourself," Jessie began, "but I'm not you, Sarah. I can't judge."

13

"I know that. You're a good woman, Jessie."

"Sarah, if there is ever anything at all, any way I can—" Jessie stopped, staring intently at Sarah as an errant shaft of light touched her cheek. She drew in a breath, closed the space between them, reached out, and jerked the bonnet from Sarah's head before she could stop her.

"My God!" Anger welled up in Jessie's throat at the sight of the blackened, swollen tissue below her eyes, the ugly red welts on her cheek. Sarah tried to turn away, but Jessie grabbed her shoulders and held her. "That bastard! Oh, Sarah!"

Sarah looked at her, the trace of a smile on her lips, a slight touch of triumph in the big, sad eyes.

She said quietly, "I knew you'd been my friend. I know when a woman won't give him what he wants."

Street pushed his platoon hard, stopping only once. They made the fifty miles by seven in the evening. A few men from Fox Troop were still around. There was nothing left to do. There were burned out wagons on the road and fresh graves. A sergeant from Fort Reno said men had trailed the raiders, but there was no chance at all they'd be found, not with the start they had. The hard trip north had been for nothing, which didn't seem to bother Street at all. If anything, Jessie decided, he had enjoyed his adventure immensely.

Jessie ate by herself that evening, and Street pretended she didn't exist.

In the morning, they moved out for Camp Supply, taking the final fifty miles at their leisure. The land they passed through now was Cheyenne and Arapaho country. Jessie saw Indians in the distance, but none came close to the troopers. The broad, open prairie baked under the summer sun. Stark, sand-colored bluffs rose in the distance. The red soil was laced with dry creek beds and shallow, eroded gullies where a few cedars survived. Once, they passed a great pile of buffalo bones bleached white as chalk. The heat seemed to suck all the color out of the sky.

They camped again that night, and they sighted Camp Supply before noon the next day. The camp lay on the near side of the Canadian. The big, sprawling stockade wavered in the heat. Jessie shaded her eyes and picked out the square redoubts over the high timber walls and saw the field guns and the bright square of the parade ground. There were barracks for the troopers, quarters for noncoms, and small, squat dwellings for mar-

14

ried officers. Sarah's new home, Jessie thought dully, God help her.

A fair-size settlement had grown up around the fort, laid out in a haphazard manner which contrasted with the precisely spaced structures built by the army. Jessie spotted a few stores, a building that might be a hotel, and several stables and barns. She longed for a hot bath and a quiet room all to herself, but regretfully set the idea aside. Bill Haggerty would have sent someone to meet her; the logical place for that was Camp Supply itself. Most likely the man had been waiting for some time, having no clear idea exactly when she might arrive.

Jessie rode down the shallow incline to the gate of the fort, trailing Street's weary troopers inside. The flat parade ground seemed to soak up the heat, warm it further in the earth's searing oven, and send it back with a vengeance. The air was stifling, almost too hot to breathe. The fort smelled of horses and dust.

Jessie guided the black gelding Morgan had lent her toward the headquarters building, leading the sorrel mare behind. A tall, stocky man in a plain black suit and string tie stepped from a shadowy porch and stalked directly toward her. Jessie glanced curiously at the man and then turned away. A thick mane of white hair erupted from under the brim of his pearl Stetson; one side of his face was hideously scarred, the skin marbled and stretched tightly, pulling the corner of one eye and the side of his mouth out of shape. Poor man, Jessie thought and wondered what could cause such an awful disfigurement.

"Jessie? Jessie Starbuck?"

"What?" Jessie turned in the saddle, searching for the man who had spoken. Her eyes found the white-haired man with the scarred face. He had stopped in the middle of the dusty parade ground to her right; his hands were spread wide in invitation and a broad grin stretched his ruined features.

"It's me, Jessie," he said softly. "I'm Bill Haggerty. Hell, I should've written you about this ugly old face. It clean slipped my mind."

"Bill? Oh, my Lord!" Jessie cried. She slid out of the saddle and ran into his arms. Haggerty swept her up, whirling her in a circle and turning the good side of his face to meet her kiss. He grasped her shoulders and held her away to look her over.

"Damn, you're your mother's child, all right," he beamed. "A real beauty. I told Alex you'd grow up to be a heartbreaker and I was right."

Jessie flushed. "You didn't say any such thing, you old faker.

15

I was—what?—ten, eleven years old when you last saw me?"

Haggerty raised a heavy brow. "A man in my business has got to learn how his stock's going to turn out," he said soberly. "If he doesn't, he isn't going to make much of a living."

Jessie laughed. "I've either been flattered or insulted. I'm not sure which."

Haggerty's smile faded. "Let me go on and get it said, Jessie, since you're too well brought up to do it yourself. I don't look much like you remember. I can see that in your eyes and it's all right. Like I said, I should've told you. Little souvenir of the fire. I've gotten used to it. Near as I'm going to. Can't recall how I used to look."

Jessie hugged him warmly again, fighting back the tears that rose to her eyes. "It's you, Bill," she said gently. "I know that. And I'm sorry for everything that happened. I know how it is to lose people you love."

"Yeah, I reckon you do, all right." His face brightened again and he showed her a broad wink. "Hell, we're both going to be bawlin' like kids in a minute. Let's see, now." He paused and squinted at the sky. "If I know women at all, I'd guess you'll be wanting to get cleaned up and do some fussin' over yourself. We'll get you into a hotel and I'll leave you alone for a couple hours. Then we'll have supper and swap some lies. First thing in the morning, if that suits you, we'll head out for my place."

"Sounds good to me," Jessie told him. "I think you read my mind. Lord, is there really any water in this country? Water that grows out of a tub—and isn't the color of mud?"

Haggerty laughed, then looked away quickly to Jessie's left. Jessie heard the footsteps behind her, turned, saw the two men approaching, and did her best to hide her surprise.

"Mr. Haggerty, you've got all the luck there is," said the taller of the two with a grin. He was a big, lanky man with muscle cording his grease-stained buckskin jacket. His eyes were the color of copper ore, his face dark and weathered. "Pretty girl rides in the gate and you've got her penned up 'fore she gets across the flat. Doesn't hardly seem fair."

Haggerty grinned and put his arm around Jessie. "That's the way it is, son. Just can't help myself. Jessie Starbuck, this fella smilin' like an ape is Matt Bilder. Scout's for the army when he's a mind to."

"A pleasure, Miss Starbuck," said Bilder.

"Thank you, sir." Jessie nodded and turned to Bilder's com-

16

panion, a man in army blues. "And are you going to introduce me to your friend?"

Bilder looked pained. "You don't want to meet him, miss. He's nothing but trouble, I'll tell you that. Miss Starbuck, Lieutenant Josh Stewart."

"Lieutenant," Jessie said evenly. Her green eyes flashed with mischief. "I assume Mr. Bilder is referring to that rather large purple bruise on your jaw. Is he correct, then? Are you nothing but trouble, sir?"

The officer cleared his throat. "A little accident, ma'am," he said soberly. "Matt here tends to exaggerate some."

"I can vouch for that," Haggerty said dryly. "Gentlemen, this lady's had a long ride, and I don't intend to keep her standin' out in the sun. Good day to both of you."

Jessie nodded at the pair, letting her gaze linger for an instant on the young officer. The two men muttered good-byes, touched their hats, and walked off.

Haggerty scowled. "I know Matt Bilder; he's all right. I'm not much taken with that officer fella. By God, if he'd looked you over another minute, I'd have plain called him on it."

"Why, Bill," Jessie scolded gently, linking her arm in his, "the man's a flirt is all. Like someone else I know."

"Humph! That's a horse of a different color. I'm ugly and old and he's not. Don't like the man at all, Jessie."

★

Chapter 3

"I'll do it," Ki said darkly, "but I'm not going to like it."

"You'll be just fine," Jessie assured him. "I'm not worried at all."

"Well, of course, you're not worried. You don't have to wear this damn thing." He scowled at himself in the mirror and shook his head. The stranger in the mirror scowled back. Ki usually wore his black hair to the top of his collar. Now, it was cut to military length. His eyes, intense and gunpowder-black, peered from under the brim of the unfamiliar hat. The eyes were slightly tilted at the corners, a gift from his Japanese mother. His cheeks were sharp planes that shadowed his face. The uniform, the hat, the new shape of his hair, seemed to obscure his Oriental heritage in favor of that of his American father. Still, he felt totally uncomfortable and out of place. Whoever the man in the mirror might be, Ki didn't know him.

"Jessie, I look about as much like a cavalry officer as I do a—a railroad president," he said in disgust. "It's never going to work."

Jessie walked around him, tapping her lips with one finger, inspecting him with a cool and critical eye. "That's not true at all. You look quite handsome, as a matter of fact. And nobody's going to know, Ki. As far as the army's concerned, you are Lieutenant Josh Stewart. Your past is a fake, but your orders are very real. We do have a few friends in high places who understand what we're up against, and Colonel Harrington did a great job. He even checked out the records of the officers at Camp Supply. No one stationed there has ever been close to Washington, D.C."

"Including me," Ki said flatly.

"Yes, but you've done your homework," Jessie said. "You probably know more about Washington than most of the people who work there."

"Which isn't saying a lot," Ki muttered.

Jessie walked to the far corner of the room and squinted at

the bright, summer sky. The parlor was comfortable and cool. Beyond the thick walls, the harsh Texas sun baked the low, rolling hills of the Circle Star ranch. She turned and faced him again.

"I know what you're thinking—you don't want me up there on my own. I don't know any other way to do this, Ki. The Starbuck holdings in land and cattle are pretty extensive—those ranchers up in the Indian Nation are going to know me or know who I am. I'm sure I've already met about half of them either here or in San Antonio or Cheyenne or somewhere else. If Bill Haggerty's right, and there is some foreign element behind those raiders, there's a good chance we're talking about the cartel again."

"Exactly," Ki said. "You're making my point for me, Jessie."

"Now, wait. If it is the cartel, they'll have agents all over the place. People close to the cattlemen, the army—God knows where. They'll know I'm up there about three minutes after I arrive, which means it isn't going to be real easy for me to dig up information."

"It also means it's not going to be real safe," Ki added. His dark eyes flashed with concern. "Jessie, what am I supposed to do if you need help? Ask my commanding officer for a leave? What if they send me out on patrol or something? I could be anywhere. They don't know I'm not in the army. They can do whatever they want to do with me."

"They might," Jessie said dryly, "if they get real desperate. According to your army records, you have spent your time running errands for generals and counting socks."

"And you don't think they're going to wonder what I'm doing at a place like Camp Supply?"

"No, not at all," Jessie said seriously. "You know as well as I do a lot of misfit officers wind up their careers at some post on the frontier. I have an idea they'll look at your record and draw their own conclusions. You obviously fouled up somewhere along the way—which is fine for our purpose. Your past will earn you some do-nothing job. You'll be inconspicuous, but you'll be in a position to learn what's going on there."

"It all sounds good," Ki said reluctantly. "It still puts you in one place and me in another."

"I'll be fine. All right?" She came to him then and gave him a friendly kiss on the cheek. "Now get on your way,

19

Lieutenant Stewart. I'm leaving the ranch for Fort Worth in a few days. I'll get in touch with you as soon as I can after I get to the Indian Nation."

Ki glanced at himself in the mirror once more, then quickly turned away. "You can say what you want. I feel like the worst damn fool in the world."

"You might get to like it, you know?" Jessie said solemnly. "A lot of men find a real home in the army."

Ki gave her a withering look. "Uh-huh. Well, you just hold your breath till that happens."

The thick walls of the small room were painted stark white. The wooden floor was worn from a thousand scrubbings and smelled of lye soap. A chair stood in precise position against the far wall. Ki was certain it had never been used. The chair was the only furniture in the room besides a small field desk and another, more comfortable chair behind it. A neatly painted sign on the inner door read:

LT. COL. GRANT L. DELONG
COMMANDING

Sergeant Major Enos McPherson stood behind his desk and carefully perused Ki's orders. He was a sparsely built man, well under six feet tall, a man in his late thirties or early forties. At first glance, he appeared nearly gaunt, and Ki wondered how many men had made that mistake to their dismay. Ki had recognized the man's power at once, the effortless animal grace, the body that wasted no motion at all. He could see a reflection of himself in the wiry, corded frame and had a fair idea what McPherson could do. His face was the color of polished wood, ebony flesh stretched tight over the prominent bones of his cheeks and brow. When he set the orders aside and looked at Ki, his features betrayed no emotion at all. Still, Ki could read the weary displeasure in his eyes.

"Sir, the lieutenant colonel's in a meetin' right now," he told Ki. "I expect he'll be tied up the rest of the day. If the lieutenant doesn't mind, I'll show him around the place and get him set up in his quarters."

Ki studied the man a moment. "I'm grateful for your help, sergeant major," he said evenly, "but if it's all the same to you, I'll save the tour till later. I've had a pretty long ride and I'd like to get settled."

"Yes, sir," McPherson said woodenly, "begging the lieutenant's pardon, the lieutenant colonel likes me to show new personnel around first thing, sir." He set his face in a respectful smile. "Standin' orders, you understand."

"All right," Ki said, making no effort to hide his irritation, "let's get it over with."

"Yes, sir, we can do that right quick." He slid from behind his desk and stalked to the door, holding it open for Ki. Ki stepped out into the stifling afternoon heat. A lance corporal snapped to attention.

"Hooper, hold down my desk while I'm gone," barked McPherson. "And don't do nothin' stupid."

"Right away, sergeant major!" The corporal fairly jumped.

Ki's horse stood at the hitching post to his left. McPherson mounted the bay gelding beside it. Ki stopped and gave the man a curious look.

"We're going to ride? I thought we were going to look over the post."

"Yes, sir, goin' to do just that," McPherson said pleasantly. "Won't take long at all."

Ki muttered to himself and slid wearily into the saddle. It was just what he needed after three days riding in the sun— more time sitting on a horse.

McPherson led him around the hot parade ground, cheerfully pointing out features such as the officers' quarters, enlisted men's barracks, the stables, the blacksmith's shop, and the sutler's store. Ki wondered if the man thought he was blind or just plain stupid. Anyone could see what the various buildings were for. He didn't need a guided tour. McPherson reached the high gates of the fort and turned abruptly left, leading Ki outside. Ki grumbled to himself, but held his tongue, determined to see the thing through. The sergeant major rode past Camp Supply's sprawling civilian settlement and then down a shallow bluff toward the river. In a moment both the settlement and the fort were lost to sight behind a thick stand of cottonwood trees.

McPherson dismounted and turned to Ki. "Would the lieutenant care to step down a minute?" he said warmly. "Real pretty out here, sir."

Ki didn't answer. "Sergeant major," he said flatly, "just what the hell is this all about? You didn't bring me out here to see the sights."

"No, sir, now that's the truth." McPherson's smile faded.

21

"If the lieutenant doesn't mind, sir, we need to do some talking."

Ki came instantly alert. He slid off his mount and faced the sergeant major. "All right. Now suppose you tell me what y—"

McPherson's fist came up out of nowhere, taking Ki almost completely by surprise. Still, rigid training came instinctively to bear, giving him the small part of a second to jerk back and deflect the full force of the blow from the side of his head. He stumbled, caught himself, and faced the sergeant major in a fighting crouch.

"Say, now . . ." McPherson nodded approval. "That wasn't bad, lieutenant. You're pretty fast on your feet."

"Damn it, man, are you crazy?" Ki blurted. He stared in disbelief. "Don't you know the penalty for striking an officer!"

"Yes, sir, I sure do know," McPherson said calmly. "Reckon I know the U.S. Army regulations backwards and forwards. Maybe sideways, too." He circled Ki, his hands cutting small arcs out of the air. "Come on, lieutenant. Let's see if you're really any good."

"I've got no reason to fight you."

"Sure you do. 'Cause if you don't, I'm goin' to knock you on your ass and stomp you good. That reason enough, sir?"

McPherson came in fast, feinted with a left, then shifted his stance quickly, and drove his right hard at Ki's belly. Ki let the blow come, moved aside at the last instant, and struck McPherson solidly in the ribs. The man's face twisted in pain. Ki moved to finish him off. McPherson suddenly turned on him like a tiger, pounding at Ki's face with a series of short, savage blows. Ki backed off. McPherson grinned and spat on the ground. The man was fast and sure on his feet. Ki felt as if he were fighting a mirror image of himself. He had to be careful, to remember to meet the man on his own terms. Yet this was certainly no time to bring his samurai skills into the open. Like Ki, McPherson had quickly sensed his own qualities in his opponent. He already knew much more than Ki cared to reveal.

Ki waited, letting McPherson take the attack, moving in and pulling back, trying to draw the sergeant major into a mistake. McPherson wasn't having any of that. He knew exactly what Ki was doing. Ki knew what had to come next— he had to turn the game, let the sergeant major pull him into a dangerous situation. McPherson feinted again. Ki waited. McPherson shifted to his right. Ki pretended to see an opening and came in slugging. A big grin split the man's features and he hit Ki solidly in the belly and followed through with a punishing blow to the face.

The blow never arrived. Ki hit the man's fist with the side of his arm, turning it deftly aside, and then brought his own fist up from the waist. It caught the sergeant major directly on the point of his jaw and lifted him off his feet. He fell on his back, turned, and came to his knees. Ki backed off and waited. McPherson shook his head and came shakily to his feet, frowning and holding his jaw.

"Lord, help me, lieutenant. You got a kick like an army mule. Damned if you don't."

"I could've finished you off down there," Ki said. "I didn't. I figure it's over."

"Yes, sir, you got it," McPherson agreed. He brushed red dirt off his blue shirt and trousers. "Fair and square for certain."

"Well, then. That's just great, isn't it?" Ki said sourly. "You lead me down to the river and we knock each other around. Now maybe you'd like to tell me what for. This some kind of custom of yours? You challenge all the new officers or just me?"

McPherson looked thoughtfully at Ki. "Why don't you go first, lieutenant. Save us both the time."

"What are you talking about?"

"Talkin' about questions and answers. Like, you comin' up here to the ass end of nowhere, reporting for duty big as you please. Records, they say you ain't done shit your whole career. Beggin' your pardon, sir, but it's so. No Indian fightin' experience, no nothin'."

"I didn't ask to come, if it's any of your concern. I go where I'm sent like everyone else."

"Yes, sir. You're right as you can be. Ain't all that unusual, seein' as how the army's got its own idea 'bout who goes where and what for. Only thing is, I watched you ride from the fort down here and you surely know which end of the mount goes first. You're used to having a saddle horn and you miss it." McPherson bit his lip and shook his head. "What I'm askin' myself is why this lieutenant is here? He's a U.S. cavalry officer who knows how to ride—but not on a cavalry saddle. He been playin' around Washington, goin' to tea parties an' such, and he can use his hands good as any brawler I ever seen. Don't make much sense, now does it?"

"I don't have to explain myself to you," Ki said coolly. "I

figure you've got a hell of a lot of explaining to do to me."

"Yes, sir." McPherson showed Ki an easy smile. "What you thinking now is here's this crazy nigger sergeant major goin' around hittin' white officers in the head. What I'll do is march in and tell the lieutenant colonel an' get this boy skinned good. Something like that, lieutenant?" The sergeant shook his head. "You think about that 'fore you do it. I got fourteen years in this man's army. I run this place for Lieutenant Colonel DeLong. He needs me. We got a real good arrangement. You—beggin' your pardon again, sir—you 'bout as useful to the lieutenant colonel as a tit on a Henry rifle. Don't mean to offend but that's the truth. What I'd do if I was you, sir, I'd say I scraped my face on a tree, somethin' like that. Case anyone should ask."

"You would, would you?"

"Yes, sir. That's what I'd do." He gave Ki a curious, knowing look. "Don't know exactly what you're doing here, lieutenant. Don't know yet, but I will. Meantime, seems to me that callin' attention to yourself, making any trouble, is probably just exactly what you don't need." He gave Ki a lazy salute. "With the lieutenant's permission, we ought to be gettin' back now, sir."

Just great, Ki thought glumly, first man I meet on the post sees right through me. I'm off to a really fine start.

Maybe, he decided hopefully, McPherson would keep his suspicions to himself. Ki figured the odds were good that he might. The sergeant was a loner, a man who didn't depend on others. He'd keep his eyes open, but he wouldn't talk around what he knew. Ki was certain the sergeant major wasn't boasting when he said he called the shots at Camp Supply. The colonel and his officers probably thought they were running the show, leaving the dirty work and the details to McPherson. McPherson wouldn't tell them any different.

Ki felt better after a bath and clean clothes. His room was small but clean—two beds, two chairs, and a window. He rinsed his face in a basin, dabbed it lightly with a towel, and gingerly touched the large purple welt on his jaw. It hurt like hell. He hoped McPherson's face was swollen like a melon. While running a brush through his hair, he heard heavy footsteps behind him, turned, and saw a tall man in buckskins entering the room.

"You Josh Stewart?" The man smiled broadly and stuck out

24

his hand. "Matt Bilder. Reckon we're sharing quarters now."

"Guess I'm messing up your privacy," said Ki.

"Forget it." Bilder waved him off. "Glad to have the company." He eased himself down on his own bed, stretched out, and put his hands behind his head. "Got yourself a bad bruise there," he said idly, staring at the low ceiling.

"Not as bad as it looks," Ki told him. If Bilder were fishing for an answer, he was plain out of luck. "You work at the fort, I guess," said Ki. "Guide, scout—what?"

"Scout," said Bilder. Something struck him funny and he grinned up at Ki. "Lieutenant Colonel doesn't need me any at all. Got three good scouts on the post. Two Osage and a Blackfoot. Only thing is, DeLong hates Indians. Doesn't trust 'em, can't stand the sight of them. Keeps me around to tell him whether they're lyin' or telling the truth." Bilder laughed aloud. "Hates Indians near as bad as he does Negro troopers. Poor bastard's in bad shape. 'Sides a handful of white officers and raggedy-ass civilians, he's plain surrounded by Negroes and Indians." He paused and looked at Ki. "You meet many fellas on the post?"

"Just you and Sergeant McPherson."

"Uh-huh. You didn't meet DeLong."

"He was in a meeting when I got here."

"He was drunk," Bilder said flatly. "Starts in around noon, tapers off at five. Sobers up good by supper. Righthand man's Captain Heywood Street. He's off in Texas now. Fort Worth. Pickin' up supplies and bringing back his wife."

"He a drunk, too?"

"Naw, just a worthless bastard," yawned Bilder. He caught Ki's expression. "You'll love it here, Stewart. Real fine place. Friendly folks, hotter'n hell during the day and worse at night. Oh, yeah. The food's damn awful."

"You sure make a man feel welcome."

Bilder sat up. "None of my business, but what'd you do to get sent out here? You don't mind me asking."

"You're right," Ki said. "It's none of your business. Real nice meeting you, Bilder." He jammed his hat on his head, stalked out of the room, and left the man looking at his back.

★

Chapter 4

If Matt Bilder were still curious about his new roommate, he kept that curiosity to himself. When they met, Ki had made it plain such questions weren't welcome—the tall scout accepted this at once. Ki found the man to be friendly and easygoing— a man who didn't go looking for trouble, but wouldn't back off if it found him.

Ki, in turn, didn't question Bilder. Talk around the post said Matt was better than most with a Colt .44 and that he'd found occasion to use one over the years. The few times they talked about anything more than the weather, Bilder gave strength to some of the stories Ki had heard. He was on drinking terms with men everyone knew—men on one side of the law or the other. He didn't brag about it.

Ki was glad to have Matt as a friend. He was one of the few people he really cared to talk to at Camp Supply. He'd seen Lieutenant Colonel DeLong from a distance; after a full week on the post, DeLong had given no indication that he cared to meet Lieutenant Josh Stewart. Sergeant Major McPherson passed along the lieutenant colonel's orders—or, more likely, Ki decided, made them out himself. Ki was assigned to First Lieutenant Jake Wallace. On paper, Wallace ran regimental headquarters for the lieutenant colonel. In reality, it was Wallace who worked for McPherson. The two kept up a fiction that it was the other way around. Wallace was overweight, ignorant, and lazy. He had been passed over for his captaincy more times than he could remember and didn't really care. Ki's job was to assist Jake Wallace in whatever way Wallace saw fit, which meant that Ki had less than nothing to do.

The men who were real cavalry officers on the post would have little to do with Ki. They were civil, but didn't go out of their way to be friendly. Ki fully understood. In the cavalry, men who rode desks were not the same as men who rode horses.

Ki visited the settlement outside the walls several times, sometimes alone and sometimes with Bilder. There was the usual collection of stores, hotels, and stables. There were places to find whiskey and whores. The officers were supposed to be discreet about this, especially since the post was right next door. Lieutenant Colonel DeLong, Ki learned, might be a drunk himself, but he abhorred all forms of vice in his officers. He was a widower with a daughter who lived on the post. Ki had seen the girl once from across the parade ground. She seemed attractive enough from afar, and Matt said that was about as close as he'd better get. All an officer had to do was look cross-eyed at Mindy DeLong, and the lieutenant colonel would make him wish that he'd never been born.

If entertainment were hard to come by for the officers at Camp Supply, it was even more difficult for the men. The Negro troopers walked lightly around the settlement, keeping to their own section of town when off duty. Any man crazy enough to enter a white saloon or try to engage a white whore was fair game for the cowhand or drifter who caught him at it.

Ki had to agree that Jessie was right. Both Camp Supply and the settlement were ideal spots for an agent of the cartel. Officers, cowhands, teamsters, storekeeps, and men who claimed no profession at all drifted in and out of the area day and night. Everyone, it seemed, knew everyone else's business. If a man wanted to know whose cattle were moving where, the direction freight wagons were going and what they carried, all he had to do was watch. Army patrols were staggered, but there was no way to hide when they came and went.

Ki heard plenty of talk about the raiders and believed about a tenth of what he heard. One rumor had it that Jesse and Frank James were the real leaders. Another said a ravishing, half-breed Indian girl ran the outlaw band. Whoever was running the show, he clearly had plenty of sources around the western half of the Indian Nation. Ki, though, was uncertain how to ferret the leader out. So far, all he'd managed to do was get thoroughly sick of the army. And Jessie, where was she? He'd been at Camp Supply over a week and there'd been no word from her at all. What the hell was she doing? *Walking* from Fort Worth?

• • •

Ki stalked out of the Cimarron Bar and started back to the fort. Darkness had set in an hour before and the streets were black. He was tired, hungry, and disgusted. For three long hours, he'd followed two men from one saloon to another. He'd overheard their talk and thought it interesting enough to listen. One had promised the other he could make some real good money if he were willing to take a chance. The other said he sure as hell was. It turned out to be illegal, as Ki had figured, but had to do with whiskey stills instead of raiders. Selling half-poisonous firewater to the Indians was a thriving business in the Cherokee Strip and farther west in No Man's Land. Stopping this traffic was one of the army's jobs—a hapless task at best, considering the size of the territory and the number of whiskey ranches in operation.

The second-rate beer he'd consumed was getting to him and he stepped into an alley to relieve himself. It was frustrating as hell, knowing he'd probably passed some of the raiders more than once during his evenings in town. He might even have talked to one. Who could say? They didn't wear signs around their necks.

Ki buttoned up, started back to the street, and changed his mind. If he remembered right, cutting through the alley would take him within a block of the fort's walls and save some time. Fine. He'd had about all of the undercover work he could stand for one evening. Jake Wallace had some harebrained idea about counting all the saddles on the post in the morning to make sure there wasn't—

Ki stopped and pressed himself flat against a rough brick wall. He'd caught a slight motion out of the corner of his eye— a figure, the silhouette of a man, standing in a doorway just ahead. A drunk, maybe, or someone like himself who'd stepped in the alley to lighten his bladder. Or perhaps a man looking to earn a day's wages the easy way.

"Bring it in here just like before without no trouble," a voice said suddenly. "I don't see any reason to change what works." The words reached Ki's ears clearly. In a moment another man answered. Ki hadn't seen the other figure, standing close to the recessed door.

"I got reason enough," the man said irritably. "You get in a routine you start a pattern. Pretty soon somebody wonders what we're doing. And 'fore you know it you got some bastard nosing around and that's it."

"You're making a big thing out of nothing. That's what you're doing. I don't see any problems here."

"Shit!" the man cursed. "That's easy for you to say, now isn't it? I'm sitting in there with my neck on the line and you're out here. Somethin' goes wrong, it's me gets it, not you."

"Nothing's going to go wrong," the man Ki could see said calmly. "You're protected. Anything happens—which it won't—you got yourself covered."

"How?" The second man made a noise. "How the hell you cover something like that? Listen, he's just as worried as I am. This thing ever comes apart he won't be able to do a damn thing. We'll be sittin' right there with a bunch of empties. There's no way he's goin' to explain that." The man paused. "He told me to tell you that last week's got to be the end of it. If you want the stuff, you hit it on the way—after it leaves us."

"No," the first man said flatly, "that's out. Absolutely. It's too risky."

"Why? We let you know when and where. What's the risk?"

"Some of your people get killed, that's what. It raises a big stink all over and we don't want it. We keep on like we are. You tell him that. You and him are both gettin' paid good money and—"

"There isn't enough money in the world to risk hanging."

"Nobody's—look, all right. Tell him to take it easy for a couple days. I've maybe got a way out that works good for us both."

"What?"

"Just tell him. I'll see about it and get to you. Come on. I got to get out of here. I need a drink and you got to get back."

Ki went nearly to the ground, ready to retreat the way he'd come if the men started to move in his direction. He breathed a sigh of relief as they left the door and walked off the other way. He could see them more clearly now. One, short and broad-shouldered in a flat-crowned Stetson. The other—Ki's muscles tightened—*an officer!* He'd only seen him for an instant but that was enough. The hat, the shape of the jacket— there was no doubt about it. The second man, the one who'd stayed out of sight in the doorway, was a cavalryman from Camp Supply!

29

Ki followed silently, keeping the men in sight. He'd already decided what to do. He didn't recognize the officer's voice, but he'd damn sure know it when he heard it again. Let him go, then. Follow the other man now; find out who he is and he'd probably have them both.

The two paused at the end of the alley, heads close together. Ki couldn't hear what they were saying. The stocky civilian poked the officer's chest with his finger, making his point clear. The officer shook his head. Whatever the other wanted he was against it. A girl suddenly came out of nowhere, crossing the darkened street. The men were so engrossed in heated discussion they didn't see her. She walked nearly to them and then stopped, head tilted slightly, palms resting provocatively on the points of her hips.

"Well, now," she said softly, "you fellas like to buy a girl a drink?"

Both men turned as if they'd been shot. The officer muttered something under his breath, backed off, and bolted out of sight.

"Damn slut," the other man blurted, "get out of here!"

"Well, you don't have to get nasty," the girl snapped. "You don't want my company just—uuuuh! No!"

The man's hand snaked out and struck her savagely across the face. The girl stumbled and fell. The man grabbed her arm and jerked her roughly to her feet, shook her hard, and hit her again. The girl cried out in fear, clawing and kicking desperately to break free. The man raised his hand, looking for an opening to get her again. Ki cursed and came out of the alley fast. The man might guess that he'd been there alone, but there was no time to worry about that. The bastard's rage was out of hand; Ki had seen it happen before. He might not stop until he hurt the girl badly or even killed her.

The girl saw him first. Her eyes darted frantically in Ki's direction. The man turned, startled. His face contorted in anger and he threw the girl roughly at Ki. Ki saw what would happen and tried to stop it. For an instant he was open, vulnerable, his hands entangled with the girl. He tried to push her away, turned on the balls of his feet, and lowered his head between his shoulders. A big fist caught him in the face and sent him sprawling. His back slammed hard against a brick wall. The girl clung to him like a tick. The man came at him, both fists swinging. Ki wrenched the girl's hand from his throat, brought his leg up fast, and kicked at the man's belly. The girl spoiled his balance—the blow struck the man's thigh and hip bone.

The man cursed and stepped back, met Ki's eyes for an instant, and then turned and limped quickly down the street.

Ki let out a breath and watched him go. The girl was clinging to his waist, her head buried in his belly.

"Okay," he told her, "it's all right." He worked his hands under her shoulders and brought her up to face him. Enormous, frightened blue eyes met his. Dark ringlets fell carelessly over her brow. Her nose and mouth were sharply defined, set in a small and angular face.

"You all right?" he asked her. "You're not hurt?"

"I don't guess," she said crossly. She pulled the torn dress over one shoulder, covering creamy flesh. Standing away from Ki, she looked him over with a critical eye. "Lord, that fella must've been plain crazy. I sure owe you one, mister."

Ki shrugged off her thanks. "Glad I could help." He searched around the alley and found his hat, brushed it off, and set it on his head. "You don't mind me saying so, miss, that's not too good an idea—walking up to folks in the dark."

"Men don't usually seem to mind," she said coolly. Her gaze traveled from Ki's dusty cavalry boots to his face. "Got a bad bruise there. Likely goin' to color."

Ki fingered his jaw and winced. "Be a good idea if I could learn to get hit somewhere else," he said soberly. "I seem to be favoring one spot."

For the first time, the girl smiled. "You do this a lot, do you?"

"Not if I can help it." He peered up and down the darkened street. "Look, if it's all right with you, why don't we walk to where it's light? I'll be glad to see you home or wherever you live." *Where you work* was on the tip of his tongue, but he stopped himself in time. The girl caught his hesitation and gave him a stony look.

"Let's just walk for now," she said. "I know a good place." Linking her arm easily in his, she led him back toward the lights of the saloons. Then, without saying a thing, she turned off to the left past rows of darkened clapboard buildings. The settlement came abruptly to an end beyond a scattering of lonely houses. The land sloped slightly toward the river. The sultry night was clear and full of stars and Ki could see the pale walls of the fort. A gully ran crookedly downhill; a line of cedars clung hopefully to the dry waterway.

"This is one of my favorite places," the girl told him. "I like to get close to water. It's real quiet and peaceful."

31

"Yeah, it is," said Ki, deciding they weren't far from where Sergeant McPherson had brought him that first day. It hadn't been all that peaceful then.

"You're new to the camp," the girl said. It was a statement, not a question.

"Yes," said Ki. "How did you know?"

"Haven't seen you is how."

"You know all the officers at the fort?" He wasn't sure just how she'd take the question, but she didn't seem offended.

"Some. By sight, anyway."

"How about the one in the alley," Ki asked. "You know him?"

"Didn't see him real good," she told him. "That other bastard, now . . ." She shook her head and frowned. "I've seen him somewhere." She looked curiously at Ki. "What you figure made him act like that? Hell, all I was trying to do was be friendly."

"I guess you just surprised him," Ki suggested.

The girl stopped. "And what were you doin' there?"

"Taking care of personal business."

"Oh." She grinned shyly and looked away.

The light in the open was better; Ki saw the girl was even prettier than he'd imagined: long-legged, slender with an incredibly slim waist, and a youthful tilt to her breasts. He guessed she was twenty, twenty-two at the most. He wondered how she'd ended up in the dreary little town that clung to the walls of the fort. She had a fresh, appealing look to her, a look that usually vanished very quickly among ladies who plied her trade for very long. He supposed she was new to the game, yet she'd been near the settlement for a while, long enough to know the officers at Camp Supply.

"You got a name, I guess," the girl said. She stopped in the shadow of the grove, leaned against a tree, and turned to face him. Her chin was tilted slightly. A light breeze blew hair across her eyes.

"Josh. Josh Stewart," said Ki.

"Josh. Like Joshua in the Bible."

"I don't know. I guess."

"I'm Amy," she said. A fetching smile touched the corners of her lips. She pressed her hands gently against his chest and then let her arms slide to the back of his neck. Dim light found its way through the leaves to dapple her face. "Guess I could

32

beat around the bush 'bout this," she said softly, "but it seems like a plain waste of time. That son of a bitch scared me out of my wits back there, Josh Stewart. I don't show my feelings a whole lot, but I'm shakin' inside and about to bust. I'm going to have to scream or do something, and I figure maybe you kinda peelin' me out of this dress and lovin' me hard would be better'n kicking trees. Might even be pure pleasure." She smiled gently. "Can't ever tell, can you?"

★

Chapter 5

"I can't think of one reason we shouldn't see whether you're right," Ki told her. He slipped his hands around the slender circle of her waist and drew her to him. Amy sighed and came lazily into his arms. Ki kissed her eyelids and the soft, downy spot below her ear. The fresh, clean smell of her hair assailed his senses. He cupped the sharp angles of her cheeks between his hands and brought her face to his. Her mouth opened eagerly, the moist flesh of her lips unbelievably tender to the touch. He explored each warm and secret hollow, drinking in the sweet taste of her mouth. When he met her probing tongue with his own, she gave a quick cry of joy. He thrust hungrily into her warmth, her lips opening wider with every touch. Amy's wiry form squirmed against him. He could feel the hot points of her breasts pressing against the fabric of his shirt. She threw back her neck, greedily drawing in his kisses. Ki ran his hands through misty hair, letting his fingers trail down the column of her throat to the curve of her shoulders. Amy's breath came in rapid bursts; a low moan caught in her throat. Ki slid his hands down her shoulders and pressed his thumbs gently on the tips of her breasts. Firm little nipples met his touch. The girl's face was slick with moisture, her skin flushed with pleasure. Her body seemed to writhe with a purpose all its own. Dark eyes held him as he found the pearl buttons of her dress. Her fingers came up to help and she laughed as they tangled with Ki's.

"Don't know who's more anxious to get me out of this thing," she whispered, "you or me."

"I figure we're even," Ki said soberly. "Wouldn't have it any other way." He helped her slip the dress off her shoulders and then freed her arms from the sleeves. In an instant she was bare to the waist. Clouds slid away from the moon and pale light licked at her flesh. Ki's throat went suddenly dry; he felt himself harden even more against his trousers. Her breasts were

34

firm and ripe, set wide apart and high. The taut, creamy globes were crowned by proud, saucy little nipples.

"Lord, I can feel you inside me already," Amy gasped. Her enormous eyes went wide; the full lips trembled, baring the tip of her tongue. "I want you in me," she said fiercely, "I want you in me something awful!"

Without taking her eyes from his, she cupped her breasts between her hands, caressing them as gently as any lover. Her palms slid over her flesh and came together, until she held each nipple between her fingers. Her eyes half closed in pleasure; her tongue flicked out to wet her lips. She stretched from the waist and groaned as Ki slid her dress over the swell of her hips and down her legs. He wasn't surprised to see she wore nothing at all underneath. He stepped back and stared, marveling at her breathtaking beauty. Her body was lean and lanky, the firm and slender form made of velvet curves and lazy angles. The narrow waist flared to the bones of her hips and then swept in a hollowed shadow to the flat plane of her belly and the proud silken mound just below. Her long legs seemed to go on forever. In the dim light beneath the trees, her flesh was highlighted by a thousand fragments of the moon. She looked at him and smiled. A tangle of hair fell onto her face. Her hand rose idly to sweep a dark lock across her shoulder and down her breast.

"My, my," she said with a smile, "you do look pleased by what you see."

"Pleased doesn't hardly say enough," Ki told her. "You're a beautiful woman, Amy, and that doesn't get it all either."

"Well, now, what a nice thing to say." Her eyes caught shards of light. She rested her hands on her hips, leaning back with the motion, thrusting her little mound boldly in his direction. She bit her lip and pretended to study him intently.

"Something's wrong here. I can't figure just what . . . Say, that's it!" Her eyes widened in understanding. "One of us is naked out here and the other one isn't."

Ki laughed aloud. He reached up to loosen the buttons of his shirt. Amy took a light step forward and stopped his hands.

"Fair's fair," she said softly.

Ki could smell the rich scent of her body. He sucked in a breath as she slipped the shirt off his shoulders. A finger trailed down his chest, the touch sweeping like a fire to his groin. Her tongue licked absently against her lips as she freed the buckle of his belt. Grasping his waist, she lowered herself slowly to her knees. He rested his hands on her shoulders as she worked off his boots, then pulled his trousers past his hips, and slipped them over his feet. He reached down and swept his hands through the dark wings of her hair.

"Oh Lordy, look what I went and found!" she whispered. Her eyes were locked on the rigid length of his manhood, now only inches from her face. Her pulse beat rapidly in her throat. Sliding her hands over the hard flanks of his thighs, she leaned in and gently kissed the swollen head.

Ki shuddered at her touch. Her tongue flicked out to tease him, to stroke him with quick little thrusts. The moist flesh of her mouth was as hot as a furnace. Ki grasped the back of her neck between his hands and drew her to him. Amy grinned and opened her mouth to take him in. Her fingers raked his thighs as she pounded her face frantically into his belly. Long hair lashed his flesh like a whip. Ki hung suspended on the high crest of pleasure; the heat of her tongue stirred every nerve in his body. Her fingers snaked past his thighs and closed gently on his scrotum. The strokes of her loving mouth became harder, faster; spasms of pleasure and pain tightened every cord and tendon in his frame. The storm churned within him, thundering through his loins. Amy groaned and writhed against him. Ki exploded with a deep cry of pleasure, filling her mouth with his warmth. Amy purred, draining the last of his strength, then slid down his legs, and sighed gently.

Ki went to his knees and took her in his arms. She shuddered and pressed her head against his chest.

"See how it works out," she said, "when everybody gets naked at once?"

"You were right," he said solemnly. "It was a fine idea. Wonder why I didn't think of it myself."

"A person keeps on learning all the time." Her eyes were focused on some point beyond the trees. Ki heard the soft sounds of the river. The moon turned her flesh a buttery gold. Once more, Ki marveled at the slender lines of her body. Her waist was so slim and fragile that he was certain he could circle it with his hands. He let his eyes drink her in—from the ripe peaks of her nipples to the dark line of down that vanished between her thighs.

"I can feel your eyes all over me," she told him. "Like you were kissin' me everywhere."

"Kissing you everywhere's just what I had in mind."

Her eyes closed to slits. "Don't see anyone trying to stop you. Don't see anyone at all."

Ki eased her down to the earth and kissed her softly, scarcely brushing her lips with his own. He bent to kiss her breasts and drew the hard little nipples into his mouth. Her breath began to quicken. Ki let his hands slide under her back to cup the swell of her buttocks. Her body jerked in a quick spasm of delight. Her breasts began to rise—slowly at first, then faster, as the heat within her grew. He flipped the coral buds with his tongue, stroking the silken tips. The musky taste of her flesh sent a sharp surge of excitement through his veins. Amy gave a harsh little cry and thrust her belly against him. Ki reached down to part the moist petals between her legs.

"Oh, Lord!" She gasped at his touch. "Get in me," she pleaded, "I just got to have you in me!"

Ki teased the plush mound with the tips of his fingers. As he stroked the feathery nest, Amy cried out and thrashed her head from side to side. Ki rubbed the sweet and tender swell. She was ready for him: sleek and wet and fragrant with desire. Ki moved between her thighs; he tried to enter her gently, but Amy wouldn't have it. Her back arched off the ground to take him in, forcing all his length deep inside her. A murmur of joy escaped her throat. Her long legs wrapped around him, urging him deeper still. Her proud mound kissed his loins. He grabbed her arms and stretched them wide, pinning her to the ground. Amy moaned as his mouth found her breasts once more. He sucked the pliant flesh between his lips, kneading the hard tips between his teeth. Amy thrust joyously against him, slender legs pounding the small of his back. Ki plunged himself inside her again and again. With each new stroke, she caressed his swelling member. The heart of her pleasure tightened about him, teasing him ever closer to sweet release. Amy trembled, her slender body singing with delight. Ki felt liquid fire begin to thunder through his loins. Amy sank her teeth into his shoulder, raked her nails across his back. The flesh of her loins convulsed about his erection, triggering explosions in them both and sending them soaring to heights of joy. She screamed as he emptied himself inside her.

"Oh, God, that was some kind of loving!" She lay limp, arms and legs sprawled in lovely abandon. The hollow of her belly heaved with rapid breathing. Her smooth flesh glistened, sleek with a fine film of moisture. Her arms circled his neck and she drew him to her, kissing him firmly on the mouth.

Her lips parted in an impish grin. "Guess I'll have to peek into alleys more often."

"That's not funny," Ki said flatly. "You could've gotten killed back there, girl."

"Yeah, I guess," she said idly.

"Isn't any guess to it. You stick to lighted streets. Hell, it's dangerous enough just—"

"Just what? Goin' around looking for men?" She shook her head and touched a finger to his lips. "You're sweet, Josh. You'd really care, wouldn't you, if something happened to me?"

"Well, of course, I'd care."

Her voice was suddenly bitter. "Not many men give a hang one way or the other, long as they get what they want."

And what do you expect, he said to himself, the kind of work you've picked for yourself? He'd almost forgotten what she was. Her loving had seemed real, her release as intense as his own. Maybe it was or maybe it wasn't. If a whore knew her business, a man didn't have much way of telling.

She pressed her hands gently against his chest, sat up, and found her dress. He watched with regret as the slender body vanished under her clothing. He slipped into his pants and shirt and sat back against a tree to pull on his boots. They didn't speak as they walked away from the river. Ki felt peculiar, uneasy. He'd paid for a woman before, but bringing up money with Amy seemed awkward. He shook the thought away. What difference did it make? If he kept quiet, she'd mention the price herself soon enough.

The moon told Ki it was late, past twelve and then some. A few lights burned in the settlement. As they passed the scattered houses and came close to the center of town, Amy seemed to grow tense, wary; her eyes darted about in the dark. Maybe it was hitting her at last, he decided. Maybe she remembered what had nearly happened here. Ki hoped that was true. A little more caution wouldn't hurt her at all.

Amy stopped suddenly, turned, and squeezed both his hands between her own. "I'm goin' to leave you here, Josh. I can make my way back by myself."

"Amy," Ki said, "it's awful late. If you don't mind, I'd rather walk you to your door."

"I'll be just fine, all right?" She showed him a quick, nervous little smile, pecked him on the mouth, and turned away, walking hurriedly up the street.

"Amy..." Ki started after her and stopped. The girl was already gone. Hell, she was even more frightened than he'd thought, so scared she'd forgotten to ask for money. Ki shook his head. If she were that scared, why didn't she want him to take her home? It was a natural thing to do, yet she'd turned him down flat.

Ki shrugged and walked on, circling the outskirts of the settlement toward the western side of the fort's high walls. There was a curfew at Camp Supply, rigidly enforced for the troopers, but more or less ignored by noncoms and officers. The front gate was closed at this hour, but there was an entry behind the stables, a place where a man could squeeze through between the timbered walls. Matt Bilder had shown him the spot after their first foray into town. An unofficial sentry was on duty between curfew and sunup. Except for those hours, the crack was wedged shut from the inside. The place was known as Post Number Nine, there being eight official sentry posts at Camp Supply.

Ki peeked through the wide crack and saw a black trooper leaning against the stable wall, a rifle cradled in his arms. He cleared his throat and the sentry came to attention.

"Lieutenant Josh Stewart," Ki said softly. "At ease, trooper."

"Yes, sir. Evening, lieutenant," the trooper answered.

Ki walked quietly behind the stables, smelling the pungent odor of the mounts inside. He wondered if Lieutenant Colonel DeLong was aware of Post Number Nine and decided he likely was and pretended to ignore it. Apparently, he ignored a great deal at Camp Supply, preferring to let Sergeant Major Mc-Pherson keep the fort from blowing away.

Ki was already thinking about the morning and what he needed to do. He'd make some excuse to Jake Wallace and find a good reason to wander around the fort. It shouldn't take long to find the officer he'd encountered in the alley. It wasn't a voice he'd soon forget. And after that, what? Nothing, for the moment. There was someone else in camp, working with the man he'd heard. Another officer, maybe. The way the conversation went, that was the way it sounded. A person with some authority. "You're protected," the man from the settlement had said, "you got yourself covered." Still, Ki reasoned, it could be someone else. There were plenty of civilians working on the post. Sutlers, teamsters, men who came and went and had business with the army. Maybe the man's job simply put him in a position to offer protection. An officer seemed like the best bet for the moment, but Ki couldn't rule anyone out. He'd have to check them all. It was someone inside, someone who had charge of something important.

What? Ki wondered. Something was moving out of the fort, into the hands of the people outside. And some kind of problem had developed. "We'll be sittin' right there with a bunch of empties." Empty what? Whatever it was, the men from Camp Supply were getting worried. They were going to stop the shipments, make the outsiders get the goods another way. Anger boiled in Ki's veins. The cold-blooded bastards! They were planning to set up their own friends—let a wagon, maybe an army supply column, fall into a trap.

He'd follow the officer, then, identify him from his voice, watch him until he led Ki to the other man inside. That wouldn't be easy. Every man on the post came in contact with dozens of others every day. Still, it had to be done. The other man, the man on the outside, wouldn't be that big a problem. His face was boldly etched in Ki's mind. He'd track down that one with no trouble, let him lead him to his friends. With luck, maybe he'd get a handle on the raiders and the traitors in the fort by the time Jessie arrived. Maybe she wouldn't have to go off on her own, put herself in danger—

Ki stopped suddenly, flattening himself against a roughly planed wall. Something moved, darted from the shadows nearby, crossing flat ground to the building beyond. A low railing, an overhanging porch. The figure slowed and walked calmly along the board sidewalk past the porch. Ki frowned and got his bearings. Barracks, officers' quarters . . .

A match flared on the dark porch. For an instant, Ki saw the lean and angular face, hands cupped about the cheroot. Good God, it was Lieutenant Colonel DeLong himself! Engrossed in his thoughts, Ki had nearly strolled right by the lieutenant colonel's quarters.

"What the hell are you doin' up at this hour?" DeLong said gruffly.

Ki tensed, thinking for a moment the lieutenant colonel was speaking to him.

"Just gettin' a little air, papa," a sweet voice answered. "Too hot to sleep, I guess."

"Well, get back in bed," DeLong told her. "I don't like you wandering around the grounds by yourself."

"All right, papa. Good night." The figure stepped on the porch, kissed DeLong quickly on the cheek, and vanished inside.

The colonel puffed at his cheroot, peering out over the moonlit parade ground. Ki stood frozen, staring in disbelief at the darkened porch. There was no mistaking the girl's voice. Her name wasn't Amy; it was Mindy. He'd been making love half the night with the colonel's daughter.

★

Chapter 6

Jessie was eager to talk to Ki, especially after their chance
meeting. They knew each other well, and Jessie had caught
the look in Ki's eyes and knew he had plenty to tell her. He
was right *there*, damn it all, and there was no way on earth
they could get together—not without making Ki's presence in
the army next to useless. At least, she mused, he was all right—
though his eyes looked bleary, as if he'd been up half the night.
Doing what? Jessie wondered. Something to earn that ugly
bruise on his jaw, no doubt.

Jessie let it go. They'd get together when they could. For
now, she'd ride to the Crescent-H with Bill Haggerty and then
find some excuse in a few days to come back to Camp Supply.

After a bath and the best meal Haggerty could drum up in
the settlement, she fell into bed and slept soundly through the
night. Camping out was fine, but there was no substitute for
hot water and a bed. Her comfort was short-lived. Haggerty's
knock roused her at five in the morning. She stumbled into her
clothes, walked down to breakfast at the café, and was on the
trail again before the sun came up to sear another day.

The Crescent-H spread wasn't far, some fifty miles northwest of Camp Supply on the Cimarron River—three or four
miles past an invisible line that separated No Man's Land from
the Cherokee Strip. You could spit into Kansas, Haggerty told
Jessie. It was a good place to settle, she knew—not far from
the army and about fifty miles farther north to Dodge City. The
Santa Fe railroad was there, convenient for shipping fattened
cattle to market.

"There's a future in this part of the country," Haggerty told
her. "Leastways there is if we don't do somethin' foolish to
ruin it."

Jessie muttered an answer and flicked her reins, gazing out
at the flat, grassy plains. The land to the west was still painted
with the end of night. Haggerty was just warming to his subject,

picking up where he'd left off the night before.

"What's going to happen is going to happen," he told her. "There isn't any doubt about that. Where there's land to be had, the Indians are going to lose. You know it, and I know it, and the Indians sure as hell know it."

Jessie caught the trace of bitterness in his voice. At supper, she'd been both pleased and surprised to learn Haggerty was one of those rare, nearly extinct birds in the West—a cattleman who truly believed the Indians had rights the same as anyone else.

"I wish I could say I thought you were wrong," said Jessie. "Lord, Bill, they've lost nearly everything they've got. The Indian Nation is all there is—there's no place else to go."

"And who's goin' to worry 'bout that? Never bothered anyone before." Haggerty shook his head. "Nobody in Washington gives a damn what happens out here. The country's growing and folks want land. Who's going to get it—some upstandin' voter or a bunch of raggedy Cheyennes and Comanches?"

It was a question that didn't require an answer, Jessie knew. The truth was hard to swallow. Dreaming that it was different wouldn't change it. The Indians had been herded over the years, uprooted from their homes and told where to settle. First, the Creeks, Cherokees, and Seminoles, with the promise that the land would be theirs as long as the sun shines and the grass grows. Then, settlers needed the land where other tribes lived, so they sent them into the Nation as well. Now, there were two vast reservations in the eastern end of the nation: the Cherokees to the north and the Choctaws to the south. And next to these two, spread between the borders of Kansas and Texas, various bands lived according to their tribe. Farther west, next to the panhandle of Texas, the Comanches, Kiowas, Apaches, Cheyennes, and Arapahoes dwelled.

A big chunk of the Indian Nation still belonged to no one at all: No Man's Land in the narrow panhandle and the Cherokee Strip to the east of that. This latter had been promised to the Cherokees from the beginning. They might even have gotten it, if some members of the tribe hadn't made the big mistake of supporting the South in the war. The government never forgave them, so the Cherokees still didn't have their land.

And, farther east still and to the south were the Unassigned Lands, a vast territory set aside for tribes who might be resettled in the future or awarded to Indians who lived in the Nation now.

No Man's Land, the Cherokee Strip and the Unassigned Lands had attracted the attention of cattlemen looking for good grass close to market. They didn't have title and didn't much care if they did for the moment. If they didn't own the land, no one else did either. They knew how to hold what they had.

And they don't have any intention of letting go, Jessie told herself. They'd get the land somehow. Whatever happened, the Indians would be left out in the cold. And beyond that, as Bill Haggerty had hinted, the takers would grow hungry again someday and look to the Indian Nation itself. Maybe sooner than people expected.

All that might never happen, Jessie reflected. If she were right, there was another hand in the game, now—men determined to sweep all the other players off the table.

They stopped at midday for a leisurely lunch; they were less than halfway to the Crescent-H, but Haggerty seemed in no hurry. The lunch didn't resemble trail fare, and Jessie wondered if the enormous roast, the baked hens, breads, pies, and bottles of wine were for her benefit or simply a reflection of Bill Haggerty's healthy appetite.

They ate in the shadow of a Crescent-H wagon, the few straggly trees offering little enough shade for stray rattlers and scorpions. Along with the wagon, Haggerty had brought five riders for the trip to and from Camp Supply. They were all armed, Jessie noted, and they kept their eyes open. It was clear enough that Haggerty and the other cattlemen in the area took the threat of raiders seriously.

"Bill," Jessie said, while making a healthy roast beef sandwich, "there's something we haven't talked about much and I guess I'm wondering why. In your letter—"

Haggerty cut her off with a look, glancing anxiously over his shoulder to see if one of the hands was around. "Sorry," he said darkly, "it's a hell of a thing, Jessie, but there's no way of telling who you can trust. I know what you're gettin' at, and there's a reason I've kept shut so far." He scowled. "I can't prove a thing, damn it. I just know it. There's outside money in this thing—foreign money, backin' up these raiders. They're after the land and they mean to have it."

"How, though? Driving all the cattlemen off the land? They've sure picked themselves a fight. There's no one more stubborn than a cowman with his temper riled. I know. I was raised by one." She grinned. "And I'm sittin' next to another."

"If that was all there was to it, you'd be right," Haggerty growled. "As smart as these raiders are, all we'd do is just sit tight and smoke 'em out." His pale eyes focused on Jessie. "I've heard things—things I can't quite figure; a word here and a word there, up in Dodge City and in Denver, from men I figure I can trust. There's people been bought off, Jessie, people in Washington and out here. Bankers. Railroad men." An angry flush turned the ruined side of his face bright scarlet. "I'm ashamed to say it aloud, but I got an idea some of the ranchers up here have got a piece of it, too—some men I been calling my friends more years than I care to count."

Jessie knew exactly what he was saying: There is more than one way to skin a cat—or grab a couple million acres of land. If the situation out here got out of hand, the cattlemen could end up the losers. The big operations already had a reputation for being greedy—a lot of that reputation was well deserved, Jessie had to admit. They didn't exactly make outsiders feel at home, and that included settlers who wanted to grow crops instead of cows.

What if Haggerty were right and her own suspicions correct? If the cartel did have a hand in this business, what better way to bring the issue to a head? Stir up enough trouble to push the cattlemen into a fight. If the cartel had bought off the right people, the cattlemen would be left out in the cold, branded as the villains once more. And once they were out of the way, the issue of untitled lands would somehow be solved very quickly. If the land came up for grabs, Jessie had no doubts at all who would end up holding the biggest pieces.

It wouldn't be the first time, she thought to herself. If there was a way to carry out such a scheme, the ruthless men she'd tangled with before would surely find it. Again, though, she had to wonder how? The cattlemen now were heroes, fighting outlaw raiders. That certainly didn't serve the cartel's interests.

Haggerty seemed to guess the subject of her thoughts. "I know why you're up here, Jessie," he said calmly. "I haven't ever asked about the men who shot your father. I won't and don't think I need to. Like I say, if a man listens, he hears things. I've heard some things about you."

"Have you, Bill?"

"Nothing I haven't forgot real quick," he said soberly. "One thing I will say: It appears to me you're your father's daughter,

45

all right." He stood and tossed out the dregs of his coffee. "Come on, I better get back on that horse 'fore I get too heavy to ride it."

The ranch house boasted a fresh coat of glistening white paint; the high clapboard walls were a luminescent orange in the setting sun. The house and most of the outbuildings were sheltered in a grove of cottonwood trees. The trees snaked down a low hill to the east and west, following the lazy curve of the Cimarron River.

Inside the house was cool, the rooms well furnished. Nearly everything looked new and Jessie suddenly remembered that this was Bill Haggerty's second home up here, that the other one had gone up in flames, his family with it. She wondered where the other house had stood. Not here, certainly, not on this site. The tall and graceful trees outside her upstairs room had been there for years.

Jessie met the Mexican household staff and pleased them at once with her fair command of their tongue. Haggerty excused himself to do ranch business and Jessie dined alone in the big dining room. She intended to wander outside and stretch her legs, but set that aside for the next day. She retired to her room.

The room was big and comfortable and had a high ceiling. Jessie turned down the kerosene lamp and perched on the side of the bed to remove her stockings and boots. Standing again, she slid the worn cotton blouse off her shoulders and pulled the snug jeans past her ankles. Crossing the room, she caught a glimpse of her naked figure in the mirror—a flash of firm, uptilted breasts; the curve of a thigh tinted gold in the soft light. She stood for a long moment at the window, staring into the night. The flat plains beyond the trees were hot and still. Heat lightning flickered to the south, a tantalizing promise of rain that would likely never appear.

A sudden weariness seemed to envelop her, a weight that threatened to bring her down. It wasn't the day's ride, she knew, or the unrelenting heat that lingered in this part of the country long after the sun disappeared. It was a weariness she carried within her, one that sleep could never cure. They were out there, somewhere, the men who had brought her to the Indian Nation. Lightning flashed again. In the sharp afterimage, she saw her father's face. She had sat beside his bed, waiting

46

for him to die, watching the life drain away from the man she'd believed would live forever.

She knew some of his story and learned the rest before he left her. A young Alex Starbuck had built a trading empire in the Pacific, helping to open the Orient to the West. There, he had come face to face with a powerful group of European traders who didn't care for the competition of an enterprising American determined to make his mark. They struck out relentlessly, sinking Alex Starbuck's ships, burning his warehouses to the ground. Starbuck was stubborn and had no intention of giving up. He struck back at once, lashed out at his foes with a fury. Men died in the war that followed. Jessie's mother, Sarah, was murdered by the Prussians, and finally Alex himself was struck down by a killer's bullet on his own Texas ranch. Jessie inherited the vast Starbuck holdings and the unending struggle against the men who were determined to take it from her. She learned soon enough that the cartel wanted a great deal more than Alex Starbuck's fortune. Their goal was nothing less than control of the United States itself, the untapped wealth of this rich, young nation.

Jessie had fought them, had taken up her father's cause. And now they're out there again. They know I'm here, and they won't leave me guessing about them for long.

Sleep didn't come quickly. She lay in her bed and watched the lightning and listened to distant thunder. Finally the storm moved on, passing by without loosing a drop of rain on the dry and thirsty land.

Jessie didn't see Bill Haggerty until just before eleven in the morning. A dark and brooding look on his scarred features, he stalked into the parlor and found her.

"I'm takin' a ride," he said abruptly. "Might be you'd like to come along. Likely, you'll learn a lot more 'bout what's going on here."

He turned and stomped off before she could answer, and Jessie followed. Four riders were waiting with Haggerty outside. They headed due south away from the ranch. The day was hot and sticky, no better and no worse than the day before.

Finally after some miles of silence, Bill Haggerty's rage subsided—enough, at least, to tell Jessie what his anger concerned.

"Rider came in early this morning," he growled. "There's

a meeting over at the Bar Double-L, Lew Lyman's place. They're goin' to talk about taking action 'gainst these raiders." He spat out the words with distaste. "You want to know what that means; it means Lew's getting itchy and wants to ride out and take a few scalps—and he doesn't much care where he gets 'em as long as it's Indian hair."

"What are you saying, Bill?" Jessie turned in the saddle and stared. "Is Lyman one of the ranchers who thinks Indians ride with the raiders?"

Haggerty forced a sour laugh. "Likely I didn't make myself clear. He's had some Cheyennes wandering north from their reservation and stealing some of his cows. A dozen cows, I guess—no more'n that. Happens all the time, but you can't start a war over that. It ain't a good thing to do. Those poor bastards get hungry like everyone else."

Jessie let out a breath. "This Lyman doesn't care if they're mixed up with the raiders or not."

"You got it straight. Oh, he'll say it's raiders he's after, but that's a lie. He got used to killing Indians in the old days an' just plain likes it."

"Good Lord! And the others, they'll listen to him?"

"Some of 'em are ready enough to listen to anybody," Haggerty told her. He squinted against the sun. "You got to remember, Jessie, a lot of these old birds are as old as I am. Isn't a one of 'em hasn't lost friends or family to the Indians."

"That works two ways!" Jessie said hotly.

"I know it does," Haggerty said flatly. "You tell these fellers 'bout loving their red brothers and forgettin' what's done—see how far you get."

At the meeting, there were nine ranchers who ran some of the biggest herds in No Man's Land and the Cherokee Strip. Their outfits were scattered along the Cimarron and the North Canadian, the Beaver Creek, Wolf Creek, and Kiowa Creek. Jessie was familiar with most of their brands, the KH, the Box-T, the Figure-4, and Anchor-D, and others. They greeted her with respect, aware that she was Alex Starbuck's daughter. They knew the Circle Star brand as well as she knew theirs. Yet Jessie sensed the restraint in their weathered faces. She was a woman, and in their minds she had no business running Alex

Starbuck's affairs. They admired her for it, but didn't entirely approve. A handsome woman ought to get herself a husband, settle down, and stay out of a man's world.

Jessie disliked Lew Lyman on sight. He was a wizened, mean-eyed man in his early sixties, a man who'd never grown out of being a bully. He scarcely acknowledged her presence and cast a sour look at Haggerty for bringing her along.

"Glad you could get here, Bill," one of the men said. "The meeting's been a little one-sided without you."

"Uh-huh, I can believe that," Haggerty said dryly. A light smattering of laughter came from the others.

Lyman showed him a lazy grin. "We got our cryin' towels out and ready, waiting for you to show."

The laughter died and Jessie could feel the sudden tension in the air. Haggerty turned on Lyman at once. "You trying to say something, Lew?" he said quietly. His words were easy, but there were sparks of fire in his eyes. He was in no mood for horseplay; Lyman didn't see this or chose to ignore it.

"Nothing, Bill, nothing at all." Lyman spread his hands. "Just figured you'd give us a little speech on the red man's plight."

"Reckon you know as much about that as I do," Haggerty said tightly.

"Well, I say we drink some of Lew's whiskey," a man broke in. "Isn't all that often he brings the good stuff out in the open."

A few men chuckled. Jessie knew the man who'd tried to break the tension between Haggerty and Lyman. She'd met him more than once with her father. His name was Art McGregor, a white-haired old cowman from the south of Texas who'd been in the cattle business as long as any man alive. He dressed like a thirty-dollar-a-month hand and could likely buy every man in the room.

A few men drifted to the crystal decanters on the table. Haggerty didn't move. He kept his eyes on Lyman.

"Lew, I know what you're trying to do," he said calmly. "You're entitled to how you feel and I wouldn't try to change a man's ways. But killin' a couple of cattle thieves isn't going to solve a damn thing and you know it."

"If you figure some better way to stop these raiders, that's fine with me," snapped Lyman.

"For God's sake, Lew," Haggerty said wearily, "half the

outlaws west of St. Louis are holed up in the Indian Nation. They steal more cattle in a week than any Indian does in a year."

"We've spotted Injuns with the raiders," said Lyman, "you can't deny that. I haven't heard anyone say they've spotted any whites."

"I've heard all that before," Haggerty growled. "Truth is, there isn't anyone I ever talked to who got close to this bunch and come out alive to say what he saw." He turned to face the others. "Hard for a dead man to recall what color the feller was that did him in."

A few men muttered agreement. Lyman colored, stood abruptly, and let his eyes sweep the room. "This the way the rest of you feel? You going to stand around and do nothing— just let these savages steal you blind and burn you out?"

For a moment no one spoke. Finally, Art McGregor broke the silence. "Lew, no one's against you on this," he said softly. "We're all in it together up here—you and me and Bill and everyone else. I've tangled with a bunch of Injuns in my time, and I don't guess I favor 'em much more than you do. But I don't see that startin' an Indian war up here's going to make things a hell of a lot better. I've got to go with Bill on that."

Most of the men in the room nodded agreement. Lew Lyman clenched his fists in anger.

"Damn. What's it going to take to wake you people up?"

"We ought to go down and talk to Lieutenant Colonel DeLong again," one man suggested. "Make him get some more troopers out here. Chasin' raiders is their job, not ours."

Lyman sneered. "Now that's a fine idea. Let's get us some more black niggers to run after the red ones!"

Several of the ranchers laughed aloud.

"Mr. Lyman, is there anyone you like?" Jessie said abruptly. She knew she ought to stay out of this, but could hold herself back no longer. "Anyone besides white men who raise cattle, I mean? Lord, mister, I'm a rancher's daughter myself. I guess I raise as much beef as any man in this room. I'm proud of what I am, I can tell you, but I don't think that makes me anything special. It doesn't give me or you or anyone else the right to go out gunning down innocent people on a hunch!"

"We aren't talking about your poor innocent redskins here, Miss Starbuck," Lyman said soberly. "We're talking about killers pure and simple. Savage thieves and murderers."

"You don't know that!" Jessie protested.

"No offense, ma'am," said one of the ranchers, "but I don't guess you've got any call to be giving out advice up here. I don't recall seein' your brand anywhere close by."

Jessie met his gaze. "You're right, mister. I apologize. You live here and I don't. That gives you a license to hunt Indians on a guess."

"Jessie—" Bill Haggerty shot her a warning glance. Jessie looked into the hard faces. There wasn't a friendly pair of eyes in the room. She flushed, swallowed her anger, stood, and picked her Stetson off the table.

"I'd say I'm sorry I interfered," she told them, "but that'd be a lie. I'm not sorry at all. Good day." She turned and stalked from the room, leaving a heavy pall of silence behind her.

They were a good half hour from the Bar Double-L before Jessie and Bill Haggerty exchanged a word. Jessie kept her eyes on the brassy sky, the low, rolling horizon. Far to the right, partially hidden in a line of scrub oak, was a small ranch house. They'd passed it on the ride out. Cattle bunched up in the trees. Jessie guessed there was water there.

"Wasn't a real good idea," Haggerty muttered finally. "Don't guess I have to tell you that."

"I've got a big mouth. I'm sorry. I shouldn't have said anything at all."

"You said a couple of things needed saying—which isn't exactly the point."

"I know the point," Jessie said bitterly. "I'm a woman. I don't know my place."

"That's some of it, yeah. You know it better'n me. Rest of it is you don't belong up here. They don't all agree with Lew Lyman, Jessie, but he's one of 'em. You faced him down in his own home and they didn't much care for that. It's okay for me to spout off. I'm the local Indian lover, but I'm a neighbor as well. You're not."

Jessie turned in the saddle to face him. "Bill, I'm really sorry. I'm your guest and I shamed you in front of your friends. I had no right to do that."

"You're forgiven," he said.

"And you're a generous man. So what happened in there after I stomped out?"

"Nothing that hasn't happened before. Me and Art McGregor convinced 'em to hold off doing anything rash for a week. Meantime, we'll send another committee down to Camp

Supply to raise hell with DeLong." He gave her a grim look. "Lot of good it'll do. Those troopers are good and they can fight—if DeLong would ever give them a chance."

"And what does that mean?"

"Means he likes to sit on his—likes to sit in his chair and keep his troops out of trouble. Any action they might run into messes up his records. And interferes with his drinking."

"Oh, I see."

"It's a bad situation, but Camp Supply's the closest post we've got. Fort Reno's too far, and the raiders stay pretty clear of th—"

Haggerty's words were lost as the sharp, flat crack of a rifle rolled over the plains. Startled, Jessie turned, heard a man cry out, and saw one of Haggerty's riders spill from his saddle. She grabbed for her Colt and wrenched it free as a second shot followed on the heels of the first. Her mount shuddered beneath her, dropped on its forelegs, and sent her sprawling. She hit hard and rolled, then raised herself on her hands and saw the horsemen atop the low hill to the west . . .

★

Chapter 7

Jessie came to her knees, leveled the pistol, and loosed three shots at the raiders. Too far. Haggerty's men returned fire; the horsemen answered with a quick, ragged volley, then jerked their reins, and fled. Bill Haggerty cursed, slid out of the saddle, and followed the riders with his rifle. Spent shells flew from his Winchester. The riders vanished.

"Damn murderin' bastards!" Haggerty bellowed. "Jack, get on their tail. Don't do something stupid; just try to stay with 'em." He glanced at Jessie and past her to the fallen mount. "You all right?"

"Yeah, fine," Jessie said shakily.

Haggerty turned over his shoulder. "Who is it got hit? He okay?"

"He's dead, Mr. Haggerty," a hand called out. "Got it right in the chest."

"Oh, Lord!" Haggerty's face screwed up in pain. He clenched his fists and walked a few paces to bend over the fallen man. Jessie raised a hand to her cheek. The boy was no more than seventeen. He lay on his back, looking straight up at the sky. He didn't look hurt at all. One of the cowhands closed his eyes, took off his own denim jacket, and laid it gently over the still face. Another man picked up the boy's hat and turned it over in his hands, not sure what to do next.

"Dick, you get a good look at them?" asked Haggerty. His eyes were as hard as glass.

"Yes, sir, I did," the man answered. "They were Injuns, near as I could tell. I'd say ten, maybe a dozen."

"That's what I saw, too," Haggerty said darkly. He shot Jessie a questioning look. Jessie nodded and looked away.

"Damn it, I'd rather eat dirt than be right about this, but I can't shut out what I saw."

"Bill, look over there!" Jessie drew in a breath and pointed to the west. A pall of dirty smoke rose straight toward the sky on the still air.

53

"It's Zack Hardy's place," Haggerty said grimly. "Had an idea that's where they were coming from. We best get on over. I'm not real anxious to see what we're goin' to find."

Jessie rode double behind Dick Robbins. Another hand, Marcus, trailed behind, leading the dead man who was draped over the saddle of his horse. At the crest of the small rise, Haggerty suddenly signaled them to stop, leaned forward, then kicked his mount hard. For a moment, he vanished in the grass. When the others caught up, he was on the ground squatting by a body in a shallow ravine.

"Got one of the bastards," he said without looking up. "Didn't think I even came close."

Jessie felt a chill as Haggerty straightened and she saw the Indian at his feet. His face was covered with blood; one arm and a leg were twisted awkwardly under his body. Black hair was parted in the center of his head and braided on either side in dirty red twists of cloth.

"Comanche, looks like," Marcus said idly.

"That's what he is," Haggerty agreed. His shoulders seemed to sag. "Get off and let's haul him to Zack's place." He shook his head with regret. "Lew Lyman's goin' to love this. Me gunning down all the evidence he needs with a lucky shot." He kicked angrily at the ground and then hauled himself back in the saddle.

It seemed only moments before that Jessie had glanced out over the prairie and seen the small ranch house as they passed, the white structure somewhat hidden in the dusty, green canopy of oak. She realized with a start that she must have been looking right at it while the raiders were there, seconds before they'd fired it. The Indians had likely spotted them riding by and then hurried up the rise to see where they were headed, maybe thinking about adding a few more whites to the score.

The house was burning with a fury, so hot they couldn't get near it. Flames licked at the trees, the dry branches popping with small explosions. Zack Hardy was in the yard, his throat cut from one ear to the other. If he'd had any weapon, the raiders had taken it or kicked it aside. His wife was in a gully by the barn. Bill Haggerty tried to stand in Jessie's way when they found her, but Jessie edged him aside, and bile rose to her throat at the sight. She clenched her teeth in anger, fighting back a low cry of sorrow. They'd pulled up her skirts, but hadn't had time enough to rape her. One shoe was gone. Her legs were caked with dust and her face was twisted in fear. Someone had stabbed her in the chest and the belly a dozen times. More than enough, thought Jessie. She was barely in her twenties, a blond girl with an angular face and a strong jaw. Except for the spreading red stain, the bright blue calico dress was perfectly clean.

"They've only been out here 'bout a year," Haggerty said distantly. "Ran a small herd, nothing much. They were good people. Come from Amarillo, I think."

"Bill," Jessie said, "the other ranches, the wagons that have been hit, is this the way the raiders have struck before?"

Haggerty squinted and then understanding crossed his features. "You mean cuttin' people up, don't you? No, it's not usual, far as I know. They likely spotted us coming 'bout the same time they got here. Didn't want to make any noise, so they used a knife."

Dick and Marcus had covered the two bodies. Jessie wiped a hand across her face. "If they hadn't fired on us, we would never have seen them at all. We might have spotted the smoke, if anyone happened to look back. The raiders would have been miles away by then. Why would they do that, Bill? It doesn't make sense."

"Damn if I know!" Haggerty flared. He blew out a breath and closed his eyes. "I'm sorry. That wasn't meant for you, Jessie."

"I know."

Haggerty stretched, wringing the tension out of his bones. "I don't have an answer to your question. Maybe the sons of bitches didn't get enough killing. I don't know. Lots of things I don't know anymore." He looked off to the north. "I had supper with Zack and Mary Ann not two weeks past. He shook his head and smiled sadly at something remembered. "That Indian I shot—Jessie, I've had me some good times in Comanche camps. I could ride right in and sit when the Comanches were killin' every white man they set eyes on. Might be I knew this boy's folks. Hell's fire, I don't like this business."

The fire burned through the grove and died out, stopping at a broad, shallow creek behind the house. It was hard to tell the charred timbers of the house and the barn from the blackened trees. Dick and Marcus found shovels outside the burned barn and buried the Hardys and the boy, Mack Turner, near the creek. Haggerty had them plant the Indian downstream. There was nothing else to be done. Haggerty said that when he got back to the ranch he'd send someone to look after the small herd and write a letter to someone he knew in Amarillo and see if there was any family there. He recalled Mrs. Hardy had said something about a sister, but he had no idea where she lived.

Late in the afternoon, Dick yelled and said riders were coming from the north. Haggerty, Jessie, and Marcus took the horses and walked them quickly down a ravine east of the grove, weapons at the ready. From the dust the mounts were raising, it was clear plenty of riders were in the party—far too many if they weren't friendly.

In a moment, Marcus stood with a nervous little grin and lowered his rifle. "It's all right," he said. "They're white."

"Isn't all right with me." Haggerty frowned once he got a look at the bunch.

Lew Lyman slid out of the saddle, glanced soberly at the house and the barn, and walked to Haggerty and Jessie. There were twenty men with him, hands from the Bar Double-L, and two ranchers from the meeting and their men.

"Zack and his wife?" asked Lyman.

"Both of them," grunted Haggerty. He stuck out his jaw and looked straight at the other man. "Guess I owe you some kind of apology. They were Indians, Lew. Comanches. I downed one of 'em."

"Christ!" Lyman looked startled. He glanced at Haggerty and Jessie and frowned. If he felt any pleasure in being right, he didn't show it.

"Miles and Yancy were leaving my place," he said. "They saw smoke and came back for me. You bury 'em?"

"Down by the creek."

"Where's the Injun?"

"In the ground. Up past the others."

"Sorry you did that. Like to see what he looked like."

"He looks like an Indian, Lew," Haggerty said testily. "You seen one before, I expect."

Lyman colored. "Whatever you're thinking, Bill, I'm not any happier about this than you are. We got three people dead. I take no satisfaction in that."

"Hell, I know you don't."

"The only good that comes of this is we know where we

stand now. We don't have to stumble around in the dark anymore, wondering who we're after."

Jessie caught the fierce light in Lyman's eyes. A chill touched the back of her neck. "Just what do you plan on doing, Mr. Lyman?" she asked flatly. "You mind me asking?"

Lyman looked at her. "I plan on putting a stop to this burning and killing, Miss Starbuck. You have any objection to that?"

"That's not what I was asking. I think you know that."

Lyman turned to Haggerty, deliberately leaving Jessie to look at his back. "I'll be getting word out to everyone I can reach. We'll meet at my place, say, day after tomorrow 'bout noon. That ought to be time enough to gather the men we need. I'm asking for every spare hand who knows the right end of a gun. I expect to see you there, Bill." He touched his hat and stalked off. Bill Haggerty stared at the ground. The two cowmen who'd ridden in with Lyman, Miles and Yancy, were walking back up from the creek. Lyman called out and stopped them. In a moment, Yancy motioned two of his hands over. The men listened and left.

"My God, Bill," said Jessie, "you know what he's going to do. If someone doesn't stop him, he'll start a blood bath right here in the Indian Nation!"

Haggerty gave her a bleary look. Jessie thought he'd aged a good ten years in the last five minutes. "I could put a bullet in his head," he said darkly. "Might slow him down some. Wouldn't stop the others."

"The first Indian he runs into is going to be one of the raiders—as far as Lyman's concerned," Jessie said hotly. "He's not going to stop and ask. Bill, we can't just sit here and—"

Haggerty's fingers closed on Jessie's arm. Jessie winced, then followed the direction of his eyes. The two hands Yancy had sent off came thrashing through the grove on horseback, whooping and waving their hands and dragging a taut rope between them. Each end of the rope was tied to one of the dead Comanche's legs. The riders dragged him out of the trees and into the Hardys' front yard and started trotting their mounts around in a circle.

"It's startin'," Haggerty said grimly. "Damn, it's startin'."

★

Chapter 8

Ki crossed the hot parade ground from the headquarters building to the supply room, giving serious thought to strangling First Lieutenant Jake Wallace. The portly officer was driving him crazy. The less he had to do, the more he wanted Ki to help him do it. After winding up the vital task of counting all the saddles on the post, Wallace, acting upon the suggestion of Sergeant Major McPherson, had decided to survey the timbered walls of the fort. The project seemed to delight him. Papers began to cover the walls of his office. With a feverish gleam in his eyes, Wallace explained to Ki how each individual timber pole would be graded according to straightness, height, and degree of decay. This information would by duly recorded, along with accompanying charts and notes, the whole making up a report that he would forward to Lieutenant Colonel DeLong. Ki knew that DeLong would never see this report, that Sergeant McPherson would toss it in the trash along with the recently completed saddle report, and then think of something else for Wallace to do. That nothing ever came of these projects didn't seem to bother Wallace at all. Putting them together was what he liked. Ki had to admire McPherson. He had an endless list of new ideas. It seemed like a hell of a way to run an army.

It was getting a little harder every day to keep Wallace out of his hair. The first lieutenant complained that he was never around; the eagle-eyed McPherson, who knew everything that happened on the post, was getting suspicious as well. He knew Ki was up to something, that his wanderings had little to do with the walls of the fort. Ki sensed it wouldn't be long before McPherson asked him what the hell was going on.

Ki was more than a little concerned. He had overheard the conversation in the alley Sunday night. On Monday, Jessie had ridden in and then left with Bill Haggerty. Ki had had no chance to talk to her at all. All that day and the next two he'd spent avoiding Jake Wallace and trying to track down the officer he'd

58

heard in the settlement. So far, he'd come up with exactly nothing. Where the hell was the man? He'd stolen a roster from McPherson's desk and gone completely down the list. The voice he'd heard didn't belong to any officer at Camp Supply and that made no sense at all. There was no mistaking the silhouette he'd seen. If Ki were right, where was he? It was Thursday morning now and he was no closer to an answer than he'd been in that alley Sunday night.

His other task, learning what shipments came in and out of the camp, presented no problems at all. McPherson kept an up-to-date list and made no effort to hide it. The only question concerned which item the inside contact was smuggling out to the raiders. Ki had no idea. Rifles? Powder? Ammunition? The whole business was beginning to get on his nerves. The answer was right there under his nose. All he had to do was find it.

Pulling a stub of pencil and a piece of paper from his pocket, Ki decided to check out the walls behind the stables while he was close. He could write up some kind of nonsense; Wallace would think he was working and maybe leave him alone a few hours.

"Josh—Josh Stewart!"

Ki stopped in his tracks and peered into the darkened horse stall. A girl stuck her face into the light and frantically motioned him in.

Oh Lord, Ki moaned to himself, this is all I need. He glanced nervously over his shoulder and ducked inside. Mindy DeLong came quickly into his arms, grinding her slender body against his and planting a wet kiss on his mouth.

"For God's sake, girl!" Ki grabbed her shoulders and held her away. "Are you plain crazy or what? You tryin' to get me shot?"

Mindy showed him a pout. "You're angry with me, aren't you? Bet you didn't even miss me at all."

"I'm not mad and I missed you," he said shortly. "I'm just a little concerned, is all."

"Goodness. About what?"

Ki looked at the dark ceiling. "Well, it might have something to do with walking down by the river with this girl who told me her name was Amy."

"Well I had to do that," she protested. "My gracious, you wouldn't have loved me up if you'd known who I was, now would you have?"

"You've got that right," Ki said soberly.

"See? I told you so. Lord, I been hot for you. You just don't know. I haven't hardly been able to eat. Do you know how much I want that thing of yours between my legs? Oh, Josh!"

Ki jumped as her hands found his crotch. He jerked her fingers away. "Now, look, Amy—Mindy. There isn't anything I'd rather do than—here, stop that!" He grabbed her hands again as she gathered her skirts and started hiking them to her waist. Mindy giggled, guiltily pressing a hand to her mouth. Ki felt his stomach go taut. He left her and peered into the dark passage between the stalls. Troopers were in and out of the stables all day. If no one had heard them, it was a wonder.

"Mindy," he said, facing her again, "I am not going to make love to you right here in the middle of Camp Supply in broad daylight. All right? It's out of the question."

"Will you meet me down at the river?"

"Yes. Okay."

"Honest?"

"Of course, I will." The look in her eyes said any other answer would be a mistake. He had never been scared of a woman, but he was plain frightened of this one.

"You'd better," she warned him. "You don't and I'll—I'll go find someone who will. I'll go poking around in alleys in the dark. You said you didn't want me doing that, remember?"

"Certainly I remember," he said calmly. "That's a dangerous thing to do."

"I don't do it a lot," she sighed. "I just get this—you know, kind of tingly feeling down there and I got to do something."

Ki swallowed hard. She was standing alarmingly close and he could smell the sharp scent of her arousal. "Mindy, you— Meeting men from the fort isn't a real good idea. They've got to know who you are. You live right here."

Mindy frowned and bit her lip. "Oh, I don't do it much with the men from Camp Supply," she said blandly. "Just a few now and then. Usually it's fellas who work for one of the cattle outfits. Besides," she said slyly, touching a finger to Ki's lips, "you don't think one of my father's officers is going to tell anyone, do you?"

"No, no, I suppose not," Ki said dryly. "I know I sure as hell wouldn't."

"Well, see?" She stretched up her toes and kissed him again.

"Good-bye. You be there, hear?"

Ki watched her disappear down the dark passage. The mounts shuffled nervously as she passed. Ki didn't blame them at all.

Straightening his shirt, he walked back into the bright light, trying to look as if he had urgent business in the stable. He could feel the sting of sweat on his face and knew it had nothing to do with the heat. The girl didn't have the good sense God gave a duck. Loving her was a pleasure, but it didn't seem all that exciting at the moment. And if he didn't show up at the river, then what? He didn't want to think about that. With a girl like Mindy DeLong, you couldn't tell what she might do.

Ki snapped a hurried salute as Captain Heywood Street stalked by. He was clearly in a hurry and hardly noticed Ki at all. Even the scowl that he wore as a permanent fixture was taking a rest.

Street had ridden in Monday from the site of the raid to the south, ahead of the supply train he'd led from Fort Worth. Ki knew Jessie had come in with his detachment and that Street had complained long and loud about her presence. Matt Bilder had pegged the man right. He was brutal and uncaring; the troopers despised and feared him, and the other officers would have nothing to do with him. The first time he'd run into Ki, he'd braced him at attention and chewed him out for a good ten minutes—for no reason at all, strictly for the pleasure. Ki had seen his wife from a distance—a scrawny, sad-eyed woman, the trace of her former beauty following her about like a shadow.

Ki left the stables behind, forgetting his good intentions. After Mindy DeLong, he'd lost all interest in counting timber. Stepping past the corner of the stables, he stopped and looked curiously at the parade ground. Something was up. Street wasn't the only man on the post in a hurry. Officers and men alike were scurrying like ants. He caught Matt Bilder's eye as the man came out of headquarters and Bilder hurried over.

"What's up," Ki asked, "we going to war or what?"

"That's close," Bilder said shortly. He jerked his head over his shoulder. "Rider came in from Haggerty's place. The raiders hit up south of the Cimarron yesterday afternoon. They killed a man and his wife and burned them out. Bill Haggerty was right close by and saw 'em. Had that pretty lady we met with him. Jessie Starbuck."

"What?" Ki stared. "Was—was anyone hurt?"

Bilder gave him an irritated look. "Didn't you hear me? Two people got killed. And Haggerty lost a man in the fight. You said a war and you're 'bout right. Haggerty and his crew exchanged fire with the bastards and Haggerty brought one down. Turns out he was a Comanche. I wouldn't believe it if it wasn't Bill Haggerty who saw it—and there's a body to prove it besides. I'd have sworn it was whites behind this business, Josh. Indians just don't figure. I can't buy it."

"I'll be damned." Ki found it hard to believe as well, especially knowing what he knew. Had he stumbled onto something that had nothing to do with the raiders in that alley? That didn't seem likely. But neither did Indians and whites working together.

Bilder let out a breath. "DeLong's goin' to have to get off his ass and play soldier and he's mad as hell about that. The rider who came in said Lew Lyman from the Bar Double-L is getting up an army of cattlemen to go out and kill Indians. Just what we need right now. And if that isn't plenty, I'll bet anything that the Light Horse is going to be buzzing around here like hornets any minute. The shit's going to fly, you wait and see if it doesn't."

"I won't argue that," said Ki. He knew all about the Light Horse. He had seen some of their riders outside the fort the day before. They were good men, sharp as they could be. Some tribes had their own law and their own courts in the Indian Nation and protected their territory with mounted troopers. The Light Horse knew its business, but their job was to police their own people—not fight the white man. Ki wondered what would happen if the ranchers' vigilantes ran into the Light Horse. He had seen mobs before and could make a good guess. An Indian was an Indian if you were looking for blood. If that happened, and something like it would sooner or later . . . Ki repressed a shudder. There were about thirty tribes in the Nation. They didn't all like each other, but none of them had any love for the race that had taken away their lands and jammed them all together between Kansas and the Red River.

Someone called out to Bilder who nodded to Ki and then hurried off to the front gate of the fort. Ki watched him a moment. Then he joined the stream of officers and men running in and out of the headquarters building. He was no longer worried about avoiding Jake Wallace. No one in Camp Supply was going to be counting timber that afternoon.

Camp Supply turned from a sleepy outpost to a bristling frontier fortress in a matter of moments. Lookouts manned the battlements and cannon were brought to the ready. A steady stream of mounted troopers galloped in and out of the main gate.

Rumors spread like a prairie fire through the settlement outside the walls. A thousand Cheyenne and Arapaho warriors had broken out of their reservations and slaughtered every man, woman, and child in Fort Reno to the south. Another thousand, maybe two or three, were headed for Camp Supply that very moment. The Kiowa and Comanche held Fort Sill in a state of siege. In less than an hour, Ki heard supposed news about the ravages of nearly every tribe in the Indian Nation. The latest, absolutely verified story was that the five tribes had taken command of the rebellion—it wasn't a pack of raiders, but a war—blockaded the railroads that ran through Choctaw and Cherokee lands, and were riding on Fort Smith, Arkansas with ten thousand warriors.

The idea of the Indians putting together any such organized campaigns—overnight at that—was ludicrous to anyone who knew anything at all about the tribes within the nation. The Comanches and Kiowas hated the Arapahoes and Cheyennes; the Pawnees remembered they had once been the most powerful tribe on the prairie and resented the Cherokees and nearly everyone else who had crowded them into a corner. The list of grievances was endless. More than that, Ki knew, each tribe contained smaller tribes and clans within it, and each small tribe had a chief who wouldn't give the time of day to other chiefs. The Choctaws, Cherokees, Seminoles, Creeks, and Chickasaws felt the whole Indian Nation belonged to them and looked upon all others as intruders, loftily setting them aside as the "wild tribes."

The people in the settlement and in the surrounding country-side weren't interested in facts. They were convinced an Indian uprising was underway and they wanted to know exactly what the U.S. Army was going to do to protect them. Some packed their belongings and headed north to Kansas. Others crowded the walls of Camp Supply and demanded sanctuary. Some people noticed that the friendly Indians who ordinarily camped around the fort had suddenly vanished, and they took this as a sure sign the rumors they heard were true. Old-timers in and out of the fort knew the Indians weren't fools and had wisely taken off for other parts.

Ki saw Jessie ride in the main gate with Bill Haggerty and a number of his men at three that afternoon. He had just gotten word that he was assigned to lead a reserve platoon, which might or might not take to the field. He wondered whose warped idea this sudden rise to command might be and guessed Sergeant Major McPherson.

Ki stalked over at once and took the reins from Jessie and Haggerty.

"Thank you," Haggerty said gruffly, letting Ki know he hadn't forgotten he didn't like him. He eased himself ponderously out of the saddle and brushed off his coat. Jessie slid down and flashed Ki a smile.

"Glad to see you're safe, ma'am," Ki said. "Looks like we might be in for some rough times."

"That might well be. Josh Stewart, isn't it? Did I get that right?"

"Yes, ma'am," Ki said without expression, "that's it."

Matt Bilder waved from the front steps of headquarters and took long strides over the parade ground to join them.

"Bad business, Bill," he told Haggerty, "the lieutenant colonel will be glad to know you're here. He's anxious to hear what really happened up there."

"The man I sent likely said all there was to say," Haggerty said soberly. "He was there."

"Miss Jessie, pleased to see you again," said Bilder. He touched his hat and grinned, holding Jessie's gaze and clearly trying to think of something to say she'd find of interest. "Well, then," he stammered finally, "if you folks would like to get in out of the sun, I'll see if I can't drum up somethin' cool to drink."

"That would be nice, Mr. Bilder." Jessie returned his smile.

"Matt," Haggerty broke in, "what's DeLong doing 'bout this, too much or too little?"

Bilder nodded understanding. "Sort of sittin' on the fence," he said wryly. "Sending out a lot of patrols and flying the colors."

"That figures," Haggerty muttered. "Guess we ought to be grateful, considering. You know about Lew Lyman, I reckon."

"I heard."

"Anyone spotted these raiders anywhere else?"

"Lot of wild stories. None of 'em true."

"Uh-huh." Haggerty ran a hand across his face. "One of my boys followed them far as he could before he lost them. Took off north, then doubled back. Might've got past Kiowa Creek and down into Texas. Not much telling."

Bilder turned and looked over his shoulder as someone shouted his name. Captain Street stood on the front steps of headquarters, gesturing him forward and studiously avoiding Jessie's eye.

"Guess the lieutenant colonel's ready to talk," said Bilder. "Josh, look after Miss Jessie here, if you will. But not too much, all right?" He grinned at Jessie again, touched Haggerty's arm, and guided him toward the building.

Ki waited a moment and then grinned crookedly at Jessie. "Looks like you got yourself an admirer."

"Looks that way," said Jessie. "So how's army life treating you, Lieutenant Stewart?"

"I'm glad to see you," Ki said dryly. "Don't go spoiling our reunion."

Jessie laughed. "Are you all right? Been in any more fights? I've been dying to ask you if you'll stop that grinning. Come on, we can get a little shade by the stables."

He ran quickly through what he'd learned, not certain how much time they'd have to talk. He told her about his encounter in the alley, leaving out the more personal segments of his meeting with Mindy DeLong. When he was finished, Jessie frowned and bit her lip.

"And you haven't been able to track this officer down? You don't have any idea who he is?"

"Not even a guess. It doesn't make sense. He's got to be here, but he's not. Now all this . . ." He shook his head. "Matt Bilder knows as much about the tribes in the Indian Nation as anyone around. He doesn't go for this idea of the raiders turning out to be Indians. Says it doesn't figure at all."

"I can't agree more," said Jessie. "And Bill Haggerty feels the same way. Only there's no denying what happened at the Hardy house. I was there, Ki. I saw the Indians, including the one Bill shot." A cloud crossed her features. "I also saw what they left behind."

"So what do we have here—a coincidence or what? A party of renegade Comanches that just happens to act like raiders? Those two I overheard in the alley, Jessie . . . I could have stumbled across something else, but I don't believe it for a minute. That was raider business I heard."

Jessie let out a breath. "You're right, of course. We've got more coincidences around here than I care to swallow. You want to add one more to the list you can put down the business with Lew Lyman. We're riding back from a meeting where Lyman's doing his damndest to convince all the ranchers to ride out after the Indians—and what do you know? Comanche raiders, just like that."

Ki gave her a startled look. "Are you saying maybe Lyman's mixed up with the raiders? Is that what you think?"

Jessie made a noise in her throat. "The Indian hater working with the raiders who can't be Indians because they couldn't handle this kind of thing? Only they are? I don't know what I'm saying, Ki. Not really. And it isn't going to matter what I think or you think, if your friend Matt Bilder and Bill Haggerty can't talk that lieutenant colonel in there into doing something fast—before Lyman and his bunch start an Indian war."

"If DeLong makes a decision that doesn't have something to do with pulling corks, I want to see it," Ki said woodenly.

"Bill said he was a drinker. He's really that bad?"

"I haven't heard any different. Every trooper in camp knows th—" Ki stopped as a ragged cheer went up from the soldiers by the gate. As he turned, the gates opened and a cavalry patrol rode in, blue uniforms sweat-stained and red with dust. In the center of the riders, three Indians staggered along on foot. Their hands were manacled to a single length of chain that led to a mounted trooper. The men cheered again, and the trooper with the chain flushed with pleasure, kicked his mount, and sent his captives sprawling headlong to the ground. The men laughed and jeered. One walked boldly forward and kicked an Indian soundly in the leg. The Indian lost his footing and fell to his knees, brought himself erect, and faced his tormenter squarely, holding himself proud as if he dared the man to touch him again. The trooper looked at him, startled. A peculiar expression crossed his features and he covered his confusion with a laugh and stepped away. The Indian turned aside in disdain and an instant later the mounted trooper jerked his chain again and brought his captives past the gate.

"I knew it," Ki said soberly. "Now we got real live prisoners to kick around."

"Ki, I know that man," Jessie said in a wonder. "He's a Kiowa and his name's White Bull. I saw him on the cattle drive!" Her fingers tightened on Ki's arm; she turned and stared at headquarters, thinking at once of Captain Heywood Street inside. "My God," she said under her breath, "of all the places that Indian could be, why did he have to show up here?"

66

★

Chapter 9

Word of the Indians spread quickly about the fort. Before Jessie and Ki could cross the parade ground, off-duty troopers and every civilian on the post swarmed around the captives. Ki edged his way through, making a path for Jessie. An officer whom he knew made way when he saw that Ki was with the beauty every man at Camp Supply wanted to meet.

"They're saying there were maybe three hundred more with this bunch, but they got away," the sandy-haired officer told Jessie. "What do you think of that, ma'am?"

"If I believed it," Jessie said dryly, "I'd say the men on this patrol are real lucky to still have their hides."

The officer flushed and looked disappointed. He hadn't thought of that.

"Uh-oh, here comes trouble," Jessie told Ki.

Ki followed her glance and saw the crowd part to let Captain Heywood Street and Lieutenant Colonel DeLong through. DeLong glanced at the Indians and frowned. Street's gaze flicked over the scene and came to rest on White Bull. Jessie caught the surprise of recognition, the dark flash of pleasure in Street's eyes.

"Well, now, what do we have here? *Sergeant!*"

"Yes, sir!" The tall, black sergeant in charge of the patrol stepped forward and went rigid. Street absently acknowledged his salute.

"Where did you find these Injuns?" asked Street. "Give me a full report."

"Sir," the sergeant said stiffly, "southwest of here on Wolf Creek."

Street looked annoyed. "And they just walked up and surrendered? Is that it?"

"No, sir!" the sergeant bawled. "They had a camp, sir. Got up and rode out when they saw us. Trooper Baxter shot the

67

horse out from under the boy there. The other two stopped to help him 'stead of running."

"The noble savage, eh?" Street looked amused.

For the first time, Jessie recognized one of the other two Kiowas. The boy the sergeant was referring to was the one who'd ridden into the cattle camp with White Bull. He'd looked frightened then. Now he just looked sullen and angry. The other Indian was thick-bodied, shorter than White Bull, and a great deal older.

Street took a step forward, studied White Bull a long moment, and smiled. "Injun, you're about a hundred miles from your reservation. You don't belong here." His smile vanished and the cords in his neck went stiff. "Where are the murdering bastards you ride with?" he snapped. "Where are they? By God, you'll tell me or I will have your filthy tongue torn out!"

White Bull's expression didn't change. Matt Bilder was standing next to DeLong and Bill Haggerty. "He's a Kiowa," Bilder said evenly. "The raiders were Comanches."

Street gave him a harsh, bitter laugh. "Don't play me for a fool, Bilder. You know better than that and so do I. The Comanches and Kiowas are thick as fleas. Besides, I never saw one Injun any different from another."

Ki glanced at the black troopers around him. Each kept his feelings to himself except Sergeant Major McPherson. His expression didn't change, but his eyes narrowed slightly and darted in Street's direction.

Street stepped back and spoke quickly to DeLong. Whatever he said, DeLong appeared to agree. Street nodded curtly at McPherson.

"Lock these prisoners up, sergeant. I'll see to them later." Street glared at the crowd and touched his mustache. "Get about your business," he said sharply, "there's nothing more to see." He turned abruptly and followed DeLong back to the building. Bill Haggerty joined them, but Bilder stayed behind. Jessie caught White Bull's eye as he passed and she was certain he knew who she was.

"What's going to happen to them?" Jessie asked Matt as he walked up. She watched the captives until they vanished past the corner of the stable and then nervously chewed at her lip. "Maybe I don't want to ask that question."

"Might be you don't," said Bilder. "With Street and De-Long, you've got maybe two of the biggest Indian haters in the U.S. Army. Those poor devils got no idea what a bad idea it was pitchin' camp down on Wolf Creek."

"One of them does," Jessie said evenly. Bilder gave her a curious look and she explained, telling him how White Bull had stood up to Street down on the Red.

"Oh, Lord." Bilder flinched in pain. "That about says it. Street'll have their hides."

"After a fair and impartial review of the facts, of course," Ki said wryly.

"Oh well, sure. By the book."

"Stewart! Over here on the double!"

Ki groaned and looked at the sky. Jake Wallace was scowling at him from the steps of the headquarters building.

"Important army business," Ki said darkly. "Guess I'll see you folks later." He turned and stalked off.

Bilder grinned after him. "Poor ol' Josh. That tub of lard's going to drive him plain crazy."

"He seems very nice," Jessie said idly.

"Who, Josh?" Bilder winked. "Yeah, he's a real fine fella, all right. Good friend of mine." He paused, then, frowning in deep thought. "Course I wouldn't want you to take this wrong or anything. I mean, Josh bein' a friend and all."

"Yes, Mr. Bilder?"

"Well, it's just he seems inclined to trouble, if you get what I mean."

"No, I'm not sure that I do."

"Fighting, ma'am," said Bilder. "Can't say for sure, but he might be a drinkin' man as well."

"Oh, I see."

"That doesn't mean he's not the salt of the earth," Bilder added quickly.

"And a good friend of yours."

"Absolutely. Yes, ma'am. That's it exactly."

Jessie made an effort to hold her somber expression. "Thank you for your concern," she said. "I will surely take care, Mr. Bilder."

"Well, that's fine. Now, if there's a way I can be of service while you're here, you just let me know what I can do, Miss Jessie." He showed Jessie a broad, friendly grin.

Jessie returned the smile. "Well, there is one thing," she said, "if it's not too much trouble."

"Just ask it, that's all," Bilder said eagerly.

"I would like very much to talk to that Indian."

"Huh?" Bilder's smile vanished. "By talkin' to him you mean—"

"I mean I want to talk to him, Mr. Bilder. I want to ask him a few questions."

"What for?"

"Could you do it? You're the expert on Indians around here. You have a perfectly good reason, seems to me."

Bilder looked pained. "Yeah, I guess I do. 'Course Heywood Street'll have my hide."

"Oh, well, then," Jessie said, "I wouldn't want that. I shouldn't have even asked."

"Just a minute," Bilder said quickly. "You're right. There isn't any reason I shouldn't try to find out all I can from these Indian raiders."

Jessie smiled. "Seems to me there's every reason you should."

"Sure sounds reasonable." Bilder cleared his throat. "Lot better'n it's going to sound when Street and the lieutenant colonel get wind of it."

Jessie rested a hand on his arm. "You don't think these Kiowas are involved with the raiders in any way at all, do you, Mr. Bilder?"

"'Course they're not," Bilder snorted. "Only thing those three are guilty of is jumpin' the reservation. I used to hang around down at Fort Sill near where the Kiowas and Comanches live. They get itchy and run off all the time."

"And the others? What about them?"

"What others?"

"The Indians who murdered the Hardy family."

Bilder shook his head. "You were there," he said plainly, "you'd know more 'bout that than I would."

"That isn't answering my question and you know it," Jessie insisted. "I saw a bunch of live Comanches and I saw one dead. There's no denying that. I am asking you what you think, Mr. Bilder."

Bilder looked at his boots. "I think something's real peculiar about this whole damn business," he said flatly. "I just don't happen to know what it is."

"Thank you," said Jessie. "That's what I want to know. Now let's go get ourselves in trouble."

The guard didn't like the idea at all. Matt Bilder gave a good imitation of a man exploding with anger and said he didn't give a damn what a U.S. Army trooper might like or not like. The guard knew who Bilder was—that Bilder went in and out of the lieutenant colonel's office all the time and that he, himself, didn't share that privilege. Backing down seemed the sensible thing to do.

The small, stone building was dark and stifling hot. Jessie nearly choked on the smell. The guard led them to a thick, wooden door and Bilder told him to leave. Through a small opening Jessie could see the three Indians inside, all sitting against the far wall. They looked up at once and met her eyes.

"White Bull, I'm Matt Bilder," the scout said. "Maybe you don't know me, but you likely know who I am."

"I know who you are," White Bull said without expression. "You hunt Indians for the yellow legs."

Jessie was surprised. When she'd seen him before, the Indian hadn't acted as if he knew much English.

"You're mistaken," Bilder said flatly. "I don't hunt Indians and never have."

"Yes, I see," White Bull said. "You look like a wolf. You live with the wolves. But you yourself are not a wolf."

Bilder gave Jessie a look. "White Bull, why don't you and me insult each other some other time? There's a lady here who wants to say something to you, so I'll just step out of the way." He leaned against the wall, pulled his hat down over his brow, and started building a smoke.

"White Bull," said Jessie, "my name is Jessie Starbuck. I know you remember me. I'm a friend of Charlie Morgan's. I was there when you and the boy here cut your steers out of the herd."

White Bull regarded her a long moment. "What do you want of me, woman?"

"I want to tell you something, first. I know you've done nothing wrong. I know you shouldn't be in here."

White Bull almost smiled. "Why should we waste time in talk? Both of us know the same things."

Jessie felt a hot flush of anger and realized he was right. White Bull was an Indian—no one had to tell him why he was jailed.

"White Bull," she began, "yesterday a band of Comanches killed a man and his wife near here. I was there. I saw them. I saw the body of one of the men who took part in the raid. The army thinks you and your friends are part of that group. I know this isn't so, but—"

71

"No, this is a lie!" For the first time, the Indian showed his feelings. He came to his feet and crossed the small cell. "There are no Comanches doing such a thing. If there were, I would know it."

Jessie could see the white anger in his eyes. She nearly stepped back from under his gaze, but managed to hold her ground. "I wouldn't expect you to trust the army," she said firmly. "I understand that. I have no reason to lie to you, White Bull. I saw what I told you. Look at me and know that I'm telling you the truth."

For an instant the Indian's dark eyes wavered. Jessie saw confusion and hesitation; the moment passed quickly, but she knew she'd made her point.

"This could not be," he said haughtily, shaking his head with scorn. "My Comanche brothers are not fools."

"I don't think they are," Jessie said. "You know about the raids, what's happening in the western end of the Indian Nation."

"Everyone knows of this." His eyes narrowed to slits. "The raiders are white. They are not Kiowas or Comanches. It is the whites who do this." Jessie started to speak. White Bull shook his head firmly. "Maybe you saw these Comanches, woman. I cannot say. The truth can look like a lie. A lie can look like the truth."

"I don't guess I know what that means."

White Bull made a noise in his throat. "When the yellow legs take us out and shoot us, you will see a lie become the truth."

Jessie let out a breath. The building captured heat like an oven. "What were you doing at Wolf Creek? Do you mind telling me that? You are far from home, White Bull."

"The old man over there is my uncle. His name is Running Wolf. He had a dream that told him there were buffalo to the north. He wanted to eat buffalo meat once more before he died." White Bull's eyes betrayed sadness mixed with fury. "His dream was wrong. There were no buffalo. I did not think there were."

"Yes, I see." Jessie looked away and then met his eyes again. "Thank you. Thank you for telling me, White Bull. If there is anything—" She stopped, knowing it was a foolish thing to say. White Bull nodded. He turned, walked back, and sat down against the wall.

• • •

Matt Bilder had business and reluctantly left Jessie on her own, getting a conditional promise that they'd get together later that evening if they could. He was persistent, Jessie couldn't fault him for that. He was a good-looking man and pleasant enough to talk to. The way his bold eyes looked her over, there was no mistaking his intentions—but Jessie decided she didn't greatly object. At least his wants were honest and out in the open. He was not like Heywood Street. Two men could be thinking the same thing or close to it; one made your skin crawl and the other started interesting feelings in your belly. It all had to do with the way things showed in a man's eyes.

Jessie laughed to herself, thinking how Matt had done his best to warn her away from his good friend Josh Stewart. She was sure Bilder would aid Ki in a minute in nearly any situation, but a woman was something else. She didn't dare tell him any different—that she and Ki had a deep and binding relationship. He was, at once, friend, brother, and protector—everything to Jessie but a lover. If she told Bilder that, she'd have to tell him a great deal more besides.

The moment Bilder left her, Jessie began stalking about the post looking for Ki. Men turned to watch her and she knew what they were thinking. A woman didn't walk in the blazing sun without a reason.

Jessie ignored them. She needed to find Ki, had to find him at once. After her talk with White Bull, they desperately needed to talk. Where the hell was he? Off with that fat lieutenant somewhere, no doubt. She didn't have the slightest idea where to look and this was something that definitely couldn't wait.

Bill Haggerty caught up with her, puffing in the heat, and drew her into the shade.

"You tryin' to get yourself a heat stroke or what?" he asked her. "Come on, I want to introduce you to Lieutenant Colonel DeLong. He and his daughter are waiting to meet you. She's made up some cool lemonade."

Jessie moaned to herself but said nothing. Haggerty guided her past headquarters building and up the lieutenant colonel's steps. Jessie stopped him and turned him around.

"Bill, it's getting near sundown. Are we planning to ride back tonight?"

Haggerty shook his head. "Naw, I figured we'd best stay in town. Get off in the morning. Still got some talkin' to do here. That all right with you?"

"Oh, that's just fine with me," Jessie said absently. She wondered what she would have said if he'd told her he wanted to ride out at once. That the sun was getting to her, most likely—that she was much too ill to ride. Whatever happened, she wasn't leaving Camp Supply until morning.

Lieutenant Colonel DeLong did his best to be charming, but the strain of recent events had taken its toll. His hands shook and his gaunt, drawn features were pale. He needed a drink badly and knew a single whiskey wouldn't suffice. Jessie wondered how long he could hold himself together.

Mindy DeLong was young and vibrant, a sensuous and breathtaking beauty. Mindy got Jessie aside and wanted to know exactly what kind of dresses ladies were wearing in Fort Worth. Had Jessie really been to New York and San Francisco? What on earth were they like? As wicked as everyone said? She herself had been to Denver and St. Louis with her father, after her mother had come down with cholera and died, but she'd been too young to have any fun and now she was stuck out *here*, in the middle of nowhere at all.

Jessie let the girl ramble on, listening with half an ear, trying to pick up the talk between Bill and DeLong. What she heard made her blood run cold and confirmed her worst fears. Damn Heywood Street! And DeLong, too, for being too weak to speak his mind. Street had totally convinced his commanding officer that the Kiowas he was holding were bloodthirsty raiders. Street intended to shoot them first thing in the morning—as White Bull himself had already guessed. It was a warning, DeLong told Bill, a warning to the other raiders that they had the U.S. Army to reckon with.

It was clear to Jessie that Bill Haggerty had done all he could to change the man's mind. This was army business, DeLong told him coolly; he'd be damned if he'd wait for some fool from the Bureau of Indian Affairs to show up. Jessie burned with anger; it was obvious the lieutenant colonel was simply mouthing the words Street had poured into his ear. My God, Jessie thought to herself, Street doesn't care how much blood he gets on his hands, as long as he gets even with White Bull for backing him down at the Red River!

She was relieved when an orderly came in to tell DeLong that a troop of Indian police, the Pawnee Light Horse, had arrived at the main gate. DeLong stood irritably and told Haggerty the damned redskins had their nerve, showing their faces at Camp Supply. He stalked out the door, bellowing for Street.

Mindy didn't seem to notice what was going on around her. Jessie excused herself; Haggerty shot her a weary look and dragged himself up after DeLong.

Outside, by the light of a dozen torches, Jessie saw the Indian riders coming through the main gate. There were fifteen or twenty, surrounded by twice as many troopers. Many of the Pawnees had shaved heads and had sprigs of spiky hair. Even, from a distance, Jessie could see they weren't happy to be here. Like the Crows, they'd learned to get along with the whites, which meant the other Indians despised them, labeling them everybody's enemy. Now, it was clear the whites weren't overly pleased with them either.

Jessie saw Bilder catch up with DeLong. Street was stalking doggedly toward the Pawnees, his hand on his sidearm as if he meant to gun them all down on the spot. Jessie walked around the edge of the growing crowd, found Ki, and waved him to her.

"Lord, I thought I'd never find you," she sighed, gripping his arm tightly. "This business of you being in the army makes things inconvenient."

"Your idea," he said glumly, "not mine. What's wrong? You act like someone set your boots on fire."

"Ki, you said there was a way in and out of the fort—a place between the timbers. You called it post something."

"Post Number Nine. Why?"

"I'll be staying in town at the hotel tonight," she told him. "Meet me at the edge of the settlement about two in the morning."

Ki stared. "For what, Jessie? What are we talking about here?"

"Getting White Bull and his friends out of Camp Supply," she said evenly. "It has to be tonight, Ki. I am not going to let Heywood Street line them up against a wall and shoot them down!"

★

Chapter 10

The air was hot and still; Jessie's skin felt moist with perspiration. Even the long night had failed to draw the oppressive heat from the earth. Walking hurriedly past the edge of the settlement, Jessie glanced at the sky and prayed the low clouds would continue to hide the moon. It was much too bright already—if the sky began to clear, she could read a newspaper right where she stood.

A dog barked in a darkened yard to her left. Another, across town, took up the call. Jessie stopped and held her breath until the hounds went silent. The high walls of the fort were just ahead. Lord, the light was too bright—she could almost count the timbers from fifty yards away! She imagined the sentries atop the walls. They would be there, for certain, every man with an itchy trigger finger, every shadow approaching the fort a Comanche raider.

Jessie tried to swallow, but her throat was too dry. She waited a long moment, watching the fort, then walked slowly forward, found the ravine she remembered from the evening before, and bent low to follow its course. The gully was masked with dry grass and wormed its way nearly to the walls. Of course, the sentries knew it was there and would watch for any movement in that direction.

Something darted across the ground just ahead and Jessie froze. A mouse squeaked once in fear; a snake silenced it quickly. Jessie felt her heart hammer. That was the way it happened. One minute you were alive and running free, the next—

She choked off a scream and shrank back. A figure rose straight up out of the ground.

"It's okay," Ki whispered sharply. "It's me."

"You scared the life out of me, friend." Jessie sank to the ground and ran a hand across her face. "Nobody saw you? Everything went all right?"

"I wouldn't exactly call it all right," Ki muttered. "I punched a guard cold at Post Number Nine and tied him up. He won't wake up for a while, but someone could come by and find him any minute. I've already done enough to get us shot and we haven't even started. This is crazy, Jessie, plain crazy."

"I won't argue that." She squinted at the fort. "We'd better get back in there. We're wasting time out here."

"Jessie . . ." Ki grasped her arm in the dark. "There's no need for you to go. I could work a lot better if you didn't. I'll get your Kiowas out and go back to bed—and wake up surprised like everyone else."

"Uh-uh." Jessie shook her head firmly. "We talked about this before and nothing's changed. White Bull sees a man in army blue comin' to set him free and that's only going to spell one thing—he gets shot while trying to escape. He won't buy it, Ki. He'd be stupid if he did. You open that cell without me and he'll try to kill you. What has he got to lose?"

Ki muttered under his breath. "Come on. Stay low and keep close. I hope DeLong gives us breakfast before he shoots us."

Jessie hugged the ground, her body pressed closely against the base of the wall. Above her and less than twenty yards away, a sentry leaned over and peered into the night. For a moment, she was certain he had looked right at her. Coming to her feet, she slipped through the narrow opening and inside. The sentry lay bound to the left, nearly out of sight in the darkness beside the stables. Ki moved like a wraith, quickly and without a sound, flowing with the shifting shadow from the clouds scudding low overhead. His samurai skills made him a part of the night itself. If they see anyone they'll see me, Jessie thought. I'll be the one who gets us caught.

Ki motioned for her to stop. Two troopers crossed the parade ground ahead. They laughed softly at some joke, paused to light smokes, and walked on.

A man stood guard outside the building. Jessie glanced at the walls for an instant. When she looked back again, the sentry was gone. A chill touched the back of her neck. Sometimes Ki frightened her. This man she knew so well, a man as gentle and caring as any man she knew, was as quick and deadly as a viper.

Ki's hand came out of the darkness, drew her inside, closed the door softly behind her. A trooper lay sprawled on the floor. A few steps farther, past a corner, another slumped on his arms across a table. Both men looked as if they were asleep. Jessie knew Ki had struck them deftly at the base of the skull, a blow that could stun a man or kill him, depending upon the way it was delivered. These two, and the man at the wall, would wake up with headaches and nothing more.

Ki took the lantern from the table, shadowed the flame with his hand, and let Jessie lead the way. A ring of keys hung on the wall and he lifted them off a peg and gave them to her. At the barred door, she whispered White Bull's name. He was already there. His dark eyes darted past Jessie, found Ki, and held him.

"I don't have time to tell you this more than once," Jessie whispered. "The man in that uniform's a friend. This isn't a trick, White Bull. You're going to have to trust me. When I let you out, just follow me and you'll be outside the fort in a minute. Now, I'm telling you again, that man means you no harm. Do you want to stay here or go? If I open this door, I'm taking you on your word."

"Why?" White Bull said sharply. "Why do you do this, woman?"

"Because the army's going to kill you," she said simply, "soon as the sun comes up. You and the old man and the boy. He's your son, isn't he, White Bull?"

White Bull didn't answer. His eyes closed to slits. Then he said, "You have my word."

Jessie opened the door. White Bull turned and spoke rapidly to the others. He came out of the cell, paused an instant, and looked into Ki's eyes. Ki met his gaze and then deliberately blew out the lantern, giving the Indian time to see what he was doing. Jessie held her breath. White Bull didn't move.

"There's a wall," Ki said softly. "That's where we're going. When we get there, you're on your own. This woman will go part of the way with you. You understand?"

White Bull grunted an answer.

"All right, let's go." Ki turned and disappeared in the dark.

Ki melted into shadow by the wall, stood a long moment and studied the night. White Bull sniffed the air. He glanced once at the sentry bound by the stables and looked curiously at Jessie and Ki.

"The sentry's at the other end of the wall," Ki whispered. "Now—go right *now*." He squeezed Jessie's arm. Jessie moved aside to let the Indians slip through the wall. She looked once at Ki and bent low, moving into the night.

Jessie held her breath, counting off the agonizing seconds in her head. The ravine appeared again and the Kiowas quickly slipped from sight. Jessie followed and found White Bull waiting.

"Why do you come?" he asked cautiously. "Why do you leave the fort?"

"'Cause I'm not supposed to be in there," she said. "Go on, now. Get out of here!"

White Bull started to speak. A rifle cracked through the night; lead whined past Jessie's shoulder.

"For God's sake, go!" Jessie said, rasping shrilly.

White Bull nodded sharply to the others, turned, and moved down the twisting ravine. Shouts went up along the wall. A rapid volley of fire lit up the night, stitching dirt along the gully.

"Over there," a trooper bellowed. "Get the bastards!" The gunfire shifted from Jessie's position. She bent low and moved as fast as she could toward the settlement. Out of the corner of her eye, she saw the Indians leap up from the depression and run south. The troopers found them at once and peppered the dark. Jessie could see the first scattered houses of the settlement. She took a deep breath and ran low, knowing she had to make it, that if they caught her in the open, wandering around in the night—

The shot gouged dirt at her feet. A second clipped the heel of her boot and sent her sprawling. She choked off a curse, came to her knees, looked up, and saw dark hooves pawing air just above her. A trooper leaned out of the saddle, rifle at his shoulder, the muzzle aimed directly at her chest.

"No, don't!" Jessie shouted.

The trooper paused, stared in surprise, and kicked his mount closer.

"Jesus Christ," he said under his breath, "Over here, sir!"

Two more mounted troopers suddenly appeared beside the first. Another horse edged around them. Captain Heywood Street slid out of the saddle before his horse came to a halt. His hair was in disarray, the suspenders of his trousers pulled hastily over his bare chest. He stopped above Jessie, pale blue eyes opened wide with disbelief.

"Well, I'll be damned," he said under his breath. "Just what in hell are you doing out here?"

Jessie pulled herself to her feet. "Taking a little walk," she said crossly, "or trying to, without gettin' shot. My God, captain, we under attack or what?"

Street's eyes narrowed. "A walk, Miss Starbuck? At three o'clock in the morning?"

Jessie thrust out her chin in defiance. "My sleeping habits are no concern of yours, Captain Street."

"I think perhaps they are," he said darkly.

"Oh, really?" Jessie threw back her head and laughed. "You got another bottle of that fine French brandy stashed away somewhere? No thanks, pal!"

Street flushed with anger. His eyes darted to the troopers around them; the men made certain they weren't looking in his direction. "Escort this lady inside," he said. "If she doesn't want to come, tie her up and toss her over a horse!" He turned away, mounted, kicked his horse savagely, and started back for the gate.

In the early morning hour, Lieutenant Colonel DeLong looked like a corpse. He sat at the end of the table and let Street do the talking. Jessie wondered what was in his cup besides coffee.

"You still contend you were taking a little stroll around the settlement, Miss Starbuck?" asked Street. "That's your story, is it?"

He stood before Jessie, hands locked behind his back. Earlier, an orderly had brought him a shirt. His lips curled slightly at the corners and his eyes flashed with delight. His expression made Jessie extremely nervous. He knew something, something that pleased him immensely; whatever it was, it couldn't very well be good news for her.

"It isn't a story, Captain Street," she said wearily. "It happens to be the truth."

"Yes, of course." Street looked up and studied the ceiling. "And you had nothing to do with the Indians' escape."

Jessie laughed aloud. "Do we have to go through that business again?" She glanced at DeLong and sighed. "How long do I have to listen to this nonsense? It's not funny anymore."

"Well, ah—" DeLong licked his lips. "It does seem unlikely that Miss, ah, Miss Starbuck here is involved, Heywood."

Street looked away, closed his eyes, then turned his attention back to Jessie. "Are you pleased the Indians have escaped, Miss Starbuck?"

"Yes. Of course, I am. I'm always pleased when innocent

men get away with their lives. You were going to murder them, Captain Street. I'm delighted that they're gone."

"Is that what you told the Kiowas when you and Matt Bilder went to see them this afternoon? That they were to be shot?"

Jessie shrugged. She wasn't at all surprised he'd found out.

Street loomed over her, palms flat on the table. "The man on duty this afternoon kept his mouth shut for a while. He thought he'd get in trouble if I knew he'd let you and Bilder in." He showed her a thin smile. "He is right, of course. But he has vindicated himself to some degree by coming forward."

"All right. We were there," Jessie said. "So what?"

"Is that when you planned the prisoners' escape?"

Jessie sank back in her chair. "Captain Street, you told me a minute ago three troopers were knocked unconscious, that they didn't even see who hit them. Do you think a woman could do that? Honestly!" She grinned and shook her head. "I confess. I sneaked up and hit them with a club and then set the Indians free. What time do I get shot?"

"Don't play me for a fool, Miss Starbuck," he said harshly. "I know you aren't in this alone. It was Matt Bilder, wasn't it?"

"I hardly even know Mr. Bilder."

"That lieutenant, then—the one you were seen with this afternoon. Josh Stewart."

"I hardly know him."

Street nodded. "What if I told you that the man who was with you has already confessed and admitted that the whole idea was yours?"

"Then I'd say you were a liar, Captain Street."

Street looked at her thoughtfully a long moment, turned, went to the door, and spoke quietly to someone outside. A short black trooper entered the room and stood at attention. He glanced uneasily at DeLong and Street, not at all used to such company.

"This is Trooper Henry Andrews, Miss Starbuck," said Street. "Andrews, tell this lady what you told me a minute ago."

"Yes, sir." Andrews wet his lips. He looked straight at the wall, avoiding Jessie's eyes. "I was on sentry duty, sir. Post Number Six. I heard a shot fired and I looked up and saw Lucas—Trooper Lucas, sir—shootin' at something outside the wall. I leaned over quick and looked out and I saw Injuns makin' for the brush."

"And what else did you see?" Street prompted.

"Sir, I saw this lady. She was with 'em."

"You're certain of that?"

"Yes, sir. When Trooper Lucas fired again, I saw the color of her hair in the light."

Street looked at Jessie. "Is this man telling the truth, Miss Starbuck? Would you care to ask him any questions?"

"No," Jessie said calmly. She looked right at the trooper. "I'm sure he's not lying, Captain Street. He's simply mistaken in what he saw." She knew the man was telling what he'd seen and wasn't at all happy with the task. How ironic, she thought. Both Street and DeLong despised every black man on the post. Now, though, Trooper Henry Andrews was telling them exactly what they wanted to hear; suddenly, he was a reliable, trustworthy witness.

"Trooper," asked Street, "are you a liar?"

"No, sir, I'm not." He forced himself to look at Jessie. "Beggin' your pardon, ma'am, but I saw you. No mistakin' that."

"Dismissed," Street said sharply, "that's all. McPherson!" He bellowed over his shoulder at the open door. "Get those two in here on the double!"

Uh-oh, Jessie told herself silently, now's when the party could get rough.

Matt Bilder and Ki came into the room. Matt stood casually with his fingers hooked in his belt. Ki stood at attention.

Street glared at them both. "One of you helped this woman free those damned savages tonight," he said between his teeth. "I am going to find out who!"

"Wasn't me," Bilder drawled. "I haven't been out of bed." He glanced at DeLong. "Do I have to stand here and listen to this fool? If I do, I'm going to have some of that coffee."

Street flushed and clenched his fists. "You will answer my question, Bilder!"

"This is, ah, just an informal hearing, Matt," DeLong muttered. He showed Bilder a sickly grin. "No one is accusing you of anything. Are you, Heywood?"

"No sir," Street said acidly, "I wouldn't think of it." He turned his attention to Ki. "And you, Stewart—"

"Guess I can vouch for him," Bilder broke in. "I been awake maybe two, three hours. Damn heat. Stewart there's been sawin' logs all night."

Jessie sucked in a breath. Bless Matt Bilder—he'd lied for Ki without blinking an eye!

"How convenient for you both," Street said caustically. "Nobody did anything." He turned angrily and poured himself a tumbler of water. Jessie looked at Ki. His eyes were locked on the wall. Bilder stared right at her and his message was clear as glass: What in hell are you up to, lady?

"Someone's lying," said Street, turning to face them again. "I intend to find out who. And you, Miss Starbuck—" He jabbed a finger at Jessie. "You are confined to this post. Under guard. If you attempt to escape, I will not hesitate to have you shot."

"I don't doubt it," Jessie said dryly.

"Seems to me, Street," Bilder said idly, "'stead of standing around here jawin', you ought to let me get out after those Indians. Those patrols of yours aren't going to find a damn thing out there in the dark—'cept a gopher hole or two."

"You aren't going anywhere," Street said tightly. "If you try to leave this post, you will be promptly arrested."

Bilder's eyes turned to glass. "I hope you try to handle that personal. I sure do."

Street glared at Bilder. The door burst open and Bill Haggerty exploded into the room. He looked at Street, dismissed him at once, and turned to the lieutenant colonel.

"I don't know what the hell you think you're doing in here, but it better come to a halt right now," Haggerty bellowed. He looked at Jessie. "You all right?"

"I'm fine," said Jessie. "A little tired is all."

"You have no right to come in here like this," Street protested. "This is a military proceeding, Mr. Haggerty."

Haggerty took a full three seconds to turn and face him. "Son," he said gently, "you open your mouth again and I will give you an unmilitary kick in the ass. Do you understand me, boy?"

Street's face fell. Haggerty ignored him.

"You figure on holding Miss Starbuck here on some damn fool charge?" Haggerty asked DeLong.

"Bill, we, ah, have certain evidence," DeLong said nervously. "She seems to have some involvement in these matters."

"Uh-huh." Haggerty leaned in close, so close that DeLong had to press himself back against his chair. "All right, now, here's what I'm going to do. You listen good. This lady walks out with me—or I walk out by myself and ride to the first telegraph I can find. What I will do there is get off about two dozen messages to senators and some of my poker playin' friends in the War Department. I'll tell them what's goin' on down here and how the drunk they got in charge *is not* running the show. I figure maybe twenty-four hours from right now you'll be cleanin' up horse shit. If that suits you, it sure as hell suits me."

DeLong's eyes went wide. He gripped the arms of his chair to keep from shaking. "Now, Bill—you, you got no call to talk to me like that—you got no right!"

"I'm leaving," Haggerty said flatly. "What's it going to be?"

"Why, ah, I suppose if you give me your word th—that Miss Starbuck will be available if we, if we should—"

Street snapped, "You cannot let that woman walk out of here!"

"Shut up, Street!" DeLong's eyes blazed with sudden fury. "I can do whatever I want. I'm in charge here, you know!" He looked at Haggerty. His flesh seemed to slide down the planes of his face. "Get her out of here," he said, his words almost too low to hear. "Get her off my post."

"Sound reasoning," Haggerty said plainly. "Jessie, unless you want to have breakfast with these gents, let's make tracks."

★

Chapter 11

Bill Haggerty kept to himself as he and Jessie rode out of Camp Supply and back to the settlement outside the gates. Jessie sensed the strain between them, that he was holding back his anger, and made no effort to draw him out. At the hotel he muttered that he'd meet her out front in a half hour and then turned and rode off to rouse his hands.

Jessie gathered her belongings and grabbed a quick breakfast at the café. First light was just beginning to touch the eastern sky. Things had been happening so fast that she'd scarcely had time to sort them out. Matt Bilder had undoubtedly saved Ki's hide, covering for him quickly in front of Street. He must have seen Ki slipping back in bed only moments before the sentries sounded the alarm. It wouldn't take much to put two and two together and guess that Ki was involved. Had they talked before Street had them brought up before him? Did Bilder confront Ki? Jessie somehow knew he hadn't. The look she'd gotten from Bilder said he had more questions than answers.

Did he do it for me, then, or for Ki? Jessie wondered. Maybe some of both, she decided. Matt Bilder was a good man. He'd follow his instincts, his loyalties to the people he liked, and look for reasons later.

Bilder could take care of himself. Heywood Street might kick him off the post, but he didn't have the power to do him harm, not without buying a lot of trouble. Street was plainly afraid of the man and showed it. Ki was something else, and that worried Jessie more than a little. The man Street knew as Josh Stewart was under his thumb; Street was determined to get someone for freeing White Bull and Ki was a likely choice. Bilder would help if he could, but Bilder might be out of a job and gone this minute. Street was clearly running the show and that put Ki in certain danger. Still, Jessie reasoned, Haggerty had put the fear of God into DeLong. The lieutenant colonel might think twice before he let Street go too far. And Ki would

85

be all right—he knew how to take care of himself, get himself out of a scrape.

Lord, I wish you were out of that place, she thought dismally, I wish you were out of there, Ki, three hundred miles from Heywood Street.

Bill Haggerty pulled his mount up beside her and scowled, carefully avoiding her eyes. "I think you and me ought to talk," he said flatly. "Seems to me there's things need saying."

"Yes, I guess there are," said Jessie.

"It's true, I take it, what Street said back there. It was you who let the Indians go."

"Yes, Bill, it was me. Street was going to shoot them. They'd be dead this minute. I'm not sorry I did it."

"Didn't figure you were." Haggerty made a noise in his throat. "Damn it, Jessie, I understand your reasons—won't even say I blame you. But it was a fool thing to do; it didn't have to be."

"Didn't have to be?" Jessie's green eyes flashed. "You mean it's all right if innocent men die?"

"I don't mean anything of the sort," Haggerty snorted, "and you know it. What I'm saying is there's more than one way to skin a cat. I was talkin' some sense into DeLong—gettin' him away from that damn Street. I was tryin' to work him toward using his troopers to keep the peace 'stead of their doing nothing at all or his lettin' Street make things worse. He's not a complete fool, Jessie, just close enough to it. I think I could've talked him out of shooting those Indians."

"You think."

"All right," Haggerty snapped, "I know I could have. I could have stopped him."

"But I didn't know that, Bill," Jessie said gently. "I still don't. I'm sorry. And I don't think you can be all that sure."

Haggerty turned abruptly in the saddle. For the first time, Jessie saw the fury in his eyes. "What we've got here now is nothing, you understand that? I threatened DeLong, scared him out of his wits, and shamed him—took everything the man had left to get you out of Camp Supply. The man's a coward and a drunk, but he isn't going to forget what I did. He won't listen to me now—he's going to listen to Street—Street and Lew Lyman, which means a lot more than three Kiowas are likely to get shot 'fore this is over."

Jessie jerked her mount to a stop. "And you're going to lay

that on me, is that it?" She shook her head firmly. "Damn it, Bill, I won't accept that. I'm grateful for what you did back there and I'm sorry I put you in that position with DeLong. But you are not going to lay the responsibility for an Indian war on my shoulders. Not on your life!"

"That isn't what I'm saying," Haggerty muttered.

"The hell it isn't."

"I don't think we're getting anywhere with this conversation. You're taking me all wrong, twistin' what I'm saying."

"No, I don't think I am."

"Who helped you?" Haggerty asked suddenly. "Matt Bilder or that lieutenant? You mind telling me that?"

"Yes, I do mind," Jessie said coolly.

"Christ, Jessie." Haggerty looked pained. "We got ourselves goin' at each other on this and I don't much like it."

"I don't like it either."

"You don't trust me—after what I said. Is that why you won't say?"

"No, that's not it at all. I do trust you, Bill. I just can't betray a confidence. I wouldn't betray yours and I won't betray someone else's. Besides, what difference does it make who helped me? And while we're at it, it wasn't me who said Matt Bilder or Josh Stewart was involved. That was Heywood Street's idea."

Haggerty's eyes narrowed. It was clear Jessie's words took him completely by surprise. "Had to be one of 'em. You don't hardly know anyone else at Camp Supply."

"I don't hardly know those two," Jessie said irritably. "That's what I kept telling Street. I sure don't know 'em well enough to ask them to take a chance on getting shot. Heywood Street was too damn stubborn to stop and think about that. Apparently, you are too." She kicked her horse and rode ahead, leaving Haggerty to watch her back.

Maybe it would throw him off some, she reflected. Or maybe it wouldn't. She did trust him, in spite of what he thought. He was a good friend and she'd put her life in his hands. But there was no need to tell him about Ki—that the man masquerading as Josh Stewart wasn't really Stewart at all. There was already bad feeling between them. Telling the truth right now would only show Bill Haggerty she'd deceived him. It would make things worse and she definitely didn't need that at the moment.

. . .

Just before noon, Haggerty rode up and reined in his horse in her path, forcing her to stop.

"Look, is it all right with you if we try to get things straight between us?" he said gruffly. "If I went too far in what I said, then I'm sorry."

"Bill, I'd like that just fine," Jessie told him.

"Good. If we got any problems, we'll hash 'em out later. I'm sending two of my boys back to the ranch to tell them where we'll be. I want to stop over at Art McGregor's spread southwest of here. It isn't but eight or ten miles and he'll know what Lyman and his bunch are up to. Art's about the only man up here in the Strip's got a lick of sense left." He showed her a crooked grin. "Besides me, of course."

"Of course." Jessie smiled, pleased that the tension had eased between them.

Two of Haggerty's hands, Dick Robbins and a man Jessie remembered only as Jack, rode off toward the Crescent-H. Haggerty led the way southwest, keeping riders off to either side to scout the land.

"Art's a crusty old bastard," said Haggerty, "only man in the Indian Nation older and meaner than me."

Jessie laughed. "I guess that's why I liked him when I first met him."

Haggerty's features tightened into a frown. "Most fellers who run cattle up here are a good bunch of men. I don't have to tell you we believe in solving our own problems. I don't say we're always right, now, but that's how it is. You saw what happened at Lew Lyman's. This raider business has got everyone on a real short fuse—and for damn good reason."

Jessie felt a chill. "They'll ride with Lyman, won't they?" she said distantly. "And the army won't even try to stop them."

"The army will decide to get movin' just as soon as it's too damn late to get started," Haggerty said bitterly. "And, yes, most of the ranchers will go with Lyman. You can bet he's got an army of his own out there right now. That's one reason I'm headed for Art's spread. Art'll know where Lyman is and how we can get to him. Him and me have still got some clout with those boys. If the two of us hit 'em together, they'll sit up and listen—whether Lew likes it or not."

"We've got to stop them in time, Bill, before they start something they can't finish."

Haggerty didn't answer. His eyes half closed and his thoughts were somewhere else.

• • •

Armed riders met them a good mile from the Box-M spread, five men with Winchester rifles at the ready. As soon as they saw Bill Haggerty, they waved him on and rode to the north. Jessie saw a few other hands on the place and guessed that most of the men were out with the herds.

Art McGregor ran twice as many cattle as any man in the Indian Nation, including Bill Haggerty himself. He looked for all the world as if he didn't have a dime and might not eat past Sunday. His house was big, sprawling, comfortable, unpretentious, and in total disarray. It was easy to see that an old man lived there alone, without a woman's hand. Haggerty had told Jessie that Art McGregor had been widowed thirty years, had loved one woman, and had never found another to take her place.

"Lyman's got 'em all riled up," McGregor reported. "Maybe two hundred men." He shook his grizzled head in disgust. "Never thought I'd have anything good to say about those Englishmen who run herds over here and ain't ever been 'cross the ocean or seen a cow. Some of them are holding off, Bill— fellers who run 'em say they don't have the authority to loan their hands to Lyman's crew."

"Well, I guess that's something," Haggerty said dryly, "not a lot, but something."

"Sounds to me as if Lyman's got more than enough men to cause trouble," said Jessie. "Lord, two hundred men!"

"It's enough," said McGregor. He told Haggerty and Jessie that Lyman was still on the North Canadian somewhere, waiting for some of the men from the far western end of No Man's Land to show. The bulk of his forces were camped to the south, maybe close to Wolf Creek.

"Word I got," said McGregor, "is that some of the ranchers got good sense want to wait and talk to the army. Lyman, of course, isn't going to sit still for that, if he can help it."

Haggerty cursed under his breath. "He'll head for the Cheyenne and Arapaho reservations, the closest Indians he can find." He exchanged a look with McGregor. McGregor nodded back.

"Be safer if we waited till morning, 'stead of looking to find Lew 'fore it's dark," McGregor muttered. "Guess safe don't count anymore, does it?"

"No, I don't guess it does," said Haggerty.

• • •

As the men saddled up, Jessie watched from the front porch, clenching her fists in frustration. Haggerty's men would go along and so would a few hands from Art McGregor's spread. If it turned out Lyman were still waiting on the North Canadian, there was a chance they could find him in the few hours left before dark. If not, they'd have to camp out and start looking again the next morning. Haggerty said he wouldn't take Jessie and that was that. Jessie protested loudly, but Haggerty wouldn't budge. She told him he was just getting back, punishing her for the incident at Camp Supply. He told her she could think whatever she wanted and he stalked off.

Art McGregor walked up beside her, cradling a Winchester under his arm. "You look like a storm 'bout to happen," he said dryly. "Lightnin' in a pretty woman's eyes scares the hell out of me. Not much else does but that'll do it."

"It will, huh?" Jessie grinned in spite of herself.

"Bill told me 'bout that business with the Kiowas," McGregor went on. "Guess you figured that. Took a lot of nerve to do that, lady." He glanced over his shoulder at the others. "Hell of a lot of nerve."

"Are you saying you approve, Mr. McGregor?"

"Didn't say that, did I?" The deep valleys in his face, the lines the sun and the years had carved out of his flesh, twisted into an expression Jessie found nearly impossible to read. "Said it took a lot of nerve is what I said, and that's a quality I do truly admire." He looked at Jessie and shook his head. "You look like your mother. I always told Alex Starbuck if I didn't have a fine woman myself, I'd go after his. He always said he'd lock up every woman on his place if he thought I was closer'n fifty miles." McGregor laughed. "Don't get too riled up about Bill. He's doing what he thinks he ought to do. And he's right as he can be, too—you got no business ridin' out on this."

"Not you, too." Jessie groaned.

"Yeah, me, too," McGregor said flatly, softening his words with a grin. "Good day to you, Miss Jessie, and make yourself at home here." He touched his hat and turned away, the worn heels of his boots making a deep hollow sound on the wooden porch.

"Mr. McGregor—" Jessie called after him.

"Yes'm?" He stopped and half turned, twisting his head to face her, revealing a smile. She saw a bullet strike him in the corner of his eye, the impact tearing away the bridge of his nose and a chunk of flesh and bone the size of a silver dollar. The force pushed air out of his lungs, twisted him on his heels, sent his Stetson flying, and slammed him back hard against the wall of his house. His slid down until he was sitting on the porch, with his legs out before him and his hands spread limply at his sides, palms open and up. His head pitched forward, blood spilling into his lap in a steady pulse.

The sound of the shot was lost in the sudden, awful volley of fire that followed. Jessie heard Haggerty bellow her name; she came to her senses and hit the floor, crawling over McGregor's lifeless legs, grabbing his rifle and throwing herself off the porch and into the dirt. One of Haggerty's men jerked his arms straight up over his head, cried out, and spilled off the back of his saddle. Another man, one of McGregor's hands, was already down. Jessie watched in horror as a man leaped off his mount and scrambled for cover. She called out a warning too late. Lead caught the man in the open, lifted him off the earth in a crazy dance, and refused to let him go until he tripped over his feet and fell in a heap.

Jessie bellied across dirt hot as an oven. White puffs of smoke drifted from a sparse grove of trees to her left. Haggerty waved her to him. He was sprawled behind a water trough near the corral. Anger twisted his features, painted the ruined side of his face deep crimson.

"The bastards are in the trees," he breathed heavily, "must've left their horses down in the gully that runs back of Art's barn. Damn it, they caught us all bunched up!"

"Art McGregor's dead," said Jessie, "three other men down I know of, don't know how many more." She pressed herself hard against the ground as lead chipped wood overhead.

Haggerty clenched his fists. "There's another over there," he nodded. "I think two of my boys got away in the bushes. Hell, I don't know." His bleary eyes locked on Jessie's. "We can't count on gettin' any help. The riders Art had out there could be three or four miles from here or more'n that."

. "Bill, if we can—" A scream cut off her words. She turned on her side and saw a man stagger away from the fence, twenty yards down the corral. He clutched his leg and tried to drag himself to cover. The men in the trees opened up, stitching dirt at his heels. Jessie knew he'd never make it. She rolled away from Haggerty, came to her knees, levered a shell in the Winchester, and started along the fence.

"Jessie," Haggerty shouted, "get down, damn it—get down!"

Jessie kept low, pressing the rifle against her breasts. Lead whined overhead. The wounded man limped for safety, his face white with fear. Jessie broke from the cover of the corral, raised the rifle to her shoulder, squeezed off a quick volley of fire toward the trees, jumped to one side, and fired again. Haggerty called out behind her. She fired until the rifle clicked empty and then leaped for the cover of the brush. From the corner of her eye, she saw the wounded man hop behind a wagon. A fresh round of fire suddenly erupted from the trees. She risked a look and saw five horses churning up dust, coming on fast over the rise. Art's riders! They were circling off east, down behind the raiders' position. The fire from the trees stopped abruptly. In a moment a line of painted ponies appeared for an instant through the branches, but then vanished over the hill.

Jessie stood. Her heart beat rapidly. Haggerty came to her and turned her around to face him. His skin was the color of ash.

"Jessie," he said harshly, gripping her shoulders hard, "that was the bravest, most foolhardy damn stunt I ever saw. They could've torn you in two, girl—standing right there in the open!"

Haggerty stalked off to help the others. Jessie stared at his back. His words seemed etched in the air and something cold touched the base of her spine. She suddenly felt hollow, as if all her substance had vanished. She saw it all in her head, remembered every second standing out there in the dust, a perfect target for the men in the trees. Haggerty was right. They could have shot her a half dozen times. Only they didn't. It couldn't possibly have happened that way; it made no sense at all. She knew, though, that it was true. *They stopped, quit firing. They saw me there in the open and they stopped and let me go.*

★

Chapter 12

McGregor's riders pursued the raiders, following them past the trees through the dry stretch of land to the north. The hands were good at working cattle; the raiders practiced another trade. The men rushed in without caution, anger overcoming good sense. The raiders let them come and then drew them into the simplest kind of trap. An hour later, three hands rode back to the Box-M. Of the five who had taken up the chase, two were dead, draped over their saddles. Another was bleeding badly and a fourth had taken a bullet in the leg. Only one was unscathed. He was a young man, scarcely seventeen. When he rode into the yard, he was bawling unashamedly, unable to stop his tears.

The three new graves brought the dead up to seven, including Art McGregor, two of his men at the ranch, and one of Haggerty's. Four men were wounded, one badly. Haggerty's hands and those who'd worked for Art McGregor stood about wondering what to do. Haggerty took command and whipped them into shape, giving them things to do. There was nothing that really had to be done, but anything was better than thinking about friends who just died.

Haggerty and Jessie left the ranch late in the afternoon, heading back for the Crescent-H. One of the men who'd been hurt stayed behind. The hand Jessie had come to know as Marcus rode with them.

Haggerty spoke little on the way; it was clear to Jessie that he could barely contain his anger and sorrow. He had tangled with the raiders twice now. He'd seen good people die and both times the raiders had struck and vanished, mocking any effort to run them down.

"Art McGregor was one of the finest men I ever knew," he said finally. "Damn it, that shouldn't have happened. It shouldn't be!"

"I'm sorry, Bill," Jessie said gently. "I know that doesn't do any good."

"No, it doesn't," he muttered, choking his reins in his fist. "Doesn't do any good."

"Can I ask you something?"

"Ask whatever you want. I don't likely have the answers."

"What are you going to do? Now, I mean. This isn't the time to say it, I guess, but I don't see any good way to stop this business before it sets the whole Indian Nation on fire."

"Maybe Lew Lyman's got the answer," Haggerty said under his breath.

"You don't mean that, Bill Haggerty, so don't say it," Jessie said sharply.

"No, I don't mean it." He turned to Jessie, his features void of expression. "Lew's doing something. He isn't just sittin' on his hands. Maybe it's not right—but what happened back there's not right either."

Jessie tried to think of something to tell him, but couldn't find the words. Instead, she kept her silence and stared out at the flat, featureless land ahead.

The hand named Marcus spotted them first—a dozen or more riders circled about the dusty arroyo ahead. He looked blankly at Haggerty, shaken by what he'd seen that day and unsure if he could face trouble again.

"Easy, son," Haggerty said quietly, "I reckon they're friends this time."

The riders saw them coming and turned; Jessie read their faces from a distance and knew at once something was wrong. As they got closer, she saw Bill Haggerty's hand, Jack. He was sitting on the ground, drinking thirstily from a canteen. His face was white with dust, his features slack and empty of all feeling.

Haggerty slid wearily off his horse, walked past the others, and bent to him. "What is it, Jack?" he said gently. "Tell me what happened. Where's Dick Robbins, boy?"

"Dick and me—Dick and me was on our way back to the Crescent-H," Jack said shakily. "To—to let 'em know you was stoppin' off at Mr. McGregor's. They hit us, Mr. Haggerty. Dick seen 'em and we tried to get out . . ."

"They killed your other hand, Bill," one of the riders finished. "We found this one walking back to your spread."

Haggerty nodded. "You and these fellows ridin' with Lyman?"

"Lew's likely at your place now. He's getting ready to start south. Bill, you and McGregor going to come in with us or not? We sure as hell need you."

"Art's through fighting," Haggerty said dully. "And I don't much give a damn, one way or the other." The riders looked startled. Haggerty stalked past them back to his horse, mounted, and kicked it savagely in the sides.

Jessie was awed by the sight. There had to be two hundred men at the Crescent-H, all of them armed and ready to ride. She knew why they were there and what they intended to do. Yet, she couldn't help the sudden surge of excitement that coursed through her veins. Someone had to stop the raiders, put an end to the killing—

Heat rose to her face and she cast the thought aside. The sound of men dying still echoed in her ears and more killing wouldn't bring them back. These men were angry and full of hate—right now they didn't want justice; they wanted blood and didn't much care where they found it.

More than twenty ranchers crowded into Bill Haggerty's parlor. The news of what had happened to Art McGregor left them boiling with a rage they could scarcely contain. Lyman, Jessie saw, made no effort to cool them down.

"Any of you boys feel like waitin' any longer?" he asked the crowd. "You want to sit down and talk things out with the Injuns who murdered Art McGregor?"

His words brought a deafening chorus of rage; they were a roomful of dark faces and shaking fists.

"Bill, you with us on this now? You need any more convincing?"

Haggerty's eyes found Lyman's. "I'm ready to track down and bring in every murderin' bastard responsible for killing my friends." His gaze swept the room. "That don't mean storming down south and wiping out the nearest reservation."

"Where in hell you think those devils live?" a cattleman yelled out. The others joined in. Haggerty tried to quiet them, but no one cared to listen.

"Hold it!" Lyman raised his hands. "I don't agree with Bill Haggerty and you know it. But there isn't a man here don't respect him and that includes me." He turned, looked past Haggerty, and jabbed an accusing finger at Jessie. "My regard for Bill doesn't include this woman," he said savagely. "Maybe some of you men don't know it, and I don't reckon Bill's going to tell you, but the army had three of the Injuns we're looking for, and I hear that one right there set 'em free!"

For an instant, the men looked startled. Then, as a man, they roared in anger and surged forward. Jessie shrank back, her heart racing. For a moment she was certain the men would take her and tear her apart.

"Get back, damn you!" Haggerty moved quickly and set himself before her.

"Damn Indian lover!" a man shouted.

"She's working with 'em," yelled another. "She's one of them!"

Haggerty didn't move. "Don't talk like fools," he told the men who'd spoken. "I'm not saying what Jessie Starbuck did was right. But those Kiowas didn't do a damn thing 'cept get themselves caught by the army. Hell, two of 'em were a kid and an old man."

"Bill," Lyman said soberly, "you ain't ever seen a redskin that's done something wrong and you know it. You're not thinking straight. If you were, you wouldn't be defending this woman."

The crowd added its anger.

"This woman you're talking about stood up to those raiders at Art's place," Haggerty said tightly. "Risked her life so a man could get to cover. Anybody who says it didn't happen is calling me a liar."

Haggerty's words quieted them for a moment. Not a man in the room cared to pick up a challenge like that.

Lyman didn't care for the sudden silence. "It isn't your word that's in question," he said doggedly. "It's what she's up to with those killers that bothers us." He gave Jessie a scornful laugh. "Firing off a couple of shots don't prove you're any angel—not in my book, it doesn't."

"Damn you," Jessie exploded. "If you're accusing me of keeping three innocent men from getting shot, then I'm guilty. You've got no right and no cause to say I've got Art McGregor's blood on my hands!"

Lyman gave her a look of total contempt. He faced Bill Haggerty and shook his head. "You do whatever the hell you want, Bill. I'm getting tired of asking you to join us. Come with us or let your friends do your fighting."

"You son of a bitch," Haggerty flared, "you better back off!" He went for Lyman, both fists swinging. Two men moved to stop him, pressing him hard against the wall.

"Bill, I'm sorry," one of them muttered, "but you're wrong in this."

Haggerty glared, straining against their grip, the ruined side of his face blood-red.

"Like I say," Lew told him, "you do whatever you want. But you listen close to what I'm saying. Your friend here isn't getting the chance for more mischief. Miss Starbuck strays a foot from this house and I'll have her shot." He caught Jessie's expression. "I mean it, lady. Just try me. I'm leaving hands here to see it's done. And don't try to interfere with this, Bill. I don't like to give orders on another man's spread, but I'm doing it. We got enough trouble to face without havin' her at our backs." He looked at Haggerty as if he meant to say more, then turned abruptly, and walked through the crowd. The men holding Haggerty let him go. He pushed them off angrily and watched his friends file through the door. To a man, they turned their faces away.

When the room was empty, Jessie looked at the floor. "I'm sorry," she said quietly. "I've put you in an awful situation. I wish I'd never come up here, Bill."

Haggerty looked at her, but Jessie was certain he didn't see her. Without a word he walked off and left her standing. Jessie heard riders mounting up. In a moment the yard outside the ranch house was empty.

Ki squinted into the harsh glare of noon. Camp Supply was twelve or fifteen miles at his back. The patrol moved steadily southeast, following the path of the North Canadian. Ki glanced back and saw Lance Corporal Daniels and four troopers behind. They formed a ragged line along the bank, caps pulled over their faces against the sun. Gnats swarmed up from the river and the horses flicked their ears and shook their heads.

Ki opened his canteen, dampened his bandanna with water, and then pressed the cloth to the back of his neck. The earth was bleached white, wavering in glassy planes of heat. There was no way to tell where the sky ended and the barren land began.

It hadn't taken Ki long to gain Heywood Street's attention. Jessie and Haggerty were scarcely out of sight before Street marched Ki out of DeLong's quarters and braced him stiffly against the wall.

"If I had my way," Street said tightly, "I would have you

97

stood up and shot before the sun got another foot higher. That son of a bitch Bilder is lyin' to save your tail. If I could prove it, I'd shoot you myself right here and now. Instead, I'm going to do something worse. I'm going to see how long I can keep you alive. Sergeant Major!" He bawled over his shoulder and then turned as McPherson came down the steps. They talked for a moment. Then Street stalked off in a fury. McPherson turned to Ki.

"Best get your gear and get ready, lieutenant," McPherson told him. "The man is sending you out on patrol."

Ki looked surprised. "That's it? The way he was talking, I figured he might toss me in a hole full of rattlers."

"Might be you'll wish he had," the sergeant major said soberly. He raised an eye at Ki. "I'll put it to you straight, lieutenant. You aren't just on patrol. You're *on* patrol."

Ki shook his head. "Is that supposed to make sense?"

"What it means is that the captain is sending you out right now. When you get back in about fifteen hours, you're going to be so hot and worn out you'll be ready to drop. What the captain's going to do right then, sir, is stick you on a nice fresh horse and send you out again. Fresh mount and fresh men. You ride all night, get back tomorrow mornin', and he'll have another horse waiting. You see what I'm getting at, sir?"

Ki let out a breath. "I understand, sergeant major. And Captain Street thinks if I don't fall out of the saddle I'll maybe run off. Is that it?"

Enos McPherson showed him a weary grin. "I don't suppose he cares what you do, one way or the other. You run off, those troopers he's sending with you will shoot you dead. He'll be givin' them orders 'bout that right now. See, he's making sure you ride out of here with some pretty mean boys who don't like officers at all. They'll be delighted to see you run off— might not even wait till you do."

Ki thought for a moment. "And if I fall off my horse in a couple of days . . ."

McPherson feigned alarm. "Wouldn't do that, sir. The penalty for going to sleep on duty's a firing squad." He looked warily over his shoulder. "Sir, you help that lady let those Injuns loose?"

"What do you think?"

"With respect to the lieutenant, I don't know what the hell to think about you. Smelled something funny the minute you got here. Don't smell any different now."

Ki faced him in the growing dawn. "Let me ask you a question, sergeant major," he said evenly. "You've got such a nose for bad smells, what else you figure stinks about here? Anything besides me bother you lately on this post?"

McPherson was a master at hiding his feelings, especially from men with rank on their shoulders. Still, Ki's words caught him unaware for an instant. Something was there and Ki saw it.

"I got no idea what you're talking about, sir," McPherson said plainly. Now, his features betrayed nothing at all. He stepped back and gave Ki a salute. "I'd watch Trooper Hayes," he added soberly. "Boy can hit a snake's ass with his weapon."

Ki led his patrol straight down the river. The idea was to make a rough square from Camp Supply southeast, turn back southwest, then angle back across Wolf Creek, and head on home. Ki had watched patrols come and go at all hours. It was a dull, plodding job. Other patrols were out now in other sectors. No one expected that they'd suddenly find the raiders sound asleep under a tree or even find any sign that they existed. So far, the raiders had left the army alone. The troopers were grateful for that. The men who left the fort prayed they'd have the most uneventful patrol on record.

By late afternoon they had completed the first leg of the square and turned away from the river. A row of dead trees and a narrow, dry gully marked a dead branch of the North Canadian. Now, in open ground, the patrol rode in a diamond, Ki at the point. When Ki saw the gully and the trees, he held up a hand to signal a halt. Lance Corporal Daniels rode up to his side at once. He was a heavy man with strong, ebony features, a thick neck, and a patch over one eye.

"Couple of buzzards circling over that creek bed." Ki pointed. "Send a man forward to check it out."

Daniels muttered an answer and jerked his mount around smartly. Moments later, a trooper trotted past Ki and made his way to the skeletal line of trees. Ki knew it was likely nothing. Plenty of things died out here.

The trooper turned and waved them forward. Ki brought the rest of the men down the shallow slope. Again, Daniels rode up beside him.

The trooper was standing well away from the gully. Ki picked up the smell. The trooper waved his hat and four buzzards squawked into flight.

"It's a horse, lieutenant," the trooper called out. "Hasn't been dead real long."

"Long enough," Daniels muttered.

"Any sign of a rider?" asked Ki.

"No, sir. No saddle or nothing."

If nothing had happened to the rider, he would have taken the saddle with him, carried it as long as he could. Ki frowned at the sight. The horse was a good riding animal, well fed and with a silky coat. What happened to it? he wondered. There was no sign at all of what had killed it. If he wanted to know that badly, he'd have to ask the troopers to try to turn the animal over.

Ki slid off his mount and walked past the dead horse to the bone-white trees. The stark column formed a crooked line along the creek bed and then vanished abruptly at a slight rise in the land to the west.

"What do you suppose happened?" Ki asked Daniels.

"Hard to say, lieutenant." Daniels shrugged and took off his cap to wipe his brow. "Cheyenne and Arapaho reservation right to the south, but that's sure not an Indian pony. They might've stole it—or shot it out from under whoever was on it."

"Then where are the tracks of who did it?" Ki wondered aloud. "As far as that goes—"

Ki stopped and went rigid. In spite of the heat, something cold touched the back of his neck. *Where are the horse's tracks? How did it get where it is without leaving any sign?*

Daniels saw it on his face and read it himself.

"Get 'em out of here," Ki said sharply. "Get them out fast!"

Daniels turned and bolted down the dry bed of the creek, snapping quick commands at the others. Ki drew the Colt from his holster. The troopers scattered; they didn't know what was wrong, but they understood the urgency in Daniels' voice. One man took the horses, while the others grabbed their rifles and formed a rough circle under the trees. It was the way the army had taught them—get off your mounts and form a covering field of fire.

Ki stared at the men in alarm. "To hell with that," he shouted. "Mount up and get out of here—do it!"

The troopers hesitated an instant, then obeyed. Ki ran across the dry bed. Daniels grabbed the reins of Ki's horse and started for him. Ki saw the blood fountain from Daniels' throat, saw the bullet's impact an instant before the flat sound of the shot reached his ears. Daniels dropped as if all his bones had vanished. The mounts tried to bolt. One squealed as a bullet found its mark. Ki braced his legs and squeezed off shots in the direction of the trees. A trooper tried to reach him, hugging his own mount and dragging Ki's horse with him. A volley of fire came from the trees and sent the trooper sprawling.

From the corner of his eye, Ki saw a gaunt trooper kneeling by his mount, calmly firing one shot after another into the trees. Hayes, maybe. The man who could nail a snake in the ass. Only this time there weren't any snakes.

Ki dived for cover as lead snapped wood at his head. The Colt was empty. No time to reload or get to his rifle. He glanced up and saw that Hayes was down. The one trooper left was riding his horse in a crazy circle, one hand clutched at his bleeding arm. Ki caught his eyes and waved him off. The trooper looked right at him.

"Go on, get out of here," Ki yelled. "Get out of here, damn it!"

The trooper turned and bolted. Bullets raised dust at his horse's heels. The trooper bent low and vanished over the rise. Ki saw two spotted ponies burst from the trees and take up the chase. He turned and ran, darting through the gully past the stark, white trees. Two riderless cavalry mounts trotted twenty yards ahead. Ki raced through the powdery soil. If the lead didn't drive the horses off—

He heard the sound behind him, turned to face it, and saw a blur of motion at his back: the blunt head of a horse; one slim leg and a bare thigh; then darkness reached out and pulled him under...

★

Chapter 13

He came awake slowly, drifting up from the bottom of a dark abyss. He dreaded reaching the top. He knew the pain was waiting there to meet him. When he opened his eyes, he saw dirt and stubby grass. The ground moved; the sight sent a sudden wave of nausea through his belly. He closed his eyes and then opened them slowly, a little at a time.

After a while, the sharp, lancing pain in his head was only a deep and throbbing presence. Without the pain he could think. He couldn't move. His arms and legs were numb—rawhide ties, probably, cutting off his blood. The world came to him slowly. The sky was a different color, which said he'd been out for some time. He smelled a wood fire. Meat. The faint odor of people, the strong smell of horses. Men were talking, their voices too low for him to comprehend.

The hurt wasn't as bad as the anger he felt within him, the anger and the shame at what had happened. He had let pretending become real. He had forgotten who he was—just for a moment, but enough. Spotting the buzzards and riding into the dry creek, he had let himself become Lieutenant Josh Stewart. The role had blinded him for an instant, dulled his senses. He had been Josh Stewart on patrol and not Ki, one trained in samurai skills that should have told him what was wrong. The skills should have told him that the horse was out of place and not lying in a natural position of death. He should also have known that whoever had left it there had backed off covering tracks, destroying the animal's tracks as well. And when he had finally seen it, had become himself again and realized the horse hadn't dropped out of the sky, it was much too late to back off, to save himself or help the others.

He opened his eyes fully and tried to guess where he was. Probably not too far from where they'd taken him, though the land up here all looked alike. Ki could guess why they'd kept him alive. The glimpse he'd seen of the horses told him Indians had ambushed his patrol. Indians, he figured, and most likely raiders as well. So he'd be the evening's entertainment, the main event. He cast the thought aside—trouble would find him soon enough.

He remembered the troopers—all dead except for the man with the bleeding arm and they'd likely killed him, too, for a man losing blood couldn't ride too far.

He heard steps, someone approaching through the grass, and closed his eyes. The footsteps came to a halt. Someone kicked him soundly in the ribs. Ki gasped and the man laughed, bent, and cut the bonds from around his legs. A foot turned him over on his back. He looked up and saw tree-trunk legs in leather trousers, saw a broad chest and an open calico shirt. The Indian's face was flat, misshapen, as if someone had hit him with a shovel.

"Get up," he said curtly. "Over there." He pointed vaguely past his shoulder.

The feeling returned to Ki's legs with a vengeance. He clenched his teeth and felt sweat coat his face. He saw they'd taken away his boots. The Indian watched him. Ki struggled to his knees, put one leg beneath him, and fell on his back. The Indian swore and kicked him again. Ki swallowed the pain and forced himself erect. His legs threatened to betray him, but he knew if he fell again the man would gladly work him over. He clearly enjoyed his work.

The Indian motioned again and Ki staggered across the clearing. The camp was in a hollow by a narrow, high-banked creek. Cottonwoods shaded the water. Some branch of the North Canadian, Ki guessed.

The Indian pushed Ki toward the others. Men watched him from a small cooking fire. The late evening sun dappled the clearing with red-orange light. There were five men by the fire, dark-skinned men with black hair to their shoulders, bands of cloth around their brows. Three were barechested; one wore a brightly colored shirt, the other a leather vest. Ki took them all in and glanced away—then looked back quickly again. Something was wrong. His eyes had said *Indian* without a thought and now he saw that wasn't true. The man who'd brought him to the fire was. The others weren't Indians at all. Hell, two of the men had light blue eyes! Their hair was long, their skin stained a coppery brown—but they were white, no question about it. From a distance no one would notice; close up was something else.

"Well, what you lookin' at, soldier?" One of the men stood, tossed a meat bone in the fire, and took a long swallow from his canteen. "See anything you ain't seen before?"

"I could use some of that water, if you don't mind," Ki told him.

The man laughed and the others joined in.

"Hungry, too, I bet. Like a little steak and beans with that water?"

"I wouldn't mind."

The man gave Ki a pained look. "Now, does that make sense to you? Feedin' and watering a dead man? Don't make sense to me."

Again, the others grinned at their friend.

"What you think about that?" the man went on. He enjoyed the taunting and wouldn't drop it. Ki saw the Indian had disappeared. "Bet you didn't even know you was dead. Bet you figured you was alive."

Ki didn't answer. He wondered how long this was going to take.

"Those troopers of yours," another man chimed in, "they ain't asked for food or water at all."

This brought a laugh and the man who was standing didn't like it. Pushing their captive around was his affair and he hadn't asked for help. Stepping across the fire, he hit Ki solidly in the face. Ki saw it coming and rolled, but the blow sent him sprawling on his back. The man kicked out at his head. Ki jerked away from the blow. The man cursed and kicked him savagely in the belly. Ki sucked in a breath and tried to fold himself in a ball. His hands were still bound and he felt like a turtle on its back. Another blow landed in his ribs. Maybe the man intended to end it right here—kick him to death on the ground. If he did, he wouldn't have to try much harder.

Ki rolled away from a brutal kick at his head, twisted on his back, and lashed out suddenly with his foot, the motion arching his body into a bow and snapping his leg like a spring. It took the man completely by surprise. He sprawled on his back and howled, clutching at his vitals. The others looked stunned. The best way to keep a man from making any trouble was to take away his boots. Most men were quite helpless without boots.

The man whom Ki had downed came to his knees, his face a mask of pain and savage rage. When he stood, he had a knife in his hand, a big blade, flat and heavy and made for skinning buffalo. He came at Ki, pushing back the pain; his glazed eyes focused on a point between Ki's legs.

"Damn you, Cleve—back off!"

The man stopped, blinked, and looked to his left. Ki turned his head and spat dirt. He had forgotten the bare legs, the patch of thigh he'd seen an instant before the darkness closed in. Now, the figure that belonged to the legs stood just at the edge of the clearing. She was tall, well over six feet. Ki had seldom seen a woman that size, much less a woman of Indian blood. She wore a dirty leather dress that had once been decorated with beads. The leather clung to the curves of her body like skin.

The man named Cleve stared at the girl, flexing the blade in his hand. His eyes flicked past her to the Indian who stood behind her.

"He's mine, Sparrow," he said harshly. "He's got it coming."

"No, Cleve."

"Listen, you got no right in this."

The girl moved, taking two long strides toward the man with the knife. She moved with a quick, animal grace, every motion betraying her strength. The point of Cleve's knife was only inches from her belly. She paid no attention to it.

"Untie his hands," she said. "Get him something to eat. I want to see him."

Cleve's face contorted in anger. "Hell, you let him loose and he's going to run!"

"If he does, kill him," the girl said simply. She turned and walked out of the clearing for the trees. If her eyes had ever touched Ki, he hadn't noticed.

He wolfed down the meat and beans and drank from the canteen they'd tossed him. The girl's mandated, brief reprise was more than welcome, but it failed to put him at ease. She had some control of this bunch; that was clear—just how much was hard to say. She'd stood up to Cleve and he'd backed off—maybe because the Indian was standing there, watching. Ki guessed Cleve respected the girl's prowess as well. Next time, though . . . Cleve wanted him dead. As long as Ki was alive, the others wouldn't let Cleve forget what had happened.

The Indian led him off through the trees. The girl was down by the creek. She had her own small fire; a blanket and her possessions were off in the brush. When Ki approached, she looked up, studied him a moment, and then gave the Indian a curt nod. The man left. Instead of returning to the camp, he walked across the creek into the trees.

The girl caught Ki watching. One corner of her mouth curled in amusement. "You are right. He is not far away. It would not be a good idea to try to run."

"Now, why would I want to do that?" Ki asked mockingly.

"Sit down." The girl's smile faded. She looked over Ki as if he might be some new bug she'd just discovered. The firelight licked at her honeyed flesh, the high bones of her cheeks. Her hair was as black as his own and hung freely past her shoulders to the swell of her breasts. Ki saw she wasn't full-blooded. Her features and the lighter cast of her skin betrayed something more than an Indian heritage. As tall as she was, she was still a perfectly proportioned woman, every curve and hollow of her body lovely to see. She was all there, everything in place. There was simply a lot more to her than Ki was used to seeing in one woman.

"Why do you think you're still alive?" she asked suddenly. "Tell me."

The question took Ki by surprise. "I don't know," he said honestly. "I don't guess it matters."

She seemed to like his answer. She shifted her long legs and sat on her thighs, hands pressed flat against her knees, her upper body leaning toward Ki.

"Your face, your features tell me you are not all white. What else are you?"

She surprised him once more. Most people ignored the slight tilt at the corners of his eyes, the sharp planes of his cheeks. He looked a great deal like any other man who'd grown up in the West.

"My mother was Japanese," he told her. "My father was an American." He saw at once *Japanese* was a word she didn't know. "I guess we're two of a kind," he added. "Your mother white or your father?"

The girl went stiff. Her dark eyes flashed with rage. "I am a Cherokee," she said sharply. "No other race has tainted my blood. I have nothing in common with you!"

"Well, then, my mistake." Ki cleared his throat. He was plainly on the wrong track.

The girl's rage subsided; there were still live coals in her eyes. "You are strong. You fight well. You kicked out very quickly at Cleve."

"I didn't see that waiting to get stomped would do me much good."

"How long have you been a soldier?"

"Nine years," Ki told her, reciting the number on his record.

"Tell me why the soldiers hate our people."

The girl sure had a way with questions. "I don't. I've known a lot of Indians from a lot of different tribes. I've got a lot of respect for some."

"Some?"

"Indians are just like everyone else. There are good ones and there are bad."

"Have you killed Indians?"

"Yes, I have." He looked right at her. "Because I had to—to keep 'em from killing me. I don't like taking a man's life, no matter his color."

"I have killed soldiers."

"I guess that makes us even."

"No." She shook her head angrily and stiffened her jaw in defiance. "This is not true. You do not belong here. You kill to take more land. We kill to keep the land."

"I can't argue that we kill," Ki said.

"Get up."

"What?"

"Stand. Get on your feet."

Ki stood. The girl pulled herself erect, moving with a quick fluid motion. Her foot swept out and smothered the small fire with sand. In the fading light of dusk, she peeled the leather dress over her head. Ki drew in a breath and stared.

"Take off your clothes," she said. "Tonight you stay with me. I can kill you in the morning."

★
Chapter 14

"Lady, you've got a hell of a way of arousing a man," Ki said dryly.

"So? Which is better?" The girl shrugged. "To take this pleasure or not?"

"I'm thinking."

"Come here. Thinking at such a time is a waste."

In the dark the girl's naked flesh seemed to shimmer with a life of its own. In spite of himself, Ki felt a swelling in his loins.

"Uh, what about that friend of yours? I know he's over there across the creek. I'm not much used to having spectators."

"Elk Ear belongs to me. He will see nothing he is not supposed to see." The girl's eyes narrowed. "He will see you if you should try to run off, though."

Ki had been considering the idea since the Indian had delivered him to the girl. But he didn't know how far he could get without a horse. When he did make his break, he wanted full darkness as his partner. He also wanted to know exactly where they kept the mounts.

"I can't imagine running off," Ki said soberly, "not while I've got such a fine looking woman to keep me company."

"Ha!" The girl cleared her throat. "A white man can't go a minute without a lie."

She came to him, then, closing the few steps between them. Her presence, the heat of her body, was overwhelming. The scent of her arousal was almost visible in the air.

Ki took her in his arms, feeling the hard, clean lines of her figure under his touch. The girl trembled; a sharp, little cry exploded in her throat. She tore at his clothes in a frenzy, ripping away his shirt and then bending to jerk his trousers down his legs. Strong hands gripped his back and drew him to the ground. She was a firm and luscious woman with a body made for pleasure. Her skin was light gold in the dark. When he kissed her, she opened her soft lips against his own and flicked her tongue hungrily into his mouth. Ki tasted every sweet hollow, stroking her mouth ever more open. Her body writhed, lashing wildly against him with a need she couldn't control. The heat of her flesh was like a furnace. Every cord and tendon in her hard, slender frame sang with an agony of delight. A fine sheen of moisture covered her skin. Her breasts were points of fire against his chest. He cupped one of the firm, lovely mounds in his hand, squeezed it, and brought the dark nipple into his mouth.

The girl shuddered, slid her strong hands beneath his own, and gripped her breasts hard, pressing the pliant flesh in loving strokes. As Ki watched, her palms slipped over her skin and came together, until she grasped each nipple between her fingers. She kneaded the firm nubs, relaxed, then squeezed them again. Her neck arched back and she smiled broadly with her pleasure.

Ki swept her hands aside and drew a musky nipple into his mouth. The heady scent assailed his senses. The girl groaned beneath him, lashing her body against his own. Her hands came up to grip his hair, to force his mouth tighter against her breast. He sucked the moist flesh between his lips, drawing a swollen nipple between his teeth. Long legs scissored about him; the girl was so strong that she nearly squeezed the breath from his body.

Ki's own hunger surged within his loins. He broke the hold of her legs and let his hand slide down the firm swell of her belly. When he touched the soft feathery edge of her treasure, she cried out and thrust her bottom up to meet him. He stroked the moist cleft, letting his fingers sink deeply in her satin flesh. Her body smoldered with heat; silken walls spasmed against him, drawing his fingers farther within her. Her hands raked his back, fighting to bring him to her. Dark eyes flashed in the night. She held him with a look of curious wonder; he saw the hunger in her eyes, hunger mixed with savage anger. Her hand reached down to find his member. When she found it, her lips stretched tight against her teeth. She muttered words he couldn't understand, arched her back, and thrust his length inside her. She shuddered and yelped aloud. Her legs gripped him hard and she threw herself against him.

Ki felt the fire churn in his belly. Velvet muscles tightened around him, heightening his desire. He thrust himself rapidly against her, so hard that the motion forced air out of her lungs.

A ragged cry escaped her throat. She shook her head wildly from side to side, whipping his face with dark hair.

Ki felt his release swelling toward a joyous peak of pleasure. The girl sucked air and clawed his back. Her teeth sank into his shoulder; the pain sharpened his arousal all the more. He pounded her again and again, each rapid thrust loosing her breath in small explosions. He felt the spasms of her orgasm grip her, felt her body jerk beneath him. She threw back her head and cried out with joy. Ki spilled himself inside her, filling her like a flood, one furious wave after another. She refused to let him go. Her body convulsed with a fury she couldn't control. Ki was drained, sated, yet the girl seemed unable to stop. Suddenly he felt the fires building within him again. He laughed aloud as her passion drew a final burst of pleasure from his loins, an agony even greater than the first.

She drew in a breath, held herself tightly against him, then sighed, and went limp in his arms. Ki pressed her within the hollow of his shoulder. He kissed her lips gently, brushing the moist strands of hair from her face. She returned the kiss quickly, then touched his shoulders, and pressed him back.

"I am surprised," she said evenly. "I did not think a soldier could give me pleasure. I have had one before. No—two. Neither was worth the time."

"I guess I'm flattered," Ki said.

The girl's eyes narrowed. "Do not take my words for weakness. Nothing is changed. I cannot leave you alive."

Ki let out a breath. "Now, why do we have to talk about that? We've been getting along fine."

She touched the side of his head. "Does it hurt greatly? Where I struck you from my horse?"

"It hurts, yeah." The girl was a wonder—what the hell difference did it make how he felt? If he cared to stay around, she'd put a bullet in his head in a few hours.

"The man named Cleve called you Sparrow. Is that your name?"

"Little Sparrow." She gave him a rueful laugh. "My mother did not think that I would grow. The name is no good now."

"Well, you sure grew."

She pushed herself up on one arm and studied his eyes. Long hair shrouded half her face. "You are a strange man. I do not think you are afraid."

"If I were, do you think I'd let you see it?"

Sparrow considered that. "No. I think that you would not.

110

Do you believe I will change my mind? That I will let you live?"

"I don't see how you can," Ki said, "not after what I've seen here."

"And what do you think you have seen?"

Ki looked up at the darkened sky, the scatter of stars through the trees. "You get your dander up too easy, Sparrow. I don't think you want to hear what I see. I don't think you'd much like it."

Sparrow's eyes narrowed to slits, her chin set in defiance. "You are afraid to tell me, is that it?" Ki's look told her she was wrong. "Go on, then. Tell me what it is I don't wish to hear."

"All right." He spread his hands behind his head. "If I were making a report back at the fort, I'd tell them they were only partially right about the raiders. I'd tell them that some Indians are involved, but not many—and those who are don't have any idea they're being used. I'd guess there's no more than a handful of Indians mixed up in the whole thing. The white men behind this business are playing them for fools."

"Stop!" Sparrow sat up straight, her face flushed with anger. "You have said enough. I will not listen to more."

"Of course, you won't," Ki said quietly. "Told you it wasn't something you wanted to hear."

"Why should I listen to lies?"

"No reason at all."

"Go on," she said, her interest obviously piqued.

"What?"

"Go on. Finish. I will hear your words—only because they will help me understand how the white man thinks." She crossed her arms haughtily over her breasts.

"I might have some of it wrong," said Ki, "but I can make a couple of pretty fair guesses. Seeing those men in your camp tells me a lot."

"What about them?" Sparrow said coolly.

"For God's sake, girl, you know what about them as well as I do," Ki said. "They're the lowest kind of life you can find this side of a snake. I've seen them before and I know exactly what they are—killers so far beyond any kind of law they can't even show their faces. They'd cut their mothers' throats for two dollars and they don't give a damn about whites, Negroes, Indians, or anyone else. The men who pay them don't have to dirty their hands—these boys like to earn their pay. And the men, the men in clean suits who are behind all this, they're worse than Cleve or any of the others."

Sparrow wet her lips. She wouldn't look at Ki. "Sometimes you have to do things to—to get where you want to go. Why should I care what they are? They kill other whites. I have never known a white who didn't need killing."

"Uh-huh." Ki made a face. "Let me guess how this works, all right? You've got a bunch of Indians who don't like being penned up on reservations. They want things the way they used to be—and they won't have anything to do with the five tribes and the way they run the Indian Nation because the tribes try to work with the whites. What these friends of yours are going to do is drive all the cattlemen and the settlers off the land, make it too hot for them to stay. Then they take over and work everything out. All they want is some of the Unassigned Lands and No Man's Land and part of the Cherokee Strip. Is that about right? Maybe a little path up past the Red River, alongside the panhandle of Texas." He saw the girl's sudden, startled look and knew he'd hit home. "They'll control the trails up to market and all the good grazing land. What your people get is a thank you and a promise—no more white encroachment on Indian land. They'll never bother you again. I expect they've told you that after this is finished the government will be so grateful that the trouble with the raiders is over, they'll back the whites working with you." Ki shook his head. He reached up and touched the girl's cheek and made her face him. "Are you looking for lies, Sparrow? That's the lie. That's the way it's supposed to happen, only it won't. It'll never be, believe me. When it's over, it's the Indians who'll be on the losing end. That's not a hell of a lot different from how it's been before. I'm sorry. This treaty you're dreaming about isn't any better than the others."

Sparrow pushed his hand roughly away. "None of this is true," she said stubbornly. "Do you think that I would listen to a soldier?" She spat on the ground. "All you know of Indians is how to kill them."

"You did listen," Ki said calmly. "You listened and you believed me. I saw it in your eyes, Sparrow. I came so close to it that you know I'm telling the truth."

"You made up things you know would make me angry. You would say anything if you thought I would let you live."

"You're dead right on that," Ki said solemnly. "Here's an-

112

other lie for you. The cattlemen are putting the blame right on the Indians. Just as I said it would happen—just as these friends of yours intend for it to happen. There's a rancher named Lyman who's gathering every fighting man he can find. They're going to ride out and put an end to the Indian trouble once and for all. They don't much care if it starts a war. They aren't thinking any straighter than you are. They want blood. I expect they'll hit the Cheyenne and Arapaho first; they're closest."

Sparrow's lips parted in alarm; then she clamped her lips tight. "We were told there would be—sacrifices by some, that men would have to die."

"Men—and a whole lot of women and children," Ki said harshly, "whoever gets in the way. When something like this gets started, nobody stops to check. People who don't have the slightest idea why someone wants them dead are going to—"

Ki sensed the girl's body go rigid—he threw himself aside and saw the quick flash of silver, felt the blade slice at his ribs, and plunge in dirt to the hilt. Sparrow cried out and tore at his eyes, jerking the knife free for another try. Ki slapped her hard across the face and sent her sprawling. Light flashed from Elk Ear's gun across the creek; lead creased his hair and Ki threw himself aside, rolled, and came to his feet running.

The girl shouted. Elk Ear's shots clipped leaves over Ki's head. Ki twisted to the right, then doubled back on his path, found the shallow creek, and ducked below its bank, following the twisted course north and away from the Indian's weapon.

In a moment the sound that he was expecting reached his ears. The others, Cleve and his friends, were on his trail. Ki cocked his head and listened: to the left; coming through the trees. He went to his hands and knees in the shallow stream, gathering a handful of round stones. The sounds of pursuit came closer and he climbed the side of the bank and rolled quickly into the brush.

He was naked, in the dark, and on unfamiliar ground. Knowing these things would make the others careless. Being naked didn't bother him at all and he liked the dark. When they'd bound him, they'd taken his boots; this might slow another man down, but Ki was delighted. His feet were hard as iron. He could handle a lot tougher terrain than this. And he was not without weapons, as they imagined. His feet, his hands, his body, and his mind—they were all weapons.

113

The weapons he liked to carry were the slim-bladed *tanto* knife and the *shuriken*, throwing stars. These things had been left at the Starbuck ranch in Texas. Both he and Jessie had agreed they were much too foreign to be in an army officer's belongings. If they were found, questions would be asked. Ki didn't need these things. He had himself. The men didn't see him as any danger. They saw a soldier, frightened and alone in the dark. They didn't know that Ki was hunting them. They thought it was the other way around.

One man passed him, crossing the creek and making noise and walking within three feet of where Ki lay hidden. Ki let him go. In a moment, another stomped by to his left. Two, then. Both behind him. Three more of Cleve's friends searching somewhere else. Elk Ear and the girl. The Indian was the one he wanted to find. Elk Ear would know how to use the dark and how to approach a man in silence. The girl, too. He had seen the way she moved, how she walked. He wouldn't sell Sparrow short.

Ki waited. In a moment he had a fair idea where they were. Cleve and two others on this side of the creek. Two more thrashing through the brush around the water. He couldn't account for Elk Ear and Sparrow. That was the way he'd imagined it would be.

Coming to his feet, he backed off and slid silently down to the bank of the creek. Earlier he had guessed where the horses would be, back near the spot where Cleve and the others had camped. The men had made the horses nervous, so they blew air and moved about, letting Ki know now where they were.

Ki made a point of going nowhere near the horses. That was where Elk Ear would be. The Indian would have the good sense to know Ki would try for the mounts. It was the thing he, himself, would do.

He heard a man coming and went to the ground. Carefully he set his stones aside. He saw a dark silhouette against the sky, a sliver of light on a rifle barrel. The man walked toward him. Ki rose straight up off the ground, the fingers of his right hand stiff and slightly bent, half fist and half claw. The blow caught the man at the point between his chin and the base of his throat, crushed the windpipe, and jammed ruined cartilage against the roof of his mouth. The man made no sound at all. Ki clasped the limp body to his chest, lowering the man and his weapon to the ground.

114

He pulled the body to cover and left the rifle where it lay. Firing the weapon would only bring the others, show them where he was. He didn't want that—not just yet.

"Harry, you there?" a voice said softly.

"Shut up, you damn fool," another answered.

Ki smiled. Two of them; crossing the creek behind him. They crossed together, one going downstream, the other climbing the bank not five yards away. Ki picked up one of his rocks. When the man was nearly on him, he tossed one of the rocks to his right. The man jerked around, swinging his pistol at the sound of the noise. Ki stood quickly, twisted on the balls of his feet, and thrust his leg out like a piston. The blow snapped the man's spine. He cried out once and the pistol exploded. Ki picked up his stones and moved off to the left. The grove of trees suddenly erupted with sound. This time Ki welcomed the noise.

Someone emptied a rifle at shadows. Another man cursed. Ki saw the man who'd gone off downstream running back toward his position, his boots splashing water. Ki pressed a flat stone between his finger, using much the same grip he employed for a *shuriken* throwing star. His arm snapped forward. The rock made a soft, whirring sound and found its mark. The man in the stream choked off a cry, groped blindly at his head, and fell face down in the water.

Ki melted into the trees, keeping low and moving as far from the trouble as he could. Three down, then. Cleve and one of his men left. Elk Ear and Sparrow keeping their silence. Would the noise draw the Indian away from the horses? Probably not. Elk Ear would guess what he was doing. Maybe he had Sparrow with him. Ki hoped she was somewhere off by herself. He'd have to kill Elk Ear to stop him. He didn't want to hurt the girl. Maybe she'd feel the same if their roles were reversed.

He stopped again. Listened. The woods had suddenly gone silent. There were three dead men out there. Cleve and his friend had surely found them. They wouldn't stomp around anymore if they could help it.

He didn't concern himself with Cleve or the other man. He would hear them coming long before they were a danger. He looked for the girl. He could find Elk Ear if he were patient, but Elk Ear wasn't like the others. He wouldn't let Ki get close.

He found Sparrow. He sensed her presence and raised his

115

head slowly and she was there, four feet directly above him, her body pressed flat against the branch of a tree. She had stopped to pull on the leather garment and she had the knife. He could see its shape against the wood. He stood, grabbed her leg, and jerked her roughly to the ground. She cried out in surprise and tried to twist herself out of his grip. Her long legs flailed the air. The knife flashed; Ki knocked it away, lifted the squirming girl up, and tossed her into the brush. When he turned, he saw a dark shape moving like a blur out of the trees. He was right. The only thing that would bring the Indian out of hiding was the girl.

Ki had only an instant to meet the charge. Elk Ear came at him low and fast, the blade in his fist sweeping out in an arc to gut him. The knife whispered across his belly. Ki leaped aside, lashed out with his foot, and kicked the Indian solidly in the ribs. Elk Ear grunted, caught his footing, and turned. Ki was already there. The hard edge of his palm struck out with the force of an axe. Elk Ear moved—scarcely more than an inch, but enough to keep the blow from cracking his skull. He spat blood, took the numbing pain, and slashed out at Ki with the knife. Ki backed off, turned on his heel, and kicked out with the point of his toe. The Indian cried out as the blow caught his wrist, sending the blade flying. Ki followed through, the kick and strike that followed a single motion. He came in close, pounding the Indian's face with a series of quick, punishing blows. Elk Ear staggered back. He was strong and fast, but Ki's fighting style was something he'd never encountered before. If an Indian fought without a weapon, he tried to wrestle his opponent to the ground, break his arm or strangle him, or snap his neck. Ki wouldn't stand still long enough for Elk Ear to get a good grip.

Ki stepped back for an instant and cocked his arm like a bow. The Indian's eyes were glazed. Ki snapped his arm forward. He heard Sparrow coming, but couldn't stop her. She screamed like a cougar, leaped on his back, and tore at his eyes. Her long legs gripped him in a vise. Ki tried to toss her off. She clung to him like a leech. Elk Ear shook his head, his features twisted in rage. Ki backed up and slammed the girl hard against a tree. The breath went out of her. She collapsed and fell away. Elk Ear was on him, the blade once more in his hand. Ki went into a crouch. Suddenly Sparrow reached out and grabbed his leg. Ki kicked her off as the Indian's blade sliced at his thigh. Ki lashed out and hit Elk Ear hard across the face. The Indian took it, whipping the knife viciously at Ki's throat. Ki kicked him solidly in the groin. The Indian folded.

Ki didn't stop to watch him fall. He raced in the direction of the horses. Someone shouted and lead snapped twice at his heels. He took the first mount he could find, jerked the rawhide halter free, and threw himself across the animal's back. The horse protested, stomping the ground and twisting, arching his neck to snap at Ki's leg. Ki dug his heels in hard, jerking the short rein to one side. The horse bolted, tearing through the trees. Low branches ripped at Ki's hide. Ki pressed his face in the animal's mane. The horse burst into the clearing. The Indian was nowhere in sight. He caught quick movement from the corner of an eye; Cleve and his man ran toward him at an angle, firing wildly in his path. Ki twisted the mount to one side, heading for clear ground. Cleve ran to cut him off. Ki cursed and turned the horse straight at him. Cleve's face went slack with surprise. He emptied his revolver in Ki's direction. Lead cut a red-hot furrow across Ki's shoulder. The frightened mount hit Cleve head on; Cleve screamed and fell beneath the hooves.

Ki didn't look back. Cleve's man fired shots in the dark. Ki clung to the horse's back and tried to guess what direction he was going.

A sentry raised his rifle, then lowered it slowly, and stared. The first dim glow of morning caught the Indian pony approaching the gate. The sentry shook his head to make sure he was seeing right. The man was stark naked. A white man without a stitch of clothing riding an Indian pony. The sentry called his sergeant. The sergeant called Enos McPherson. McPherson took one look, muttered under his breath, and got Captain Heywood Street out of bed.

Ki rode through the gate and slid wearily off his mount. His body was spattered with dried blood; his rear end was raw from the pony's back. Street put his hands on his hips and looked at Ki with open disgust.

"You got nerve to come crawling back here," he said sharply. "I'm damned if you don't."

"Captain," Ki said evenly, "can you hold off for maybe a

117

minute? I've got something you've got to know. About the raiders. If you'll—"

"Sergeant Major!" Street bawled over his shoulder. "Lock up this murderin' deserter this instant. I don't want to see him or hear him and I don't want anyone going near him. And you better have a firing squad roster on my desk in ten minutes!"

Chapter 15

Jessie could scarcely contain her anger and frustration. When she'd first seen the Crescent-H, the long halls and cool, high-ceilinged rooms had seemed open and inviting. Now she felt as if she were an animal in a cage, the walls closing in around her. In the fading light of day, she stepped outside on the broad, front porch that spanned the width of the house. Lew Lyman's riders were there. Three of them, some two hundred yards away across the flats. She circled the house and found two more. Five, then. They didn't look menacing at all; they were cowhands, not gunmen. It didn't seem likely that they'd follow Lyman's orders, shoot her down in cold blood if she tried to ride out. They weren't the kind of men who would relish such a task. What had Lyman told them, that she was a turncoat, that she was working with the raiders? That the blood of men they knew was on her hands?

Men do things in sorrow and anger they later regret. She reminded herself the riders that had left the Crescent-H only hours before were decent men. Yet the first Indians who happened to cross their path were as good as dead.

Damn Lew Lyman! Jessie clenched her fists at her sides and felt the blood rush to her face. Turning, she stalked into the house. Bill Haggerty had made himself scarce all afternoon, letting her know he didn't want to see her. Well, to hell with that, she decided grimly. He could tell her to his face what he was thinking.

Jessie burst into Haggerty's study without knocking. He was sitting at a desk and didn't bother to look up.

"You can pretend I'm not here if you want," Jessie said tightly. "That doesn't mean I'm not. I intend to talk to you, Bill. You want to sit there like a stump that's your concern."

Haggerty turned in his chair. His eyes seemed to bore right through her. "I don't see as how you and me have got a whole lot to say," he said.

"Looks to me like there's plenty to say," Jessie told him. She walked to the sofa and perched on the edge, clasping her hands to her knees. "Let's start with those guards of mine out there. That suit you just fine, does it? Lew Lyman setting up sentries around your house?"

Haggerty waved her off with an angry gesture. "You figure that's going to rile me, lady, you're on the wrong track. Those men out there don't mean a damn thing to me."

"It's all right with you."

"No, it's not all right and you know it. But I'm not going to go out there and shoot 'em down 'cause I don't like it. I'll settle with Lew Lyman—not them."

Jessie looked at him. "And if I decide to ride out of here, Bill, then what? You and your hands just look the other way? If they shoot me down on your spread, it's okay? You'll settle later with Lyman?"

Haggerty sat up straight. "Don't you go puttin' words in my mouth," he said sharply.

"Then say it, damn it!" Jessie flared. "Look me right in the face and say it. You washing your hands of this or what? If you want to squat here in your chair and let that mob go on a killing spree, you do it. I'm not going to stand still for it."

"And just what do you figure you're going to do? Ride out to the rescue, is that it?" Haggerty almost laughed. The scorn in his voice as clear.

Jessie stared, puzzled at his expression and the sound of his voice. "What's wrong with you, Bill? I know you're not real pleased with me right now, but that's not important. You're not talking like yourself. You act like you're off somewhere and what's happening out there's got nothing to do with you. Is that it? Lyman wins; it's over?"

Haggerty pulled himself erect, stalked to a far corner of the room, and poured himself a stiff shot of whiskey. He downed it and looked out at the night.

"No," he muttered almost to himself, "it's not over." He turned and gave her a cold, penetrating look. "You think you're the only human being in the Indian Nation who's got any concern for what's happening around here, Jessie? Well, by God, you ain't. The minute that army of Lew Lyman's left my yard I sent riders out of here in four different directions. One to Fort Reno and another to Fort Sill where there are officers with more sense than Grant DeLong. I sent another man up to Dodge City to talk to the federal marshal and to get a telegraph message off to Judge Isaac Parker at Fort Smith. There are other messages going to the War Department in Washington and one to the President. I got another hand on his way right now to Fort Elliott southwest of here in the Texas Panhandle. I'm not exactly squattin' in my chair, as you put it," he said sourly. "More'n that, I'm riding out of here myself after midnight, soon as I get all my hands back in from the range. We can't stand up to Lyman's bunch, but we'll be there. I don't think Lew or any of the others has got the gumption to gun me down."

Jessie looked at her hands. "I'm—sorry, Bill. I owe you an apology. Again."

"Don't go to the trouble," Haggerty snapped.

Jessie stood. "I don't guess you think much of me, do you?"

"I don't see much sense in pursuing this."

"Well, I do. Look—I'm sorry some of the things I've done and said have rubbed you the wrong way. But I don't much feel like taking it any further. Getting down and crawling just isn't my style. I let those Kiowas go and I'd do it again. I stood up to Lew Lyman. But I am not guilty of anything and you're acting as if I am."

"You want to know why I'm actin' like I am?" Haggerty's eyes turned to slits. "If you're so dense you can't see it, why I'll tell you. I been straight with you all the way. I wrote and told you what I thought was goin' on up here. I've shared everything I know with you. What I got for that, Jessie, is you going around behind my back—first pullin' one thing and then another. Trust don't work that way, damn it. You like it all going in one direction and that won't cut it. Not with me, it won't."

Jessie felt the color rise to her face. "All right," she said soberly. "You've made your point, and I can't say as how I blame you. You're talking about the Kiowa business, right?"

"Mostly that, yes. I figure there's a lot more goin' on that I don't know about, too. If you want to hold your cards close, you go right ahead. Just don't expect any better from the rest of the players."

Jessie nodded. "Maybe I should have said something sooner. It was loyalty to someone else that kept me from it—not disloyalty to you. It never was that." She took a deep breath and went on. "Lieutenant Josh Stewart. That's not his name. His name is Ki. He's worked for me and been a good friend for a number of years. When I decided to come up here, it seemed like a good idea to have someone on the inside of things. If the people who are involved in this are the ones I suspect are in it, they know me too well."

Haggerty frowned. "So you got this Ki fellow into the army. And he's the one helped you with the Kiowas."

"Yes."

"And you didn't think you could trust me with that?"

"Bill, let me finish, all right? I told you that it wasn't a question of trust." She took another breath. "Before I got to Camp Supply, Ki overheard a conversation in the settlement by the fort."

Haggerty raised his brows in interest. "What kind of a conversation?"

Jessie remembered Ki's words as well as she could. When she was finished, Haggerty closed his eyes and ran a hand across his chin. "So someone in Camp Supply is working with the raiders, waylaying shipments of some kind. I don't guess I'm real surprised. And he doesn't know more than that? He's got no idea who?"

"No. Nothing. And now he's in a hell of a lot of trouble back there. You can see why I didn't want to leave and why I've got to get back as soon as I can."

"Sounds to me like that man can handle himself pretty good in a pinch." A slight grin creased Haggerty's features. "Said I didn't much care for the man when I met him, didn't I?"

"Yes, you did. You were suspicious of him for all the wrong reasons, Bill." She paused to gather her thoughts. "There's something else. But let me ask you this, first. You said once you thought maybe some of the cattlemen up here might be working with the raiders, with the foreign element behind them."

"Yeah, I did. That wouldn't surprise me much either, much as I hate to say it."

"Do you think it's Lew Lyman?"

"Pretty obvious choice, considering," Haggerty said soberly. "Hell, I don't know, Jessie. Like I say, he's a damn good choice. Maybe too good. It could be someone else is kinda eggin' him on, using the way Lew just naturally is. I've known the man a long time. He doesn't need any help bein' Lew Lyman. He hates every color of skin 'cept his own." He stopped and looked curiously at Jessie. "That isn't what you were gettin' at, though, is it? There's something else on your mind."

"Yes, there is. It doesn't make sense, but I can't forget it. At Art McGregor's place, Bill, when I tried to help that man get to cover, it was something you said yourself—how easily I could have been cut right in two by the raiders' fire. You were right. Only nothing happened. They didn't shoot at me at all. They just stopped. Nobody fired a shot."

Haggerty looked puzzled. He seemed to be waiting for Jessie to finish. When she didn't go on, he gave her a sober shake of his head. "I think you're making more out of that than there is. You said it—it don't make sense."

"Bill, it happened. I saw it."

"Won't argue with you," he said flatly. "And I don't see those bastards stoppin' to tip their hat to a lady." He came to her and gripped her shoulders. It was the first time she'd seen a smile on his face in some time. "Everything straight between us now? We all right?"

"Everything's straight. You understand why I did what I did, don't you, Bill? Maybe I should have done it differently."

"That's all over." He waved her words aside. "Why don't you go up and get a little rest? Isn't anything going to happen around here for a few hours."

He tried to move away, but Jessie held him. "When you ride out after Lyman, we're not going to go through any nonsense about me staying here, are we? I've got to go back to Camp Supply to see about Ki. I don't care how well he can take care of himself; I have to know he's all right."

Haggerty frowned. "You know 'bout how popular you are over there with DeLong and Street?" He shook his head and backed off. "Never mind. Damned if I'll try to stop you. I'll even send a couple of boys with you. Jessie, you're as stubborn as your father, and that's the truth!"

Jessie felt as if a great burden had been lifted from her shoulders. The rift with Bill Haggerty had troubled her greatly. She liked and respected the tough old cowman and earnestly wanted his respect. And, personal feelings aside, she needed his help, not his enmity and anger. The sooner she got to Camp Supply, the better she'd like it.

She thought again of the actions Haggerty had taken, sending riders to Dodge and to the army posts. Before long, federal lawmen and soldiers would be swarming into the Indian Nation. Not soon enough, though—not soon enough to stop Lew Lyman from making a tragic mistake. Only Bill Haggerty could stop Lyman. She was certain that Bill's presence would make a difference. The men who'd left the Crescent-H were eager for blood. But by now they might be thinking twice about what they planned to do.

Sleep was out of the question. Jessie paced the floor and then changed into a worn blue cotton shirt and comfortable denims. The night air was cooler for a change, so she laid aside a light leather jacket next to her Stetson. She placed the Colt and a handful of extra shells in her saddlebag and stuck the ivory-handled derringer behind the buckle of her belt. On her hands and knees she searched for her boots, found them under the bed, and sat down to pull them over her stockings. The right boot hurt, so she took it off, carried it to the lamp, peered inside, and then felt in the heel with her fingers. A piece of leather had worn loose and projected upward like a rock. That wouldn't do—half a minute on that and she'd be limping like a cripple.

After searching about the room, she decided she'd left her knife somewhere or lost it. She sat down on the bed and removed the other boot, opened the door, and walked quietly down the hall. Haggerty wasn't likely resting. Even if he were, she wouldn't disturb him padding in stocking feet down to the kitchen for a knife.

Downstairs, there was just enough light from the front window to let her make her way down the hall. The kitchen was past the parlor and the big dining room with the heavy oak table and chairs. After stopping briefly just inside the kitchen door, she felt her way. There was nothing like groping around in someone else's kitchen. If she remembered correctly, the cook kept the knives in a big earthen crock on a table next to the oven. She felt her way carefully along the table—stopped suddenly and gripped the wooden rim with both hands.

"Don't much care if they do; that's how it's got to be done. You take care of it now."

"Yes, sir. It'll get done; don't you worry."

"Don't tell me not to worry. At this stage of the game, I'm damn sure going to worry."

Bill Haggerty and—the second voice? One she'd heard before, one of Bill's hands, someone around the ranch. Jessie felt awkward. The men were just outside and to the right of the open kitchen window. If she tried to back off, they'd likely hear her. What would Bill think, finding her sneaking around in his kitchen? She decided the best thing was to wait, do nothing at all, and hope they'd go away and let her leave.

"You want me to handle it personal or what?" the man asked.

"Hell, no, I don't," Haggerty snapped. "Let our man at the fort do it. That's what he's gettin' paid for. Just get it done fast. That bastard works for the Starbuck woman, and he's on to something about the goods. I don't know what and I don't care. I don't like leavin' loose ends."

"What about her?"

"You got plenty to do; don't you worry about her. I'll handle her. I got that under control."

Haggerty—Bill Haggerty! Jessie's blood turned to ice. *My God, no. It can't be!*

She backed off quietly, fighting the panic that threatened to overwhelm her. Got to get out. Easy, just take it easy. Her foot hit a big copper pot and sent it clattering across the floor. The noise sounded like a cannon going off in the kitchen.

"What the hell!" Haggerty bellowed in surprise. Suddenly a shadow filled the door to Jessie's right. In a single motion she jerked the derringer from her buckle, thumbed back the hammer, and fired. The man in the doorway howled. In the bright flash from the muzzle, she saw his hands go up to his face. Haggerty cursed, threw the man aside, and came at her. Jessie backed off and squeezed the trigger again. The shot echoed loudly in the confined space. Haggerty grunted and grasped the sides of the door with both hands. Jessie turned and raced for the front of the house.

"Stop her," Haggerty roared at her back. "Damn it, somebody stop her!"

Jessie pushed the screen door aside and bolted off the porch. A cowhand ran out of the bunkhouse to her right, stopped, and blinked into the dark. Another followed on his heels.

"Mr. Haggerty, he's been shot," Jessie cried out. "Help him, please!" She pointed toward the house.

"Jesus!" The pair ran for the house. There were two horses at the hitching rail in front of the yard. Jessie loosed the reins, threw herself onto a dun-colored mare, and kicked it swiftly in the sides. The mare whimpered and ran. Haggerty yelled from the front porch, shoving his men aside. A Winchester roared and Jessie felt lead whine past her cheek. She bent low in the saddle and urged the mount on. From the corner of an eye, she saw the riders coming up fast on her left, and she knew Lyman's sentries had stayed awake.

★

Chapter 16

The torn denims they gave him were too big around the waist. Ki solved that by making a belt from a strip of the equally large shirt. He remembered the cell. The last time he'd been there, he and Jessie had freed White Bull and the others. He wondered where the Kiowas were now. Maybe they'd come back and return the favor.

A guard brought him water, day-old bread, and a tin plate of beans. Ki finished off the food and water, then curled up in a corner, and went to sleep. Samurai training enabled him to grab sleep whenever he could, to relax his mind and body, and to make a few minutes of rest do the job of several hours. When he woke, he guessed a little more than a half hour had passed. He felt better. He was stiff and sore from fighting his way out of the raiders' camp and the long ride back to Camp Supply. Bareback was supposed to refer to the horse, not the rider, he thought bemusedly. Elk Ear's knife had brought blood, but the wounds looked worse than they were. Next time they brought him water he'd try to soak away some of the dried blood. He'd been too thirsty to waste the water they had already brought.

Some time before eight an officer he barely knew came by to take his statement. For the court-martial, the man explained, some time before the day was out.

Captain Street was wasting no time. Ki learned the charges were desertion and cowardice under fire. Wasn't it a little unusual, Ki asked, to specify the charges before Street knew what had happened on the patrol?

The officer frowned at that. "Oh, he already knows what happened."

Ki sat up straight. "The trooper got back? He's alive?"

"He got back, all right," the officer admitted.

"Well, my God, man, if someone talked to him you know!"

The officer looked away and cleared his throat. "Lieutenant,

126

the trooper said that when he rode off everyone was dead, except you—that you were running down the creek bed."

"And what else? He's got to have said more than that."

"That's it. He died right on the parade ground, bled to death from a bullet in his arm."

Ki let out a breath. He was sorry that the trooper hadn't made it. Still, it did seem that he could have lasted another minute, long enough to straighten things out. But would that have made any difference? More than likely not. Street was just going through the motions. Evidence or no evidence, he was determined to line Ki up against a wall.

He told the officer what happened—including his information that the raiders, for the most part, were white men disguised as Indians. The officer dutifully took down everything Ki said. Ki had no hope at all that anyone would read this document. His court-martial was nothing more than a farce on the way to a firing squad.

The man thanked Ki and departed, leaving Ki with another piece of depressing information. Matt Bilder was no longer on the post. Street had talked DeLong into giving the scout his walking papers. He had left while Ki was on patrol. So much for his only friend at Camp Supply. He hadn't even had the chance to thank Matt for lying.

"Josh—Josh, over here!"

The familiar voice brought him to his feet. He moved to the small barred window at the back of his cell and saw Mindy DeLong's pretty face staring in.

"Oh, Josh, I'm so sorry about what happened! Are you all right?"

"I guess so, Mindy." Her hand found his; it was soft and cool to the touch. "I appreciate your coming. I don't want you getting in any trouble because of me."

Mindy bit her lip. "Josh, I'm not worried about me. It's you they're goin' to shoot. Everybody on the post is talking about it."

"That hasn't happened yet," Ki told her. Tears filled her eyes and he squeezed her hand again. "Don't count me out too soon. A man isn't dead till they plant him in the ground."

"Don't talk about things like that," the girl groaned. She leaned in close to the bars. "I spoke to my pa. I told you were a good man and he didn't have any cause to let that damned ol' Street have at you."

"And what did he say?"

"He kinda got real mad, I guess, and wanted to know how come I knew you in the first place. Of course, I couldn't very well tell him that. He'd likely come down here and shoot you himself. I don't guess I made things any better. I'm sorry. I'll keep trying. They just can't shoot you. I won't let 'em!"

"Thanks, Mindy. I'm grateful. Don't you get yourself in any trouble."

She looked at him longingly once more, then turned, and scurried off past the stables. Ki watched until the slender figure vanished. The sight brought a pleasant memory. He pushed the image aside. This was definitely not the time for dreaming. If he intended to see another sundown, he'd have to come up with more help than the colonel's daughter could offer.

With Matt Bilder gone and Jessie totally unaware of what had happened, the list of those who could help was pared down to nothing.

A wagon was being loaded by the stables and Ki watched. Troopers hitched four animals to the wagon, while others loaded the bed with kegs and flat wooden boxes. The morning sun already scorched the sky and sucked color out of the ground. The troopers' blue uniforms were soaked black with sweat. When the loading was complete, a tall, lean man came into sight, stalking past the stables toward the wagon. He walked past the team to the bed, stopping every few feet to tug on the ropes that bound the load, testing to see that they were secure. He wore butternut trousers, a red cotton shirt, and suspenders. His spare features were hidden under the brim of a frayed straw hat.

Ki saw the sergeant major come up behind him. He stood by the horses, hands hooked under his belt. The civilian clearly saw him, but pretended he wasn't there.

"Reckon my boys know how to load a wagon," the sergeant major said flatly. "You don't need to worry 'bout them boxes coming loose, Mr. Beamer."

The man named Beamer looked up and gave a nasty grin. "Well, now, that's comforting to hear. Long as this here's my wagon and I'm doing the driving, I'd like to see for myself, if you don't mind."

"Yeah, well you do that," the sergeant major said. He muttered under his breath and walked off.

Ki scarcely heard him. He gripped the bars of the window, staring with disbelief at the man by the wagon. Something cold touched the back of his neck. The voice, the man in the alley. Ki knew he wasn't mistaken. Beamer was the man who belonged to that voice! He had worn army blues that night, but this was the same man. There was no question at all in Ki's mind.

He saw at once what had happened and cursed himself for being a fool. He'd been looking for a man in army blue, one of the officers at Camp Supply. Beamer was a civilian, a man who'd contracted his services to the post. He could come and go as he liked during the day. There was another man, someone else in the fort working with him. Ki had learned that much in the alley. So if Beamer needed to get in touch with his friend after dark when the main gate was shut, he simply traded his butternut trousers for military garb and slipped in Post Number Nine—like any other officer coming in late from a night on the town. Sentry duty was casual at best; Ki knew that from his own experience. A trooper would think twice before he challenged a white officer coming in a little tipsy, his hat pulled over his face. What did the sentry care which officer it was?

The wagon loaded with goods. Where was it going now? Ki wondered. Beamer wouldn't likely be taking the load himself unless it was something he considered important.

"Last week's got to be the end of it. If you want the stuff, you hit it on the way. After it leaves us . . ."

The words Beamer had spoken in the alley seemed to hit Ki right between the eyes. The shipment was leaving now. It had to be something like rifles, powder, and ammunition. The raiders knew it was coming. Every trooper escorting the wagon would die. Beamer would survive. Since he was taking the wagon himself, he was very likely fading out of the picture, his role at Camp Supply finished.

Ki gripped the bars in frustration. Beamer stepped up and took his seat, released the brake, and shook the reins. The team jerked to a start and disappeared. A moment later, four black troopers guided their mounts around the corner of the stable. Another horse passed them and took the lead. Ki stared in dismay. Jake Wallace! Good God, the patrol roster had to be down to nothing if they'd pried First Lieutenant Jake Wallace away from his charts and counting chores and set his portly frame on a horse. A seasoned cavalry officer would stand less than half a chance when the raiders struck. Poor Jake wouldn't know what hit him.

129

Wallace and the troopers disappeared, leaving Ki to watch their dust. Ki ran across his cell and started pounding on the heavy wooden door, shouting for his guard.

A trooper peered through a small opening and frowned. "Lieutenant, sir, you goin' to have to stop makin' all that racket," he said. "Just can't have that in here."

"I've got to talk to Sergeant Major McPherson," Ki said sharply. "Get him over here as quickly as you can!"

The guard gave him a dubious look. "What do you want to see him for?"

"Damn it." Ki fumed. "This is important. Get him over here. Please don't waste time asking questions. I have got to talk to McPherson!"

The guard showed him a sad, understanding smile. "Beggin' the lieutenant's pardon, but there ain't much of anything you got to do, sir, 'cept sit in there quietly till they get ready for you."

"Listen—listen to me!" Ki demanded.

Ki kicked the door with his foot and kept shouting. The guard didn't return. No one paid him the slightest bit of attention. From the shadow of the sun outside his window, Ki guessed it was close to ten in the morning. He sat in his corner and did a samurai breathing exercise. It helped, but not much. Every minute that passed, Jake Wallace and his troopers came that much closer to being dead. For that matter, so did he. If the court-martial convened that afternoon—and Ki was certain it would—Street would have him tried, convicted, and shot before supper. He'd likely beat Wallace to the grave.

The noonday meal failed to arrive. Ki decided unruly prisoners didn't eat.

Late in the afternoon, a key rattled in the door. Ki came to his feet at once. The door swung open and Sergeant Major McPherson stepped inside. A trooper held a rifle on Ki. McPherson waved him off.

"Leave me be," he told the guard. "I don't reckon the lieutenant's goin' to eat me up or nothing."

"You took your sweet time," Ki said glumly. "What time is it, by the way?"

"'Bout four," McPherson told him. "You gettin' eager for the festivities to start?"

Ki muttered under his breath. "If you're talking about my so-called court-martial, the answer is no. I'm not eager at all.

Whether you know it or not, you've got another festivity taking place this afternoon. About now." He looked McPherson right in the eye. "The wagon that left here this morning with a man named Beamer—where is it supposed to be going?"

McPherson raised a brow. "You get me over here to talk about wagons?"

"Damn it!"

"Where it's going is down the North Canadian. Boys from Fort Reno going to come up halfway and meet it."

"You know what's in it?"

"What's in the wagon? Course I do. Nails and shovels. Got 'em in from the railroad at Dodge last week. Lieutenant, what in hell you askin' me all this for?"

"No." Ki shook his head firmly. "It's not nails and shovels. It's rifles and ammunition. If you don't believe me, check the arms room and you'll find they're not there. That wagon won't even get close to those troopers from Fort Reno. Beamer's working with the raiders. They've been gone six hours and that means those troopers are dead and the raiders have the wagon."

McPherson's ebony features went hard. "Lieutenant, I know you're countin' hours and I don't guess I blame you for coming up with whatever you can—"

"Sergeant Major, I am not coming up with something!" Ki said sharply. He dug his nails in his palm, forcing the calm back into his voice. "What I'm telling you is the truth. Go check those guns. They aren't there, I promise you that."

McPherson bit his lip in thought. "I figure I'm going to find in that arms room what's supposed to be there. On the other hand, I can't see what it'd get you if I find out you're a liar in about five minutes from now."

"Yeah, well, that's worth thinking about, isn't it?"

"Beamer working with the raiders?" McPherson shook his head. "Just how you figure that?"

"You see my report? The one they're supposed to read before they shoot me?"

"I saw it."

"It's the truth. Those raiders are white. They ambushed us, took me prisoner. I got away. I'm guessing there are other bands like the one I saw. White men who look like Indians from a distance. A couple of real Indians in with 'em. They strike from a number of locations all over the western half of the Indian Nation. You recall that Comanche Bill Haggerty shot a couple of days back, when the raiders killed the Hardy couple and burned them out?"

McPherson nodded. "If I recollect, that was real enough Injun."

"It was. Now that I know how the raiders operate, I can make a good guess about that Comanche. They had the poor son of a bitch along for that purpose—to get killed. I'm not sure how they did it. They could have shot him themselves at the right moment."

"So, accordin' to you, everyone sees a dead Injun and figures all the rest are redskins, too. Stands to reason, if any of this is true. It gives that mob of ranchers 'bout all they need."

Ki ran a hand through his hair. "Sergeant Major, I asked you once before if anything smelled funny to you on this post. You said no, but your eyes said something else. Damn it, you keep your hand on everything that happens in this place. You know something's wrong. Now I'm telling you what it is."

McPherson's glance didn't waver. "How do you know I'm not in it? Whatever it is we're talking about, I mean. If a fella knows as much as I do, he's the logical man, I'd say."

"You're right. He is. Only you're not it. Someone's working with Beamer, but it's not you. Whatever else you are, you're all army. I can't see you knifing your own troopers in the back."

"If I'm army, you sure as hell ain't," McPherson said narrowly. "I reckon I got that one right from the start. Just what exactly are you, mister?"

"That would take more time than we've got," Ki said plainly, "especially since that stuff's missing from the arms room. Are you with me?"

McPherson looked right through him. "That ambush of yours—it happen like you said in that report?"

"Yes, it did."

"That boy who made it back—did he run out on you? You didn't make that real clear."

Ki shook his head. "He didn't run off. He wanted to stay. He looked right at me and I told him to go."

McPherson nodded and bit his lip. Ki could read the pain on his features. "If I prove you right, I probably got me some more dead boys out there. I ain't real sure I don't want to see you a liar."

Ki waited. "When you look, check for boxes that are supposed to be empty. The conversation I overheard said something about empties. I didn't understand what they meant."

McPherson showed him a wary look. "Now what conversation'd that be? I don't recall us talkin' about that."

"Tell you later. Just check it out. If I'm wrong, you've got a front row seat at my execution."

"Got that anyway," McPherson said dryly.

"You've got a—" Ki stopped as a key turned in the big wooden door.

"I'll call you when I'm ready, boy," McPherson snapped over his shoulder, "and I ain't ready yet." Irritation crossed his features. The door swung open. Ki stared. McPherson caught his expression and twisted about in alarm.

"Mindy, no!" Ki cried out.

Startled, Mindy DeLong swung the shotgun up from her waist. McPherson simply turned right into the blow. The barrel hit him solidly across the brow. His eyes rolled back and he sank down limply to the floor.

"For God's sake, girl, what are you doing?" Ki groaned.

"I'm rescuing you," Mindy said fiercely. "What's it look like I'm doing?"

Ki crossed to her quickly, jerked the weapon out of her hands, and peered into the hall. Two guards were face down on the floor, hands clasped tightly behind their heads.

Ki's mind raced. He searched for answers that didn't exist. The only right answer lay unconscious at his feet. When McPherson came to, he could find every rifle ever stolen from the army. He could stand up for Ki and say what happened was a mistake. Maybe he would and maybe he wouldn't. It didn't much matter because Heywood Street wouldn't care one way or the other. Ki had tried to break out and never mind who'd helped him. Mindy would get a scolding. Street wouldn't wait for the trial to shoot him.

"I guess you got this all figured," Ki said tightly, "how I get out of this place in broad daylight?"

"I don't know what you're angry with me for," Mindy said. "You act like I did something wrong."

"Mindy," Ki said as he grasped her shoulders, "do you have horses? Did you think about horses?"

"'Course I did. And I got it set up to go out the back gate. Isn't hardly anyone there this time of day." Before Ki could stop her, she started out of her dress. Underneath she wore a trooper's blue uniform. She filled out the blues in a startling manner, like no soldier he'd ever seen.

"I didn't get one for you," she told him. "Figured you could strip one of the guards."

Ki stared. It suddenly occurred to him what she was doing. "Mindy, you're not going with me. You can't."

"Who says I can't?" She set her chin firmly in defiance. "You just try to get out of this place without me, Josh Stewart!"

★

Chapter 17

Jessie hugged the neck of her mount and kicked the animal into a run. Two of Lyman's men jerked their horses about quickly, turning down the rise to cut her off. Gunfire lit up the night from the front of Haggerty's house. One of Lyman's riders cursed. He forgot about Jessie at once, reined in his horse, and blazed away at the house with his rifle. Lead was coming in his direction; he didn't waste time asking why or whether the bullets were meant for him. His friend pulled up beside him, slid out of the saddle, and emptied his pistol.

Jessie urged her horse off to the right, out of the line of fire and toward the trees that lined the bend of the river. Another two of Lyman's men were off to the east, but neither looked in her direction. They were racing through the dark, intent on helping their friends. Jessie breathed a silent thanks and guided her mount through the trees. Gunfire echoed behind her. She was safe for the moment, but they'd sort out the confusion soon enough. A five minute head start, no more than that— then every rider Bill Haggerty could put in a saddle would be on her trail.

Jessie hesitated at the bank of the river. In the pale glow of the moon, the shallow water was black; pale patches of silver picked out the lazy current. Dodge City was maybe sixty miles north. She could get help there, help from the law and access to telegraph wires. For a small moment she was tempted. She needed help and plenty of it, but knew there wasn't time. Haggerty's words had been clear: Get rid of Ki. Ride to Camp Supply and make sure he never tells what he knows. The stark memory of Haggerty's voice chilled her blood. She could scarcely believe his treachery. Bill Haggerty—in God's name why? What could twist a man like that and make him turn on his friends?

There was no time now to look for answers. She had to get to Ki and warn him, get him out of Camp Supply. Leading her horse into the river, she crossed to the north bank, rode a quarter mile, then crossed back again. Tracking her wouldn't be easy in the dark. If they did pick up her trail, maybe they'd think she'd headed north. Maybe the small deception would buy her time.

And when she got to Camp Supply? Jessie didn't let herself think about that. Who'd listen to such a wild, incredible accusation? Captain Street, Lieutenant Colonel DeLong? Matt Bilder would try to help, but Street hated Bilder and had poisoned DeLong's whiskey-soaked mind against him.

Coming out of the trees, she saw them—ten, maybe fifteen riders etched against the night sky. They were four hundred yards to the south and heading east toward Camp Supply. Haggerty wasn't a fool. Muddying up her trail had been useless. All right. She'd stay parallel to their course, then circle around, try to get ahead, cross their path, and make a break for the fort. Not much of a plan, but they'd left her little choice.

She urged her mount off to the north, staying to the shadow of the trees. She would keep to the river as long as she could and use the extra darkness to hide her.

In a moment she glanced back to check her pursuers. Her heart nearly stopped. Nothing—they were gone! She reined in quickly and peered into the dark. The long line of horses had broken up, turned, and headed back in her direction. Jessie's throat went dry. They weren't headed for Camp Supply at all. They knew she wasn't ahead of them. They were spreading in a wide half circle to cut her off, to snare her like a fish in a net.

She forced her rapid breathing back to a calm and easy pace as Ki had taught her: Let the inner mind work; let instinct and reason merge as one. If Haggerty were trying to net her from the south, there was another trap waiting to the north. Riders would be circling down from the river at her back, cutting off her retreat. The jaws of the trap would close, and she'd be caught in the middle. Still, she reasoned, they couldn't cover every foot of ground. What path would they leave open? Which way would they ignore?

The answer came to her at once. The one that wouldn't concern them, the one a frightened woman on the run would never consider. Jessie turned her horse in a tight circle and headed back the way she'd come, back to the Crescent-H. She could hear riders splashing across the river. The others were gaining ground to her left. The dim lights of the house appeared ahead.

Suddenly she swung her horse south, forcing the mount forward at a killing pace, sweeping thoughts of gullies and unseen holes out of her mind. She pushed the mount hard until the animal's labored breathing told her that she'd be on foot before long if she didn't stop—on foot with a winded horse and in her stockinged feet. She thought about her boots, still sitting beside her bed in the upstairs room at Haggerty's house. Her boots; her saddlebag with the .38 Colt tucked neatly inside; her jacket draped over a chair. All she had with her was the ivory-handled derringer and that was empty. She wondered idly what kind of damage she'd done. The man with Haggerty had brought his hands to his face—powder burns or a bullet in the head, hard to say which. She'd hit Haggerty, she knew, but not enough to stop him. The little .41 calibre weapon was deadly enough—if you were close and if you happened to hit something vital.

Jessie slid wearily out of the saddle and started leading the mount to the south. The earth wasn't bad, but if she hit rocky ground she'd never last. She had no illusions about herself.

The sudden change in light caught her attention and she glanced over her shoulder in alarm. A dark gray smear touched the eastern horizon. Morning was coming a great deal faster than she liked. Grass and clumps of brush nearly invisible moments before stood out now against the ground.

Jessie picked up her pace; the mount protested, but she forced it along. Daylight seemed to rush into the sky, pushing the night to the west. Ahead, an irregular line of shadow hugged the horizon, as if the darkness refused to flee this particular corner of the world. Jessie stopped, puzzled, and then suddenly realized the shadows were trees. She breathed a sigh of relief. It had to be the North Canadian. The river ran parallel to the Cimarron, a dozen or so miles south of Haggerty's ranch.

Jessie looked back for signs of pursuit. Now that it was light, they'd spot her tracks at once. She forgot about her feet and pulled the horse hurriedly toward the trees.

Riders appeared abruptly; one moment there was nothing and then they were there, wavering out of bright planes of heat. By the sun, Jessie guessed it was eight or a little after. She'd been in the safety of the trees for a half hour. Cursing her luck, she backed the horse up to better cover. A few minutes more and she would have been gone, the horse rested and bearing her east to Camp Supply.

Two riders, three. That puzzled her a moment. Why not more than that? It came to her then that they'd split up in the predawn hours, heading out in different directions from where they'd lost her.

The men were some six hundred yards to her left. In a moment they'd find the spot where she'd led the horse into the river to cover her tracks. Once they knew that, they'd cover both banks to see where she'd ridden back out. They'd send the third man down the river itself. She'd tried to lose them once by doubling back and they wouldn't likely forget that trick.

She walked the horse through the brush as quietly as she could, then splashed through the shallows away from her pursuers. Fear knotted up in her belly and she fought to keep her calm. She couldn't stay in the river. She'd have to break free and take her chances on the flats—outrun them if she could. Next to no chance at all and she knew it. The horse wouldn't hold up.

To hell with it, she thought angrily. It's that or let them take me.

She urged the mount out of the river, doing her best to keep from silting the water and leaving a trail. Branches brushed her legs. A locust chattered in the still and humid air. Keeping to a point midway between the harsh, open country and the edge of the river, she waited and listened, letting the horse move a slow step at a time. Through the dappled light of the trees, she caught a quick blur of motion to her right. A rider was in the open, leaning intently out of the saddle and searching the trees. Jessie stopped. When he was gone, she turned back, following the direction he'd come. She didn't dare wait longer. The second man was coming up the river. He'd see her, spot her almost at once. Time to try it, then. Dig in your heels, break free, and give it your best. Now . . . now!

The horse trembled and shifted nervously to the left. Jessie cursed the animal under her breath. No time for that kind of nonsense, friend! Out of the corner of an eye, she saw a dark shadow rise swiftly out of the brush, saw a face in a blur as a hand closed roughly over her mouth and jerked her out of the saddle. The other hand grabbed the animal's bridle and held on. Jessie struggled as he held her against his chest; she clawed at his face and kicked her legs.

"Quiet down, damn it—shut up!" he said harshly.

Through his fingers she saw a knife catch silver from the sun. The horse squealed and bolted as the blade pricked sharply at its flanks. The animal crashed wildly through the brush for the river. The man pushed Jessie to the ground, driving the air out of her lungs. A shot rang out and then another. A man shouted. A rider splashed through the river. Another moved swiftly past the northern bank.

The man's grip relaxed. He turned Jessie up to face him.

"Bilder!" Jessie stared. "What are you doing here?"

"Tryin' to keep us both from getting holes in our head at the moment," he said. He stood, helped her up, walked to the edge of the trees for a moment, and returned.

"Come on, let's go," he said. "It'll be about a minute 'fore those boys find out that horse of yours doesn't have a rider."

Jessie started to protest, wondering just where they might be going on foot. Bilder walked ahead, spreading branches aside. Jessie stepped back, startled. A gelding stood in the trees; she could swear it hadn't been there an instant before. Bilder stepped up into the saddle and helped Jessie climb on behind him. The scout kicked the mount into a run. Jessie wrapped her arms around his waist and held on. She didn't ask questions.

He took them back west, riding the horse full out and staying close to the trees. After they'd covered a good two miles, he turned abruptly and headed due south. Jessie looked at the ground on either side and understood. The earth was churned up, scarred with the marks of cattle. A herd had passed by in the last few days. One of the cattlemen moving his stock to better range or maybe taking them to Dodge. When the men came back from chasing her horse, they'd find no trace of Bilder's mount. They'd lose precious time beating the brush, figuring Jessie was still alone and on foot.

"Matt, we've got to talk," Jessie said. "I have to go to Camp Supply. I've got to get there right now."

"What you got to do is hold on till I get to where we're going," Bilder said. "Then you can tell me all about it."

"Matt—"

Bilder simply ducked his head into the wind and kicked the horse harder.

The sun was past its midway point in the sky. A parched row of trees followed a narrow trickle of water.

"It's Kiowa Creek," Bilder told Jessie. "Tail end of it, at least. It runs northeast up to where we were on the North Canadian. We've come about fifteen miles. Right down there over your back is Texas."

"And where's Camp Supply?" Jessie asked.

"Thirty-five, forty miles due east."

Jessie's heart sank. Forty miles might as well have been a thousand. Haggerty's men had had plenty of time to ride to the fort.

Bilder caught her expression. "I think you and me got a lot of talking to do, lady."

"I told you," Jessie said shortly. "I've got to get to Camp Supply—if it's not too late already. Ki's in a hell of a lot of trouble. Bill Haggerty sent word to someone, I don't know who, at Camp Supply. They're going to kill him!"

"Whoa, hold on." Bilder looked puzzled. "Bill Haggerty's going to do what? And who's this Ki fellow?"

Jessie hadn't realized the name had slipped out. "Ki's Josh Stewart. He's not really in the army. He's a good friend and he works for me. It's a long story, Matt."

"Uh-huh, I'll bet. Can't wait to hear it."

"We don't have time!" Jessie protested.

"We got time, all right," Bilder said. "The two of us been riding this horse hard and fast. I'd like to make sure we get to use him a little more."

Jessie knew he was right. She'd nearly run one horse to death already. Bilder led the mount to water, and Jessie told him how she happened to be running from Haggerty's men. She told it all, leaving out nothing. He heard the story of her father's fight with the Prussian cartel and how the cartel had finally murdered him on his own Texas ranch, leaving Jessie to take up the battle.

Bilder found it hard to believe Bill Haggerty was involved with the raiders. He knew the man and trusted him.

"I can't hardly believe it either," Jessie said firmly, "but it's true, Matt. A lot of things I didn't understand are falling into place. I know who it was I overheard talking to Haggerty outside the kitchen window. His name's Jack and he's one of Bill's top hands. Remember that raid on Zack Hardy's place—how Haggerty just happened to get off a good shot and kill that Comanche? I'm certain that raid was all set up. And it was this Jack that Haggerty supposedly sent off to trail the raiders. Killing that Indian and proving Lyman's point was about all Lyman needed to stir up the other ranchers."

"Yeah, that'd about do it," Bilder agreed.

"And then Haggerty arranged another raid, while I was with him at Art McGregor's. Right before that, he sent this Jack back to the Crescent-H. He said he wanted to let folks there know we were stopping off at the Box-M. I'll bet the real purpose of that ride was for Jack to set the raiders on Art's place. He even killed a hand just to show there'd been trouble. Then he arranged to be staggering out on the flats. That's where some of Lyman's men found him."

Bilder looked grim. "All this is hard to swallow, damn it. I don't much like it."

Jessie met his eyes. "Matt, it bothered me when I realized the raiders had a chance to kill me at McGregor's place. Only they didn't." She felt a sudden chill and hugged her arms. "The only reason they'd leave me alive is if Haggerty'd given them instructions not to shoot me."

"You got any idea why?"

"Yes," Jessie said soberly, "I do. He wants to use me for something. I don't know what, but that has to be it. He got me up here using bait he knew would draw me in—that the raiders had foreign backing. The man's got gall, I'll hand him that. He wanted me here, Matt. I just don't know why."

"Sounds to me like he might've changed his mind," Bilder said dryly, "about keeping you alive."

Jessie shook her head. "Don't get me wrong—he never planned to keep me alive. He just wanted me around where he could do me in when it suited his plan, whatever the hell that is."

Bilder didn't answer. They walked back from the creek and sat in the shade. Matt built a smoke and Jessie pulled burrs out of her stockings. When she was finished, she looked up curiously at the scout.

"Just what were you doing up there on the North Canadian?" she asked. "I can't believe you just happened to pop out of the ground when you did."

Bilder looked at his hands. "Yesterday morning after you and Josh—you and this Ki set those Kiowas loose, Street got DeLong to fire me and kick me off the post. I wandered around some, thought about going down to Texas, then, uh, sorta headed back up toward Haggerty's place."

"Just sorta headed up there, huh?"

Bilder studied the sky. "Maybe I was—I kinda wanted to see you again, I guess. Make sure you were all right."

Jessie saw the color rise to his face. She smiled and laid a hand on his arm. "You don't have to be embarrassed about that. I would have been glad to see you too, Matt—even if you hadn't turned up when you did."

"You would, would you?" Matt didn't look at her.

"Yes, I would. You going to tell me you didn't know that?"

Matt cleared his throat, started to say something, and changed his mind. "I saw those three fellows trackin' you and worked my way up behind them. I didn't know what they were up to, but it looked like you could use a little help."

"Thank you, Matt." She looked up into his eyes. "For that and the other favor I owe you—covering up for Ki about those Kiowas."

Bilder shrugged. "Didn't know what he was up to, but I figured he had some reason. Anyway, if Heywood Street's down on a man, that's good enough reason to be for him." He nodded thoughtfully and wet his lips. "One thing you ought to know, Jessie: When I left, Street was sending your friend out on patrol. He'll keep him on a horse and try to break him until he figures the best way to get rid of him, legal like. If you're right about Haggerty getting word to his contact at the post, might be Ki's better off than you figured. The more he's away from Camp Supply, the better. Isn't likely anything'll happen to him on patrol."

Jessie sighed and leaned back against a tree. "There's hope in that, I guess. I wish I were there, though, Matt—instead of sitting out here. I know what I'd do if we had two horses. I'd go on up to Camp Supply and take a two-by-four to Street— while you rode fast for Fort Reno or maybe up to Dodge."

"Well, one horse is all we've got, and he isn't going to make that forty miles to Camp Supply without stopping. So I guess we better start moving. I doubt if those riders'll find their way down here, but they might."

Bilder led the gelding out of the trees into the afternoon sun, mounted up, and stretched out a hand to help Jessie. She thought about Ki, told herself that he was all right, that nothing would happen, that Haggerty's men would reach the fort while he was still out on patrol.

And Haggerty himself, she wondered, what does he have planned? What's he doing right now? Lew Lyman's makeshift army was on the march, which was exactly what Haggerty wanted. Whatever the cartel's ultimate goal might be, an Indian slaughter would get things rolling very nicely. Jessie clenched her fists in frustration. It might be happening right now and there was nothing at all she could do to stop it.

It was close to three in the afternoon when Matt suddenly reined the mount in hard. "Get down," he said calmly, sliding out of the saddle. "Just stay close and don't talk."

Jessie slipped to the ground and looked curiously at the scout. His features were taut, intent. Without looking in her direction, he handed Jessie the Winchester from his saddle and jammed a Colt .44 in his belt. They had left Kiowa Creek an hour before and headed east. The land here was parched, the flat prairie broken by harsh red scars of raw earth. Ahead, at the base of a small eroded bluff, a clump of stunted foliage struggled to stay alive.

Bilder motioned Jessie to move slowly; holding the reins, he circled the clump of trees and worked his way to the right, keeping the bluff to his back. In a moment Jessie saw a wagon, tilted at an awkward angle a few yards from the trees. The front axle had snapped in two. Wooden crates and kegs had been opened and scattered about.

Bilder let out a breath, studied the ground, and squinted into the west. "It's an army wagon," he said soberly. "I know it. It's run by a feller named Beamer out of Camp Supply. Whoever got it took the team or let it loose and took whatever was in those boxes. There were other horses here. None of 'em shod."

"Indians?"

"Maybe." Bilder's face was grim. "If there were troopers with this wagon, they didn't leave sign. That ain't good. There isn't a place in this direction that wagon would be heading, Jessie. That means someone hauled it from somewhere else. They likely killed the troopers and brought the wagon here. Shit!" He kicked angrily at the dirt.

"How long ago do you think it happened?" Jessie asked.

"Not long. I'd guess an hour, maybe two. No more'n that." He led the horse past the wagon toward the base of the bluff. "Took off that way, headin' northwest. Yeah, look there." He

143

pointed at the ground. "They did use the team horses. Likely loaded 'em up with what they took after the wagon broke down. You can see where th—"

"Matt!" Jessie screamed out his name as an apparition rose straight up out of the ground. In the smallest part of a second, she saw the hatred in the Indian's eyes, the terrible bloody tears that crossed his chest and face. He grasped the branch of a tree with one hand, holding a revolver in the other and aiming it straight at Bilder. Jessie jerked the rifle to her waist as Matt turned, clawing for his Colt. The Indian squeezed the trigger, three rapid shots in a row. Matt stiffened and slammed back against his horse, the Colt firing wildly into the air. The horse shrieked and went down as Jessie pumped one round after another into the Indian's body, firing until the rifle clicked empty.

★

Chapter 18

"Oh, Matt, you're hurt!" Jessie stared in horror, tossed the rifle aside, and then ran to him.

"Never mind me, damn it!" Bilder rolled on the ground, his face the color of ash. He gripped his leg and Jessie saw blood pour through his fingers. "Take my gun and make sure that bastard's dead," he said through his teeth. "Go on—do it!"

Jessie nodded, picked up the weapon, and turned to the trees. The Indian was dead. Jessie didn't doubt it for a moment. Still, she forced herself to bend down and look him over carefully. Her quick volley had struck him three times, twice in the chest and once in the throat. Before that, though, someone had worked him over badly, carved him up with a knife and left him for dead. Lord, she thought in wonder, how did he manage even to get off a shot at Matt?

He was a big man with broad shoulders and flat, ugly features, a face now contorted forever in pain. Jessie stood, turned away from the sight, and started back to Matt. Something caught her eye and she stopped. A patch of color, off to her left. Gripping the Colt, she pushed branches aside and walked into the trees. When she saw the thing she stood there and looked, puzzled, her eyes trying to turn it into something she understood. When the image reached her brain, she choked off a cry, stumbled back, and retched on the ground. The spasms wouldn't stop. Even when her stomach was clearly empty, the pain continued to wrack her body.

Bilder looked up and saw her as she came out of the trees. "Jessie, what is it?" His eyes went wide with alarm.

Jessie didn't answer. Bilder's horse was dead. She pulled the canteens off the saddle, opened one, wet her face, walked shakily back to Matt, and sat down beside him.

"How bad is it?" she said calmly. "Let me have a look at that, Matt."

"Jessie—" He touched her face and turned her to him.

"I'm all right." Jessie bit her lip and looked at his leg. He had the trousers ripped to the knee and was pressing a bandanna to the wound.

"It's a woman," Jessie said without expression. "An Indian girl, I think, though it's hard to tell. There's nothing left of her, Matt. It looks like animals got to her, but that isn't what did it. God, they just cut her to pieces like meat. She's—oh, Matt!"

"All right," Matt said gently, "that's enough. Damn, no wonder he started shooting. I guess he figured maybe they were coming back."

"They thought he was dead. They ruined him—did things to him. He didn't have any idea who we were or much care."

Jessie shook her head and brushed hair out of her face. "That leg looks bad, Matt. I don't like it."

"It ain't good," he said soberly. "Fractured or maybe broken. Bullet hit the bone right below the knee, chipped it some, and went on through."

She washed the wound clean, managed to stop the bleeding, and then bandaged it with strips of Matt's spare shirt. The worst part was getting off the boot. Even cutting it free with a knife caused him pain. Jessie tore boards from the empty boxes and made a splint, binding it firmly with leather strips. When she was finished, Matt's face was peppered with sweat. She helped him up, got him to the shade of the overturned wagon, then left him, and made her way past the bluff, searching for a better place to stay. Buzzards were starting to circle overhead. Even if she had a shovel handy and had the stomach for burying the two bodies, there was nothing she could do about the horse. The buzzards would flock to the site and they couldn't stay close to that.

Trees hugged the base of the bluff and she found a good spot some fifty yards from the wagon. Getting Matt there was a job. They made it, four or five steps at a time, Matt clinging to Jessie and trying not to pass out. Jessie got their gear from the horse and found jerky and biscuits in Matt's saddlebags. By the time they were settled in, the sun had dropped behind the bluff.

Matt leaned against a tree and watched her pad about the small clearing, wincing now and then as a foot found a sharp stone.

"We're a fine pair, you and me," he grinned. "One of us a

146

cripple, the other without any boots."

"And no horse. You forgot about that."

"I didn't forget. Just don't much want to think about it."

"How far do you think we are from Camp Supply?"

"Twenty, twenty-five miles. Pretty fair walk—you barefoot and me on your back."

"That's a problem, all right," Jessie agreed. She sat down beside him and offered another piece of jerky. Matt made a face, but bit off a chunk and started chewing.

"You're worried about that friend of yours," Matt said finally. "I figure he'll be all right. I truly do."

"I'm worried about him—and a half dozen other things besides."

"That's it? Hell, I thought of ten things right off."

"Don't," Jessie said dryly. "I don't need any help."

The shadows were crawling rapidly across the small clearing, the night closing in. Jessie leaned in against Matt's shoulder. His body felt good against her back.

"That doesn't hurt, does it?" she asked.

"Didn't get shot in the chest," Matt told her.

"The leg easing up any?"

"It's settlin' down. Throbbing some. I don't reckon it's a break, or if it is, it's not a bad one."

"Good. Then you can carry me."

"Not just yet."

For a long moment, Jessie sat in silence and looked out at the night. She tried not to think about what lay just beyond the trees, past the dark shadow of the bluff. Matt slipped his arm about her shoulder; the gesture seemed natural and reassuring, as if his warmth could somehow ward off the awful chill of death.

"Thank you for coming after me, Matt," she said softly. "I'm real glad you were there."

"My pleasure," he told her.

She said ruefully, "I didn't bring you a whole lot of luck." Without thinking, she turned in the curve of his arm and kissed him lightly on the cheek. Matt looked at her curiously, as if the kiss had caught him by surprise.

"Don't look so startled." Jessie smiled. "I imagine you've been kissed once or twice."

"Not by you I haven't. I've sure as hell thought about it some."

"Oh? Have you now?"

"Uh-huh. Only it wasn't exactly a kiss on the cheek I had pictured."

"What kind of kiss was it?"

Her eyes met his and held them. His lips brushed the corners of her eyes, trailed down to her cheek, and found the softness of her mouth. Jessie sighed and opened her lips to his caresses. She watched a vein pulse rapidly in his throat, felt the hot touch of his breath against her skin. His mouth stroked her gently; she welcomed the hard, probing thrust of his tongue. He drew her close and ground his mouth against hers, forcing her lips fully open. The tip of her tongue flicked out to meet his. The taste of his mouth sent a hot wave of desire coursing through her. She cried out, clinging to him with a sudden, desperate hunger and need. A great feeling of wonder and relief spread through her body and left her shaken. She understood the hunger and the fear that rode along with it. The smell of death still clung to her flesh. She was alive, grateful that it had happened to someone else and not to her. The thought brought a quick feeling of shame, sorrow, and regret. She swept the feelings aside.

No, damn it, I can't help that—I'm not ashamed to be alive!

Matt pushed her gently away, grasping her shoulders hard. Jessie felt the tears scald her eyes.

"Jessie, Jessie . . ." He soothed her with his words. His fingers touched her cheeks, brushed away the tears. He caressed the curve of her neck and let his hand brush the hollow of her throat. He stopped near the firm swell of her breasts.

"Matt, it's all right," she said quietly. "I want you to. I need you to touch me." She covered his hand with her own and slid it into her shirt, her eyes meeting his with warm assurance.

Matt drew in a breath and cupped the tender, pliant flesh.

"My God, Jessie." A moan came from deep within his chest. "This is sure a hell of time for me to come up a cripple!"

Jessie grinned, gently pressed his hand, then drew away from his grasp. "Guess a girl has to be a little helpful to a man in your condition. Just hold still."

She turned and straddled his thighs, resting her knees on the ground and taking care not to touch his bad leg.

"There," she said, "maybe this'll help some." She gave him a sly grin. "Course I can't do everything for you."

Bilder stared and wet his lips. "Like I said, lady, I got shot in the leg. Nowhere else."

He reached out and opened the buttons of her shirt, working at the task until a thin line of creamy white skin reached from her throat to the circle of her waist. Laying his rough palms at the base of her throat, he moved his hands outward until the fabric slid off of her shoulders. The shirt hung provocatively on the tips of her breasts. Jessie looked down at herself, smiled at Matt, and drew her shoulders together, baring herself to his eyes. Tossing fiery hair off her shoulders, she cupped the swollen globes in her palms and lovingly offered them to him. She watched as his eyes drank her in; she saw the tanned flesh of his cheeks go taut with hunger. A cry choked in his throat and he clutched her breasts in his hands; she saw the sudden pain as he tried to draw her to him.

"Hey, now, just hold on there," she scolded gently. "I said I'd help, didn't I?"

Moving off his thighs, she kneeled by his shoulders and helped him edge his back away from the tree.

"There, that's some better," she said finally. "Just lie flat on the ground and don't try to do anything at all."

"Not doing something's real easy at the moment," he complained.

Jessie stood and pulled the tails of her shirt from her waist and let the garment fall, then bent and peeled the denims down her legs, and slipped out of her stockings. When she was through, she stood above him, legs spread slightly apart, hands crooked boldly on the wings of her hips.

"Well, what do you think?" she grinned. "Everything suit you all right?"

Matt swallowed hard. "Lady, I never saw anyone like you in all my life."

"'Course you have to say that. Being a cripple and all, you sorta have to take what's close to hand."

"Yeah, well that's so," Bilder agreed.

"Hey, you want that other leg broken too?" Jessie laughed. "Wouldn't be any trouble."

She could feel his eyes trailing over her flesh, touching the smooth flanks of her thighs, the length of her legs. She wanted him to see her; she relished his desire. Turning slightly at the waist, she drew in the curve of her belly and thrust out her upturned breasts.

"You said that you'd been thinking about me, Matt," she said. "This what you been thinkin' of? Is it?"

Matt didn't answer. Jessie knelt by this chest and unbuttoned

149

his shirt and then helped him slide his hands out of the sleeves. The sight of him naked to the waist stirred feelings deep within her. He was lean and hard, solid flesh molded in slabs of muscle on his shoulders down to his chest and to the flat plane of his belly. When she was finished, she freed the buckle of his belt, loosed the buttons of his trousers, and slipped them carefully past his hips, making no effort to take them farther.

"Oh, Matt!" Jessie bit her lip and sighed with pleasure. "There isn't anything wrong with the rest of you, that's for certain."

"Sure as hell better not be," Matt told her.

His manhood stood boldly erect, slightly curved and hard as iron. The sight left Jessie breathless. She reached out, hesitating at first, and then clasped the stiff member in her hand.

Matt let out a deep, satisfied groan at her touch. The heavy scent of his manhood assailed her senses. Sweeping coils of coppery hair across his thighs, she gently kissed the dark matting below his belly, then touched her tongue lightly to the base of his shaft. Matt sighed as her lips moved like a whisper over his length. The tip of her tongue flicked out to tease him. She kneaded him with her mouth, relishing every touch that brought the slickness of his flesh against her lips. Matt's hands tangled in her hair as he pressed himself firmly into the heat of her mouth. She stroked him faster and faster, feeling the mounting hunger in his loins. His breath quickened; Jessie felt her own excitement smoldering in her thighs.

Suddenly Matt cried out between his teeth and Jessie thrust him deeply into her mouth. He filled her like a flood; hot fluid surged. Jessie laughed, pulled away, and came up on his chest and into his arms. Matt reached out and drew her to him, covering her face with kisses. Jessie tossed back her head and he brought her breasts hungrily into his mouth. Jessie trembled at his touch. He grasped the creamy globes, flipping the pert nipples with his tongue.

Jessie arched her back like a cat and thrust her bottom into the air. His tongue kneaded the hard little buds into satiny mounds of pleasure. Jessie ground her breasts against him; she cried out with joy as his teeth nipped playfully at her nipples. She felt his hand slide over her flesh, past her belly, to her thighs, and to the lush swell of her bottom. His fingers brushed the feathery edge of her treasure, teased the silken nest.

Jessie closed her eyes; her lips stretched tightly against her teeth. His fingers stroked her trembling flesh aside, probed gently into the hot and sugary warmth.

"Oh, Matt, yes—yes!" Jessie cried hoarsely. She thrust her firm mound against him, forcing his fingers deeper inside her. Her body twisted in a sleek and sensuous curve. Matt's touch churned fires within her. She grasped his shoulders tightly and dug her knees into the earth. Matt's hand snaked quickly between her thighs to grasp his member. Jessie knew the sudden wonder, the excitement of what was to come. She longed to feel his hardness surging inside her, pressing her satiny walls. Matt held back, teased her with his touch, caressed her wet flesh with the tip of his shaft.

"Matt, now," she pleaded, "get inside—me—now!"

Matt groaned his pleasure, grinding his erection roughly against her. Jessie cried out. Her hair clung moistly to her face. She spread her legs wide to force him closer. Matt held off another instant—then, without warning, he rammed his manhood deeply inside her.

Jessie shouted her joy, lashing her body against him. She pounded his loins in quick, savage strokes. Matt gripped her slender waist in both hands. Jessie's whole body shuddered. Her head snapped rapidly from side to side, whipping fiery hair across her face. She plunged his manhood inside her again and again.

"I'm there," she gasped, "I'm *there*, Matt . . ."

The power of her orgasm wrenched every fiber of her being, tore her apart, and left her shattered. Matt gave a deep bellow of pleasure and filled her again; his heat coursed through her in one great explosion after another, triggering Jessie once more and sending her soaring.

With a final, sharp cry of pleasure and pain, she eased her legs and she slipped off his chest; she turned and gasped for air.

In a moment she twisted on her belly and looked at Matt. "You all right? It didn't hurt or anything, did it?"

Matt laughed and kissed her hard on the mouth. "Jessie, if my leg fell off, I didn't feel it. If you want to know the truth, I don't much care."

"Not now you don't," she said solemnly. "You might care plenty in the morning." She stood, searched about, and found their blankets.

"By God, I guess this leg-breakin' business is all right," said Matt. "I got me a lovin' woman and a nurse all in one. If you could rustle up some fried chicken, you'd be perfect."

"I think maybe you got a fever, mister. If you want a late supper, it's jerky and water."

Matt made a face and drew her to him. "You talked me out of it. Remind me, though, to get some fried chicken first chance we get."

"I'll do that." Jessie snuggled in close. "What time you think it is?"

"Nine, maybe. You got another engagement?"

"You think I need another engagement?"

"Isn't any man in his right mind goin' to comment on that."

Jessie gave him a laugh. "Well, I don't. You're quite enough, Mr. Bilder. And then some."

"That's a relief to hear."

Jessie peered at the sky. "Matt," she said soberly, "you think maybe I ought to start out and try to get help? While it's still night, I mean. I could get part way by morning, maybe find somebody."

Matt made a noise in his throat. "You'd be walkin' on hipbones 'fore you got five miles."

"Well, now, maybe I would and maybe I wouldn't," Jessie said boldly. "I've been barefoot before."

"In a creek, maybe. Not walking on hard earth for twenty miles."

"I didn't say I'd like it. We've got to do something. We can't very w~ll stay here."

Matt yawned. "We'll do something, Jessie. We just won't do it tonight."

"You going to sleep?"

"Thought maybe I would."

"Yeah, well . . ."

Matt opened his eyes. "Something the matter?"

"No. Everything's fine."

"Well, go to sleep then."

"I will. In a minute. I just—Oh, Matt! What's that?" She sat up straight and stared into the dark.

"What, what is it?" Matt came up on his arms, searching for the Colt by his side.

"There's something out there," Jessie said warily. "I saw it. Just then."

"What kind of something?"

"I don't know. Something. Something big. Look, there it is again!"

Jessie pointed into the trees. Something moved. She could

see its pale shape, probing through the brush. An instant later she saw another, and then another—heard them all around her, thrashing boldly about in the dark. Suddenly, an enormous head thrust itself through the trees, a rust-colored head with placid eyes and wicked horns.

"Oh, for God's sake!" breathed Jessie.

Matt exploded into laughter. "It's cows." He grinned. "We're right in the middle of a herd of cattle!"

★

Chapter 19

Matt couldn't stop laughing. Jessie scampered around naked scattering cattle out of the clearing and trying to poke a leg in her denims at the same time. After finding her shirt and slipping it hastily over her shoulders, she glared down at Bilder.

"I'd wipe that grin off my face if I were you," she said. "A man who can't pull up his own pants'd be smart to mind his manners."

"Can't help it," said Matt. "Never had a herd of cattle come through my bedroom before."

"Guess you've led a pretty sheltered life. Grit your teeth now and raise your rear end."

Matt sucked in a breath as she pulled his trousers back up to his waist. "Damn! You were a lot gentler takin' 'em down," he complained.

"You were a lot more interested in something else," she reminded him.

Matt started to speak and then turned as a voice called out from the dark.

"Hey, someone in there? Who's that?"

Matt gripped his Colt as a horseman rode through the trees. He relaxed as he saw the young cowhand, a lanky boy who looked all of fifteen.

The moon was bright enough for the boy to see. He gaped openly at Jessie, who had hurriedly fastened one or two buttons, leaving the lovely swell of her breasts nearly uncovered. Lying on the ground at her feet was a man with no shirt at all, the buckle of his belt undone. The sight made the boy squirm. He figured this was someplace he wasn't supposed to be.

"'Scuse me, folks," he said lamely, quickly taking off his hat, "didn't mean to come bustin' in on your camp. These here cows, you see—"

"That's perfectly all right," Jessie told him. "We're real glad to see you. What outfit you with?"

"Circle-Bar-D," the boy said, "from down past San Antone."

Jessie laughed aloud. "And Charlie Morgan's your trail boss, right?"

The boy's mouth fell open. "Yes, he is, but how'd you—" He stopped, leaned forward in the saddle, and took a closer look. "Lord help me, it's Miss Starbuck, ain't it? You come up the trail with us. Ain't this something!"

"Friend of yours?" Matt said under his breath.

"We could do a lot worse," said Jessie. Then she turned back to the boy. "Where's Charlie? Is he close?"

"Back a ways, I guess. The main herd's up from here, likely near the North Canadian. Bunch of fools spooked the herd and about a quarter of 'em took off east. That's what we're doing, picking up the stragglers. Mr. Morgan's fit to be tied."

Jessie exchanged a quick look with Matt. "What spooked your herd? What happened to scatter the cattle?"

The boy's eyes went wide with excitement. "Guess you folks ain't heard. Bunch of ranchers come down on a camp of Cheyennes and went right onto the reservation. Hear tell it was a awful fight. Some Indians got killed and the rest are on the run."

"Oh, Lord!" Jessie's heart sank. She dug her fingers into Matt Bilder's arm. "We're too late. It's happened. Lyman's started his war."

It took four men to get Matt on a horse. The boy, whose name was Toby, rode off to find Charlie Morgan. By the time Jessie and Matt were a quarter mile west of the bluff, Morgan came riding out of the dark. With him were five hands and a whole squad of troopers from Camp Supply. Jessie recognized Lieutenant Banes, the officer who'd been with Heywood Street when she joined the drive out of Fort Worth. Riding just behind him was a black sergeant, a man who wore a thick white bandage about his head in place of a cap.

Charlie Morgan gave Jessie a curious smile. "Nice to see you again," he said dryly. "You just catchin' a little night air?"

"Something like that, Charlie," said Jessie.

Lieutenant Banes glanced at Jessie and turned on Matt. "Bilder, what's this all about?" he demanded. "What are you doing out here?"

"Breakin' my leg," Matt told him. "What are you doing out here, Banes?"

"Lieutenant," Jessie broke in, "is it true? Lew Lyman's bunch has attacked the reservation?"

Banes frowned. "Yes, ma'am, I guess they have. Look here, miss—"

"Lieutenant Josh Stewart, what's happened to him?" Jessie asked. "Is he all right? Where is he?"

Banes' face went tight. "Just what do you know about Stewart?" he asked. "If you've got any information about him, you'd better let me hear it right now."

Jessie looked delighted. "You don't know where he is? Then he's not at Camp Supply!"

"He escaped, ma'am." Banes gave her a withering look. "You might ask the sergeant major here 'bout that."

"What?" Jessie looked anxiously at the sergeant major. "He did what?"

"He's all right as far as I know, miss," McPherson told her. He gave Jessie a long and searching look. "Beggin' your pardon, but unless I miss my guess, what he's doin' is looking for you."

"Oh, God." Jessie's throat went tight. "Matt, he'll go straight to Haggerty's place. He doesn't know!" She turned to Charlie Morgan. "Charlie," she said firmly, "unless you've got a camp close by, I'm declaring one right here. We've got a lot of talking to do and not much time to do it."

"Talk about what?" Banes said irritably. "I don't see what there is to talk about."

"Just listen to the lady," Matt said wearily. "You're likely to learn something, Banes."

Matt sat on the bed of one of Charlie Morgan's wagons, his leg propped on a wad of canvas. Jessie stood beside him on the ground. Making her story as short as she could, she told them all what she'd learned about Haggerty. She left out any references to the cartel, knowing her story was bizarre enough without that. She told them how Matt had led her away from Haggerty's men, told how they'd been attacked by the Indian, and told Lieutenant Banes what he'd find with the wagon if he sent men back to the bluff—the bodies and the empty crates from Camp Supply.

Banes, who'd been looking dubious and unconcerned up to now, stood quickly and took notice, his face drained of color.

"My God!" Banes glanced guiltily at McPherson and looked away. McPherson's face showed no expression; his eyes said,

I told you so. "It doesn't have to be the same wagon," Banes muttered, "could be something entirely different."

"Yes, sir," McPherson said woodenly. He sent a lance corporal and a trooper riding back to the bluff.

"Go on, tell 'em, sergeant major," Banes said tightly. "But I still don't believe this cock-and-bull tale."

Jessie looked puzzled and McPherson turned to face her. He told her what had happened in the cell and what the man he knew as Josh Stewart had revealed about the raiders—the white men and the Indians who rode along with them. "They took him," McPherson explained. "The raiders got him and he fought his way out and came back to the fort. But no one believes what he told me." His eyes flicked almost imperceptibly to Banes.

Jessie looked squarely at Banes. "It's the same two Indians," she said. "You know that, lieutenant. For some reason the raiders killed them after they got the arms. Don't be so damn stubborn."

Banes flushed. "Seems like too much coincidence, I'll grant you," he said stiffly, "but I can hardly credit a man who attacked Sergeant Major McPherson and abducted the lieutenant colonel's daughter."

"Sir," McPherson said coolly, "beggin' the lieutenant's pardon, but I told you and everyone else that that isn't the way it happened."

Banes gave him a wary look. Things were happening faster than he liked. It was hard to keep arguing while people kept throwing facts in his face.

"I can't afford the time for more talking," Jessie said. "If Ki's headed for Haggerty's, he's walking into trouble. I've got to get back there fast."

"Ki?" McPherson looked blank. "Who we talkin' about now?"

Jessie didn't answer. "I'd like to borrow a horse if you can spare one, Charlie. That's two I owe you now. And if you've got a hand with a pair of small feet, I'll give him a decent price for his boots."

Matt looked alarmed. "Jessie, I know how you feel, but you can't go riding up there to the Crescent-H. It would be a good idea if you had some help."

"If I can get help, I'll take it," Jessie said flatly. "I'm going, Matt."

"Not without me, you're not," Matt told her.

"Reckon I'll ride with you," said Morgan. "My main herd's up where you're going. Toby and one of the other boys can get these strays movin' again."

"Charlie, this isn't your fight," she said warmly. She looked directly at Banes. "It is yours, lieutenant. Are you going to volunteer or do I have to ask?"

Banes looked startled. "Lady, the lieutenant colonel would have my hide," he protested. "I'm supposed to be hunting for that bunch that's killing Injuns—and findin' that fool daughter of his at the same time. I can't do both with eight men!"

"Supposed to be help comin' up from Fort Reno, sir," McPherson reminded him.

"Supposed to be is right," Banes muttered. "Way things are going . . ."

"The colonel's daughter," Jessie said, "is with the man I'm going after—and likely in a lot of hot water if we keep standing around here jawing. Give me four of your men, lieutenant. Three, even. If you do find Lyman's bunch, eight men aren't going to make much of a match against a hundred. He's—"

Jessie stopped. The thought suddenly struck her; it reached out and held her in a cold grip of fear. "Lord, that's it," she exclaimed. "That's it; that's what he's going to do!" Her eyes went wide and she whirled on Matt. "That's what the weapons were for—the ones the raiders took from the wagons. Haggerty will use every man he's got, bring them all together for this. That's how he's going to do it, Matt. While Lyman's out looking for blood, Haggerty's raiders will hit every ranch from No Man's Land to the Cherokee Strip. Don't you see? Every able-bodied man is riding with Lyman. Haggerty will burn the ranchers out and kill everyone in sight." She turned and looked at Banes. "I don't care if the whole United States Army rides up from Fort Reno. If Bill Haggerty gets away with this, Lyman and his men will start a blood bath on the reservations that no one will be able to stop!"

"Christ," moaned Banes. "I don't like this at all, lady. There's too much happening at once."

"Ain't likely going to get better," McPherson said soberly.

"Lordy, Josh," Mindy DeLong groaned, "I can't sit this horse any longer. I just got to stop and rest up."

"We already rested," Ki told her.

"That was about three hours ago, Josh!"

"One hour, Mindy. That's all."

158

"I'll bet it's more'n that." The girl sulked.

Ki didn't answer. He guessed it was close to midnight or a bit later. He had to agree with Mindy. It did seem as if they'd been riding forever. They left the fort well before sundown, riding out the back gate as easily as Mindy promised. Ki was more than a little surprised—and grateful—that the fort was likely the sloppiest he'd ever seen. DeLong didn't care one way or the other and his feelings filtered down to the lowest ranks. Even Enos McPherson's iron will couldn't shake Camp Supply out of its lethargy.

In spite of Mindy's objections, they rode hard until sundown, heading northwest along the banks of the North Canadian, trying to cover their tracks, hitting the open prairie after dark, and cutting up north as if he intended to cross into Kansas. An hour of that and he turned once more over hard, rocky ground that wouldn't likely hold tracks and then started due west for the Cimarron River. From Jessie's description, he was sure he could find the Crescent-H without any problem.

Trouble found them right after that. Ki had felt an itch at the back of his neck and turned in the saddle only to see horses coming right up on their tail over the moonlit plains. He cursed and signaled Mindy to kick her horse into a run. He'd figured on the army's trying to track him until the light played out and then taking up the chase the next day. He guessed at once what had happened. Some enterprising officer had brought along the fort's best Pawnee scout. Against all reason, the Indian was hunting him in the dark.

Ki holed up on a small branch of the Cimarron River, waiting in a sandy thicket for the scout to lead the troopers somewhere else. Once, the Indian came within ten yards of their hiding place. If Mindy decided to scream or the horse blew air or stomped the ground, it was over. He wondered if Heywood Street was riding with the Pawnee.

Finally the scout gave up. In spite of Mindy's objections, Ki waited another half hour before he'd allow them to move.

Now, with any luck, they'd stumble on Bill Haggerty's spread at any moment. Jessie had said it was on the southern bank of the Cimarron River. If he couldn't find a ranch with those directions, he'd better give up.

"I still don't know why we're going up here," Mindy complained. She gave Ki a narrow look. "You know Miss Starbuck pretty well, huh?"

"I told you I did, Mindy."

"How well's that, Josh?"

"Not what you think it is."

"Huh! I bet."

"You met her. I thought you said you liked her."

"I didn't know you knew her, too. Did you really help her let those Indians loose?"

"We don't have the time to talk about that."

"Oh, well, sure," Mindy said acidly. "We don't ever have time to talk about anything I want to talk about."

Ki wondered what Enos McPherson was doing and if he blamed him for what had happened. Maybe. Even if he didn't, he couldn't be real pleased with getting a crack on the skull. At any rate, by now he knew Ki hadn't lied. He'd know the guns were gone, that the story about Beamer working hand in hand with the raiders was true, and that Beamer's raider friends had hit the wagon.

And if he does believe me, so what? Ki thought glumly. Who's going to credit a story like that? Heywood Street? DeLong, whose daughter was riding beside him up the Cimarron River?

"There, through those branches," Ki told Mindy. Reining up under some trees, he pointed at the dim yellow lights due west.

"You think that's it? Lord, it better be."

"That's it," Ki said. "Can't be anything else. Now, if the army hasn't sent a patrol up to Haggerty's, we're all right." He kicked his horse lightly and flicked the reins, moving out into the open.

The ranch house was brightly lit; a lamp glowed in nearly every window. Several horses were hitched out front.

"Hold it, mister," a voice said harshly, "right there." The sound of a rifle's lever action followed the words.

Ki stopped. A man came out of the darkness on his horse. Two more joined him.

"I came to see Jessie Starbuck," Ki called out. "She's staying here with Mr. Haggerty. Tell her Josh Stewart from Camp Supply is here."

The man in the dark seemed to hesitate a moment. "And who else is that?"

"Miss Mindy DeLong. Look, we're a little beat from riding. All right if we get down?"

"Yeah, sure, that'll be fine." The man gave Ki an easy laugh.

Ki slid out of the saddle and helped Mindy. A man took

their horses while the others dismounted and led the way to the house. They were being real careful, Ki noted. One man stayed behind them, still holding his rifle at the ready. Ki didn't blame them, considering the way things were up here.

He squinted at the light in the hall. One man vanished for a moment, then returned, and nodded Ki and Mindy through the door. Bill Haggerty stood in the center of a well-appointed parlor. Ki saw his left arm was in a sling.

"By God, Lieutenant Stewart." He grinned expansively at Ki, as if he'd just learned Ki was his long lost brother. "Can't tell you how glad I am you're here. Yes, sir, I surely am."

"I'm glad to be here, Mr. Haggerty," Ki said. "Uh, is Jessie around? I'd like to see her if I could."

Haggerty didn't answer. Something seemed peculiar about his smile. It wouldn't go away. Ki took another step into the room, past the small entry and into the parlor proper. He saw the men seated on the overstuffed sofa and the chairs around a small table. There was whiskey on the table and crystal glasses. Three of the men he didn't know. The others were Cleve and Beamer. And Lieutenant Jake Wallace. Jake was still fat. But he no longer looked stupid or confused. He didn't look like a man who counted saddles.

Chapter 20

Jake Wallace gave him a shy, almost boyish smile. "Hello, Josh. How are you?"

"Fine," Ki said tightly, "how are you, you son of a bitch?"

Haggerty liked that. "Old army friends. That's good."

Cleve looked at Ki with silent fury. He still had a reminder of their encounter, an ugly purple bruise on the side of his face.

Ki turned on Haggerty. "Where's Jessie? What have you done with her?"

"I haven't done anything," Haggerty said dryly. "She decided to leave. Real sudden. She gave me this before she went." He nodded at his wounded arm. "Surprised to see you here, Miss DeLong. How's your father?"

"Josh, what's going on here?" Mindy clutched his arm. "I don't like it here at all!"

Haggerty almost smiled. "He doesn't know what's going on, miss. He's trying to figure that out." His eyes went hard. "Jessie and I had a nice little talk about you before she learned that she should have kept her mouth shut. I know who you are. You don't have to play soldier anymore."

"I don't guess I'll miss it." Ki shook his head at Haggerty. "I can't figure a man like you. You've got two of everything there is and you're selling out your friends to get more. What the hell for?"

Out of the corner of an eye, Ki saw the man behind him and to his right lower the barrel of his rifle—an inch or so, and then another.

Haggerty laughed. "You're way over your head, boy. I haven't got time to straighten you out."

"You had time to betray Jessie," Ki said quickly, intent on holding the man's attention, "time to sit still for the murder of men who respected you more than any other man in the Indian Nation."

Haggerty looked pained. "What are you trying to do, start

me bawling over a bunch of damn fools? I don't give a shit wh—"

Ki moved. Twisting on the balls of his feet, he bent slightly at the waist and turned on the guard with the rifle. The stiffened tips of his fingers struck the man's belly like a knife. He gasped and doubled up. Ki jerked the rifle out of his hand; in the same motion, he swung the barrel at the man behind Mindy. The weapon caught him on the chin and sent him flying. Mindy screamed, stumbled, and fell as the man whom Ki dropped slammed into her legs. Men shouted at Ki's back. Ki was already in motion. He brought the rifle about and started firing. Jake Wallace screamed as lead caught him in the chest. A man Ki had never seen before went down. Men scattered and dived for cover. He saw Haggerty move in a blur and swung the rifle around to drop him. Cleve—where the hell is Cleve? Ki thought as he quickly squeezed off another round and saw it shatter a window at Haggerty's shoulder. Haggerty stretched out with his good arm, found Mindy, and pulled her to him, jerking her head roughly against his chest.

"Go on, shoot," he bellowed, "you do and you get the girl!"

Ki took a step back; he sensed someone behind him, felt Cleve's hot breath on his neck. Then the awful instant of the explosion in his head . . .

Jessie forced herself to hold back her horse, to push aside the temptation to let the animal run. McPherson rode beside her, one trooper was behind him, and two more were ahead in the dark. Charlie and others rode just behind Jessie. Banes had taken the others and turned west, hoping to pick up Lyman's bunch at dawn and to meet the men from Fort Reno—if, indeed, any help was coming from that direction. Jessie didn't care for the young officer, but she sympathized with his dilemma. If help came at all, it probably wouldn't arrive from his own commander at Camp Supply. There was no telling what DeLong might do—send more men to Banes, commit the whole regiment to chasing down his daughter, or drink himself into a stupor.

"We ought to be close," Jessie said. "I figure six, eight miles at the most."

"Likely right," Morgan agreed. She saw him look over his shoulder into the dark. Six hands from the herd rode behind him. They had found the main herd and passed it a good three miles back. The animals were all safely across the North Canadian River and heading north. Morgan had told her he intended to keep the herd moving. Driving cattle at night was sometimes a risk, but getting out of the Indian Nation into Kansas as quickly as he could seemed a sound idea at the moment. The cattle were moving northeast, away from Jessie's group heading for the Crescent-H. She thought about Matt, propped up on his buckboard and trailing along with the herd, and probably cursing a blue streak this very minute. She'd had to threaten to shoot him in the other leg to keep him behind.

"Sergeant Major McPherson," Jessie said, "if you've got thoughts on this, I'd sure like to hear 'em. We could use a little military strategy right now. I don't have the slightest idea what we'll find, but I figure there's more of them than there are of us."

"Yes, ma'am, I expect you're right," McPherson told her. "Army hardly ever has just the right amount of men—too many or too little's the way it is." He looked thoughtfully at Jessie. "Beggin' your pardon, Miss Starbuck, but there's a couple of things we don't know about this business. We don't know how many there are and if that's where they'll be."

"They're there," Jessie said firmly. "I think Haggerty's going to gather his raiders and send them out at first light to burn every big ranch he can find." She gave a bitter laugh. "We could sure use Lyman right now—only he's off chasing the wrong enemy, while Haggerty's burning him out."

McPherson said, "It doesn't make sense at all."

Jessie noticed the restraint in his voice. McPherson refused to let down his guard, and Jessie didn't blame him for that. He wasn't used to a white woman noticing that he existed, much less asking his advice.

"I'm glad you're here," she told him. "I mean that, sergeant major. I'd rather it was you than Lieutenant Banes, to tell you the truth. I guess my luck isn't all bad tonight. At least Heywood Street isn't here." She grinned at McPherson. "I'm not complaining, mind you, but I can't figure why he sent Banes instead of coming himself. If I know Street, he'd want to be first in line for Ki's head."

"There's that name again," said McPherson.

Jessie looked at him. "That's his name. It's not Josh Stewart. I'm sorry, there wasn't time to go into everything back there. I will whenever we can."

"Yes'm," McPherson said dryly, "I'm lookin' forward to

that. I suspect it's a real interesting story. What I've heard so far sure is." He pushed his mount a little harder. "Captain Street isn't here because he wasn't on the post when your friend got loose. A trooper said he went off to the settlement outside the fort. He didn't show up all afternoon." A slight grin creased his features. "DeLong was madder than a wet hen. Wanted the captain's hide right then. He sent me and the lieutenant out to get that girl of his. When Captain Street gets back from town, he's likely to find the lieutenant colonel can still do some officerin' if he has a mind to."

"Good," Jessie said firmly, "if I ever saw a man who needs a swallow of his own medicine, it's Heywood Street." She looked off into the dark, thinking of Ki. And Lew Lyman, somewhere off to the south, what was he doing now?

"How bad was it," she asked McPherson, "Lyman's attack on the Cheyennes? Were there many killed?"

"Could've been worse, the way I hear it. They hit a camp some twenty miles northeast of the Antelope Hills. It was a huntin' party, no women and children. Ranchers made a lot of noise and the Cheyennes took off. About ten or fifteen dead. A lot more hurt."

Jessie closed her eyes. "Lyman will be more careful next time. He'll hit harder. He'll make sure."

"I expect he will." McPherson sat up straight as one of his troopers came out of the dark at a full gallop, reining in fast.

"The house we're looking for is straight ahead, sergeant major," he reported. "Left Harry there to look 'em over."

"How many do you think, trooper?"

"Plenty," the man said. "Couldn't get in close, but they got a corral that's full of horses. Injun ponies. I couldn't see the men that goes with them. They got riders circling around. But they're there."

Morgan pulled close to Jessie. "If they're ponies, then you were right," he said grimly. "Haggerty's still going to play his Indian game. The man's got gall, I'll hand him that. He knows you're free and you won't keep quiet about what you know."

"What difference does it make?" Jessie said harshly. "Next couple of days there's going to be blood all over this prairie unless we stop it. Indians, cowmen, settlers—whoever gets in the way. Who's going to worry about what I've got to say, Charlie? Haggerty knows that. He'd rather I was dead, but it doesn't much matter. If he gets this thing started, he's got a

165

good chance of winning all the chips."

Morgan muttered under his breath and turned his horse back to talk to his men.

"Trooper figures fifty to seventy-five horses are penned up back of that house," said McPherson. "I count eleven of us. I reckon, though, we got 'em right where we want 'em."

Jessie grinned. "Yeah, I guess we do. Time for those military tactics of yours, sergeant major."

McPherson looked at his hands. "If that friend of yours and Miss Mindy came up here like you figured, then Haggerty's people most likely got 'em. I guess you've thought of that. When the shootin' starts, being in there isn't going to be good at all."

"No," said Jessie, "it won't be good at all." She looked into the night. It seemed much cooler than it had a moment before. "Come on, sergeant major, we'd best get to it."

Ki woke up to the sound of screaming.

At first he was certain the screams were his own. His head felt like a melon someone had dropped from a third-story window. He opened his eyes and saw Mindy. Mindy was screaming. She was lying on the floor, her hands tied up behind her head. Cleve had ripped her trooper's shirt down to the waist. He held a buffalo skinner's knife in his fist. He squatted next to Mindy, a big grin creasing his ugly face. The tip of his blade flicked playfully at Mindy's breast.

"Damn you," Ki shouted hoarsely, "leave her alone, Cleve!"

Cleve looked up. A curious frown began to form on his face. He looked hurt that Ki had interrupted. Flipping the knife lightly in his hand, he slammed the butt hard into Ki's jaw.

Mindy screamed again and Ki spat blood. "I stepped on you with a horse," he said tightly. "What the hell does it take to kill you?"

Cleve cackled and showed Ki his dirty teeth. "More than that." His smile quickly faded. "I ain't forgot about that horse."

Ki glanced up and saw he was tied too, his hands bound to the heavy metal leg of the kitchen stove. There was a high window to his left. The sky showed the faint gray smudge of a false dawn.

Cleve was busy with the girl. He ran a hand roughly over her breasts and squeezed a nipple. "Damned if you ain't sweet as candy," he sighed. "I like more meat on my women, but I ain't all that particular." His eyes flashed at Ki. "That Sparrow,

166

now. She was something, I tell you. Course you'd know all about that. She was fine stuff once we got her quieted down some." He cocked his head and grew thoughtful. "Ain't near as pretty as she was when you saw her."

"You son of a bitch!" Ki muttered.

He was sure Cleve would hit him again, but his interest seemed to have shifted back to Mindy. He poked the knife under the waist of her army trousers and began slicing the fabric past her belly. Mindy groaned and tried to pull away. Cleve straddled her legs to stop her. After driving the knife into the floor, he tore at the cloth with his hands until he had it well past her thighs.

"Lordy, look at that!" Cleve wet his lips. He stroked her plush mound with his fingers. "That's fine. Ain't ever seen better."

The door across the room opened quickly. Cleve jerked up, yanked the blade from the floor, and turned to face the intruder. He was angry.

"Put that thing away and get out of here," snapped Haggerty. "You've got business to do."

"Aw, shit, Mr. Haggerty," Cleve protested. He got to his feet, glanced narrowly at Ki, and stalked out.

Haggerty's eyes flicked appreciatively over Mindy and then dismissed her. His coat was gone and he was strapping a .45 rig around his overly ample belly.

"Going to leave you folks to yourselves," he said simply. "Got things to do." His gaze rested on Ki. "Mister, if I had the time, I'd take pleasure in watching Cleve work you over. I'm not real pleased with your part in this."

"I'm not real happy about yours," Ki told him.

Haggerty grinned. "Well, it's good you still got your spirit. That shows character in a man."

Ki looked past Haggerty. A man walked down the hall. He carried a large tin and poured liquid on the floor. In a moment he was gone, leaving the strong smell of kerosene behind.

Haggerty caught Ki's expression and looked amused. "Guess I forgot to mention that all the ranches around here are going to have bad fires—mine included. This whole end of the Indian Nation's going up in flames today, son. There's going to be hell to pay."

"And you're the man who'll straighten it all out," Ki said soberly.

"Well, now, that's it exactly." Haggerty seemed delighted.

"I'll be the voice of reason after the storm. Course your friend Miss Starbuck, now, she's goin' to be a big help." He saw Ki's curious look. "Why do you think I got her up here, friend?" he asked quietly. "Keeping her alive's more useful than putting a bullet in her head. I already got those ranchers thinking that Jessie Starbuck may be working with the raiders. She let those Kiowas loose, after all. When this is all over, solid proof will turn up in the right places. Jessie started an Indian war to drive out the cattlemen and settlers. The ranchers are branded killers and the Indians, too. You'll never see another savage step a foot off the reservation. People won't stand for it—be terrified of lettin' the devils loose. And Jessie Starbuck, trying to use her fortune and her friends in high places to get all the land she can for her own use." Haggerty smiled again. "The newspapers'll love it. Nothing readers like better than catching a rich person tryin' to steal."

Ki shook his head. "You don't think Jessie's going to sit still and let you blame her for what you're trying to pull yourself?"

Haggerty looked bored. "The man pointin' the finger first is the fella folks always believe. That's how the world works. You aren't going to have to worry about that, though, are you?" He glanced once more at Mindy and nodded approval. "Fine looking woman. Damn fine looking." Without glancing at Ki again, he turned away.

"Haggerty!" Ki shouted.

Haggerty turned in irritation.

"Just tell me why," Ki said angrily. "What did they give you? What turned you around?"

Haggerty looked at him. It was a peculiar, distant look, as if Haggerty were already somewhere else. "You've got a nice way of putting it," he said calmly. "Nothing turned Bill Haggerty around. I'm not Bill Haggerty. I'm the man who took his place, the man who looks like Haggerty'd look if he'd survived that tragic fire that took his family." He touched the ruined side of his face. "Got this when I helped burn one of Alex Starbuck's ships." He looked at Ki, but his eyes were somewhere else. He turned and then stalked out of the kitchen into the hall.

"Jesus Christ," Ki said under his breath.

"Josh," Mindy cried, "what the hell is going on here? I don't like this. I want out of this place. You get me out of here this minute!"

"Mindy, just take it easy, all right? We've got—"

A deep, muffled roar came from another part of the house. Ki felt the hairs on the back of his neck rise. He knew exactly what had happened: Someone had tossed a match into Haggerty's house.

★

Chapter 21

Jessie knew McPherson was right. Approaching the house from the front would give them away before they could ever get close. The troopers had spotted four riders, but that didn't mean there weren't more. The long way around took time and Jessie anxiously scanned the approaching dawn as they made their way through the trees, coming up on the house with the Cimarron River behind them.

"That long building past the house is the bunkhouse and those shacks are for storing equipment," Jessie told the others. "At least, I think that's what they're for. I didn't get to walk around much when I was here."

"That's the barn, then, about forty yards to the east," said Morgan.

"Right. And the corral's close to it. You can't see it because of the edge of the trees."

"Told you what my man said," McPherson said quietly. "There are plenty of horses in there. He got close enough to see that. Where are the men who belong to those horses?"

"The bunkhouse?" Charlie suggested tentatively.

Jessie shook her head. "Too many of 'em. My guess is they're hanging around between the corral and the house. If they're riding out at first light, they'll stay close."

McPherson looked thoughtfully at Morgan. "Be helpful if those fellas were on foot."

Morgan's mouth curled in a smile. "You got a point, sergeant major."

"I told you we had a military strategist with us," Jessie said.

McPherson made a face. "What you got, ma'am, is a man who can do sums. I know how many times eleven goes into that bunch up there. Mr. Morgan, you want me to take the horses?"

"I'll take them," said Morgan. "I'd rather you give cover. I can hit a snake in a jar, but that's about it. Besides, sergeant major, you got the wrong colors for this job: black skin and blue uniform. I doubt they'd make the army feel welcome."

"You're right about that color problem," McPherson said dryly. "If things get hot out there, it's going to be hard to see which white men to shoot."

Charlie grinned. "I got some sacking in my saddlebag," he told Jessie. "Might be a good idea if we had some armbands or somethin' the sergeant major here can see."

Jessie looked at Morgan. "I'm going with you, Charlie."

"Hell you are," he said flatly.

"I've got a job to do that's personal. If Ki's in that house, I intend to get him out. I won't endanger you or anyone else doin' that."

"You just figure on walking up there, huh?"

"That's what you're going to do."

"'Course no one's likely to notice you're a woman."

"I'll put my hair up under my hat, Charlie."

Morgan cleared his throat. "Maybe it ain't a real proper thing to say, but it wasn't so much your hair I was worried about. Hell, come on—let's get to it 'fore it's noon."

Jessie stood by the corral, leaning idly on the fence, pretending to talk to one of Morgan's men named Tom. Morgan was on his belly beneath their feet. The three had come out of the trees, keeping low for the first few yards and then walking in plain sight as if they might be coming out of the bunkhouse or somewhere right of the main house. The gate was on the far side of the corral. As Jessie had guessed, a great many of Haggerty's raiders were bunched in that spot and close to the barn. She could hear them and see them in the dim light. A number of the men lit smokes.

Charlie had walked along until he found a few boards he figured he could maybe work loose with a little help. While Jessie and Tom stood guard, he slipped down and started to work.

The first thing they'd noticed was that the horses were all saddled; the raiders had let them loose in the corral as they rode in, which was easier than trying to tie that many animals to a fence.

Tom peered across the corral and looked at Jessie in alarm. "Charlie, you going to do anything down there you better get on it. Those fellers are startin' to stir."

"I'm going as fast as I can," Charlie cursed. "Don't exactly

171

have a tool shop down here to work with."

"How long, Charlie?" Jessie asked.

"Five minutes, maybe. I got a couple of half-rotten boards nearly off. If I was Bill Haggerty, I'd fire the men let these fences get like this."

"I'm going," Jessie said flatly. "I've got to get to that house before hell breaks loose out here."

"I don't like it," Charlie muttered.

"I don't like it either," said Jessie.

She left Tom and Morgan, stuck her hands in her pockets, and walked casually toward the house. She patted her jacket and felt the reassuring bulk of the Colt she'd borrowed from Charlie. Several men were standing near the barn. Two more made their way down to the corral. Jessie slowed her pace until they passed.

Don't stop, she told herself. Keep going; just keep going.

There were lamps in the upper story and near the front of the house. The back was relatively dark. Jessie angled in that direction, recalling the layout of the parlor, the dining room, the hall, the kitchen, and the study. And after she got inside—what then? If they had Ki and Mindy DeLong, where would they be?

"Let them be all right," she muttered under her breath, "let them be in there and let me find them."

A man appeared abruptly around the corner of the house and came straight for her. Jessie ducked her face under the brim of her hat. There was nothing to do now but keep walking.

"Hey, where you think you're going?" the man called out. "You people aren't supposed to be up here."

"Yeah, sorry," Jessie muttered, lowering her voice as best she could. She turned and stalked toward the barn.

"Wait a minute; hold it right there," the man said. He started toward her; Jessie kept going, snaking her hand under her jacket to grasp the Colt.

"Damn it, I told you to stop!" the man bellowed.

Jessie turned on her heels. "You want me?"

"I said for you to—"

Glass shattered: A bright ball of fire exploded from the far side of the house. The man glanced at the fire, then looked at Jessie, saw her features in the sudden brightness, and stared.

"Son of a bitch," he said tightly, clawing for his gun.

Jessie shot him in the chest. He stumbled back and looked surprised. Jessie didn't give him a second look. She turned and ran for the house, ducking into the hall that led to the kitchen. It was already heavy with smoke. She coughed and swept the crook of her arm across her face. The smell of kerosene reached her and a chill touched the back of her neck. When the fire hit the hall—

"Jessie, Jessie, over here!"

Jessie stopped and whirled to the right, straining to see through the smoke.

"Ki—oh, my God! Hang on!"

She went to him quickly, grabbing the knife from her belt and slashing the leather cords that bound his wrists. Ki took the knife and freed Mindy.

"Here, get this on," Jessie told her. She tore off her jacket and wrapped it around Mindy's naked shoulders. Mindy convulsed in a spasm of coughing. Ki helped her up and lifted her in his arms. Jessie led them through the thickening smoke to the back door. Outside, she sucked in air and nodded at Ki. They started for the darkness of the trees and the river.

"Jessie, get down!" Ki shouted.

Lead ripped at the walls of the house. Jessie leaped for cover. Ki pressed Mindy against the ground. The gunfire found them again, forcing them back toward the smoke.

Jessie spotted men by the barn, turned, leveled the Colt in both hands, and squeezed off two shots.

"We can't stay here," Ki told her, "we're—Jessie, here they come!" He jerked his arm toward the barn. Four men came at them in a crouch. Two more joined them, angling down from the side of the house. Jessie bit her lip and leveled the pistol again. A bullet tore through the crown of her hat. She snapped off a shot. A man howled and grabbed his belly. Another threw his arms up and fell on his face. A man twisted on his heels and scrambled for cover. Jessie stared at her Colt. One shot, three men down. Ki called out and she looked up and saw McPherson and one of his troopers coming toward them from the corner of the bunkhouse, Spencer rifles firing. The men in the open ran for the barn.

McPherson frantically waved Jessie and Ki to him, then knelt, and sent another volley after the raiders. Jessie ran toward him and Ki followed, pulling Mindy along.

"Get it moving, lieutenant," McPherson said out of the corner of his mouth. He loosed another round at the barn. His trooper shouted and fired toward the corner of the house. Jessie spotted Haggerty, gritted her teeth, and fired in the man's direction. Haggerty saw dirt explode at his feet and backed off. Flames rose high in the sky from the house. More glass exploded from the windows. The trooper cried out and fell on his face. McPherson stood, tossed his weapon to Ki, and threw the trooper over his shoulder. Jessie picked up the man's Spencer and helped Ki lay a covering fire. They made their way to the bunkhouse—pausing to fire, then running, then pausing to fire again.

McPherson shouted and Jessie turned. Horses were spilling out of a narrow break in the fence. Charlie Morgan ran for cover; Tom turned and loosed parting shots over his shoulder.

McPherson stopped in the cover of the bunkhouse and gently laid his burden on the ground. Jessie looked at the trooper and then saw the rage in McPherson's eyes.

"He's dead," the sergeant major said flatly.

Saddled horses ran wildly for the trees—all in the wrong direction, Jessie noted grimly. They could use the mounts themselves, but there was no way to stop any of the frightened animals. They poured through the fence and fled the flames.

Gunfire blossomed from the corral. Another volley burst from the side of the house. "We can't stay here," Ki said, "they've got us from two directions."

"Can't get out, either," McPherson said darkly, "unless we can back those boys off. A lot of horses are loose out there, but they got plenty left."

Jessie could see the mounted men gathering by the barn and the far side of the corral. In a moment they'd move in, attacking both sides of the bunkhouse. It was only forty yards back to the trees and the river—and the horses waiting for them there—but the fire had turned the landscape bright as day. There were four of Charlie's men and a trooper in the trees; McPherson had told them to hold their cover fire as long as they could. No one had counted on the conflagration.

McPherson guessed Jessie's thoughts. "We'll have to try it 'fore those fellas get moving. Our boys can't make it to us; we'll have to get to them. If the raiders box us in here, we're dead."

"We're sure as hell dead if we go out there!" Morgan snapped.

"Yes, I know that, too. If you got a better idea, I'm sure listening."

"If I did, you'd hear it," Morgan muttered.

"Look!" Ki grabbed Jessie's arm. "Here they come!"

Jessie's heart nearly stopped. Horsemen had circled and

were coming at them from the far side of the bunkhouse. Charlie and Tom ran to answer their fire. Two guns, Jessie thought desperately, won't stop them for a minute.

In the same instant, riders came at them from the other side, sweeping past the corral between the fence and the trees.

McPherson grimly checked his weapon. "All right, let's take all we can."

The raiders came straight for them, guns blazing. Jessie, Ki, and the sergeant major waited. Behind them, they could hear the other bunch laying down a withering volley at Morgan and Tom.

Suddenly, bright blossoms of fire erupted from the trees, a volley that took the raiders by surprise. Men spilled out of their saddles; frightened horses shrieked and turned, bunching up the raiders in confusion.

"Fine flankin' maneuver." McPherson grinned, getting off a shot of his own. "Damned if it ain't!"

While the raiders tried to bring their ranks under control, Charlie's hands and the lone trooper crashed through the brush, each rider holding the reins of a spare mount and firing. They raced for the cover of the bunkhouse. The raiders fired, but the men kept coming, eating up the yards of open ground. They made it halfway before the raiders got their bearings. One of Morgan's men spilled from the saddle. And then two more nearly at once.

"Oh no!" Jessie cried.

The trooper paused to grab the reins of a riderless horse, then raced for the safety of the bunkhouse. McPherson ran toward him to grab the mounts.

"Over here, give us a hand!" Morgan shouted. Jessie ran to the far side of the bunkhouse. Ki closely followed. A second bunch came in fast. Morgan, Tom, Jessie, and Ki fired into their ranks. The raiders faltered, came at them again, and then scattered.

"They'll be back," Ki said tightly. He turned back to the far side of the bunkhouse.

"We got five horses now," McPherson said harshly, "and we lost three men in the trade. I don't figure that's any bargain!"

"Get everybody up," Morgan snapped. "Ride double, whatever you have to do. We can't take another charge from two sides. I'd rather get killed on a horse than standin' here."

"That way," Ki pointed. He grabbed Mindy and helped her on a mount. "They'll come from that side of the bunkhouse like they did before—the other bunch will hit us from the corral. Best thing we can do is try for this side of the house. We'll have a fair start, at least for the first few yards. It might be enough."

McPherson looked at Morgan. Both men nodded agreement.

Six people had to ride double. Morgan and McPherson took horses for themselves, leaving them free to cover the others from either flank as best they could. A trooper shouted at McPherson. Jessie saw the raiders starting for them from the right.

"Let's go," Ki called out.

They kicked their mounts hard and burst from cover. An angry shout went up from the raiders by the corral. Blinding flashes of gunfire lit the night. Jessie heard a rider cry out. She held to Tom and saw one of Morgan's men spill from the saddle. Ki and Mindy were just ahead. Charlie and McPherson returned fire.

"Uh-oh, here come the others!" Tom called out. Jessie looked to her right and saw that the raiders who were headed for the bunkhouse had spotted their flight. They wheeled their horses about, joining the men from the corral. The sight brought a lump of fear to Jessie's throat. Twenty, thirty men, maybe more, etched against the pale light of dawn.

Another man dropped from the saddle just ahead. Tom jerked his reins to avoid the riderless mount. Jessie looked back and saw the man stumble to his feet. Haggerty's riders rode over him without stopping.

We won't make it, Jessie thought grimly. There's no place to go, nowhere to run.

"Jesus, what's that?" Tom stiffened in the saddle and jerked his arm to the south.

Jessie sucked in a breath. In the indistinct light of morning, it looked as if the prairie were coming alive, rolling itself up in a wavering line and racing straight for them, churning up dust and leaving the earth bare in its path. Ki shouted something she couldn't hear. He kicked his mount hard and bent to the saddle, Mindy clinging behind. He raced for the river. Charlie Morgan waved at Jessie and pointed frantically in Ki's direction.

"God A'mighty," Tom said, "it's the herd—someone's stampeded the damn herd!"

Jessie stared. She could see them now, hear the deep, menacing thunder of their hooves, see the darting shapes of Morgan's

176

riders who'd stayed with the cattle. They fired their guns in the air and drove the herd ahead. Jessie tried to guess the distance to the trees. Tom whipped his reins hard across the frightened mount's neck. The cattle bawled with fear as the hands forced them on, a thousand shaggy longhorns, moving like a solid deadly wall.

Ki and Mindy broke through the trees and disappeared. Jessie saw McPherson, racing his horse a scant ten yards ahead of the herd. She risked a look over her shoulder. The raiders had wrenched their horses aside, fighting desperately to break through their own ranks and flee the pounding hooves. The cattle turned in a tight circle from the trees, churning like water around a bend and heading straight for the raiders. Tom gathered in his reins and kicked the flanks of his horse; the animal shrieked and leaped through brush and into the trees.

Out of the corner of an eye, Jessie saw a buckboard wagon and a team hard on the heels of the herd. Matt Bilder whipped the horses and shouted at the top of his lungs, one splinted foot lurching crazily in the air.

Ki knew the others were there.

He could hear them all along the river. Once, McPherson shouted from the northern bank of the river, a quarter mile to Ki's right. A single shot rang out.

Ki guessed it was close to eight in the morning. The sun was blazing hot, even in the cover of the trees. A riderless horse splashed through the shallows. The horse had a furrow across its flesh where lead had plowed through hair.

Once he saw one of the raiders limping painfully downstream. He had a bullet in his leg and the wound colored the water pale red. Ki left him alone. He was unarmed. If he got by Charlie's men, McPherson would find him. The sergeant major was prowling the river like a cat. He'd lost all the troopers he'd brought with him. He wasn't a man looking for peaceful solutions.

Ki stopped and listened. He heard the sound again. Someone running clumsily through the brush. In a moment he knew the sound came from his side of the river. He waited. A locust chattered above. The locust suddenly went silent. A man came into the open, looked carefully in every direction, and studied the river. He was covered with mud and dust. Ki smiled. The man started forward and Ki stepped from behind the cover of a tree. Cleve turned and saw him. His eyes went wide and he jerked the revolver from his belt. Ki moved aside. Cleve fired wildly in Ki's direction. Three shots. One thunked into a tree. Cleve ran. He saw Ki coming behind him, turned, and fired again. Four. Five. Ki kept coming. Cleve stumbled and fell, splashed through water, and scurried up the far bank of the river. Ki walked toward him at a slow and even pace.

"Damn you!" Cleve shouted hoarsely. He squeezed the trigger again. Ki didn't bother to move. Cleve's jaw went slack. He stared wildly at Ki, raised the pistol, and squeezed the trigger. The gun clicked empty. Cleve cursed and tossed the weapon aside. He jerked the buffalo skinning knife from his belt, crooked his arm, and sent the heavy blade flying. The blade whistled straight for Ki's chest. He moved on the balls of his feet, bent his body at the waist, and kicked out with his left foot. The knife spun high in the air, sunlight flashing off its steel. Cleve followed the knife's arcing path with disbelief. The blade dropped into the water. Ki left it alone. Cleve backed against the sandy bank of the river. His lips twisted flat against his teeth; he watched Ki with narrowed, feral eyes. Ki crossed the shallow water. Cleve doubled up his fists, stooped in a wolflike crouch, and came at Ki, swinging. Ki kicked him savagely in the belly. Cleve doubled up, staggered back, and retched down his shirt. He shook his head and came at Ki again. Ki slapped him across the face.

"Think about Sparrow," he told Cleve. "About Elk Ear. About all the others."

Cleve came at him in a rage. Ki took a blow against his shoulder, reached out, grabbed Cleve under the chin with two fingers, and lifted him off the ground. Cleve swung his arms in the air and kicked out at Ki's chest. Ki held him in the air and didn't move.

"You son of a bitch," Cleve shrieked. "What are you? Fight me like a man!"

"I will," Ki said quietly. His fingers began to tighten. "Bring me a man and I will fight him."

★

Chapter 22

Jessie crossed the parade ground toward Enos McPherson's office. A storm had rolled in swiftly from the west, soaking the parched land and leaving a fresh, unfamiliar smell in the evening air.

Every hitching post at the fort was lined with horses and there were more mounts crowding the stables. Riders had been pouring into the fort for the last three days. Besides the men from Fort Reno and Fort Sill, officers and troopers were on hand from as far away as Dodge City and Fort Elliott. Among them were serious men with eagles and stars on their shoulders and young lieutenants trailing at their heels. To add to the confusion, there were men from the Bureau of Indian Affairs, representatives of the tribes, and a handful of federal marshals. As far as Jessie could tell, the men who'd converged on Camp Supply shared two things in common: They were angry and they disliked each other intensely. Whatever had happened up here—and they weren't yet sure just what that was—it wasn't their fault.

Jessie walked up the steps of the headquarters building and went inside. Enos McPherson's desk stood in its usual position. There was a blank, slightly faded rectangle of space on the inner office door, where the sign bearing Lieutenant Colonel DeLong's name used to be. He was gone. The army had acted swiftly, packing him up and getting him off the post in record time. They didn't want him talking to curious reporters and men from unfriendly government agencies. The last thing the army wanted was attention. They wouldn't charge DeLong for what he'd done or hadn't done at Camp Supply—the less said and done the better. He would be unceremoniously retired and quickly forgotten.

Jessie was pleasantly surprised that Mindy DeLong had come through her father's ordeal with flying colors. Apparently her harrowing experiences had had their effect. Whatever the reason, she had turned from a frivolous girl into a woman. Her father was a broken man. He needed her now and Mindy was there to lend him her strength. When the pair left Camp Supply, it was Mindy who was clearly and lovingly in charge.

McPherson was gone from his desk. Several officers and troopers waited in the outer office, perched on hard chairs. The hearings in DeLong's former office showed no signs of letting up. Jessie had done her share of testifying, as had Ki, Matt Bilder, and everyone else concerned.

The door opened and a group of solemn men filed out. Finally, Ki appeared with Enos McPherson.

McPherson nodded and gave Jessie a half salute.

"Anything new in there?" Jessie asked.

"Just goin' over the same old thing," the sergeant major said soberly, "like a dog chewing on a bone."

"I think I'm finished," Ki told her. "They can't think of anything else to ask me."

"Good. I'm about ready to get out of this place."

"See you folks later," McPherson said. "I got work to do." He raised a brow at the pair. "Covering up trouble's a hell of a lot harder than gettin' it started. Sure is interesting, all the things we're finding out didn't ever even happen."

Jessie grinned. When she and Ki were outside, she looked back over her shoulder at the building. "If the army had more men like that, I think I'd sleep a little better at night."

"Never happen," Ki said evenly. "If the army were like Enos, they wouldn't need all the colonels and generals strutting around. They'd have to go out and find honest work."

Jessie laughed. McPherson had come out of the fray a hero and had a medal to prove it. He had stubbornly refused to accept it until the troopers who had died received the same honor. They'd wanted to give Ki a medal, too—until they found out he wasn't in the army. They didn't know what to do about that and wanted the officer's hide who'd given him false papers. Jessie quickly straightened them out. If they wanted to cause trouble, they'd end up mighty embarrassed, she lied, since the man who'd helped Ki get in the army had sent him to ferret out the raiders. It was a good story and almost true. The army was ready and more than willing to buy it. Anything to avoid opening another can of worms. They had all of those they could use.

"McPherson told me they got Beamer this morning," Ki said, "ran him down about halfway to Dodge. He'll hang along with the others they rounded up who didn't get caught in the stampede. Some of those bastards will never get caught, but not too many." Ki was silent a long moment. "Kind of wish I hadn't shot Jake Wallace in Haggerty's parlor. I'd have liked to see him hang next to Beamer. I guess that doesn't make any sense, does it? Wanting a man to be alive so he can hang."

"I think it makes sense, all right."

"It's mostly me," Ki admitted. "I don't like thinking it was Wallace working with Beamer. I wrote him off as a fool."

"They say anything else about Haggerty?"

"No. Nothing." Ki gave her a long and thoughtful look. "There's a general in there, Jessie. He got in just this morning. I don't know where he's from, but I know who he is. He belongs to them. The cartel. The first time he looked at me I knew it. He kept waiting to hear what I was going to say."

"He's already read my testimony, then," Jessie said hotly. "He ought to be happy with that." She wasn't at all surprised that the Prussians had gotten their man to the scene quickly. The man pretending to be Bill Haggerty was dead and buried— what they'd found of him after the herd had gotten through. He was dead and the cartel wanted him to stay that way. They didn't have to worry. Jessie and Ki had agreed there was little use pushing the matter further. Matt, the only other person who knew the truth, was willing to do whatever the two wanted. It was a bitter pill for Jessie, but there was nothing else to do. There was no evidence to link Haggerty to the European cartel. Bill Haggerty was a respected rancher who'd gone bad and backed the raiders for his own enrichment—period. The idea that he wasn't Haggerty at all, that the cartel had murdered Haggerty and his family and sent a man with a ruined face to take his place—it was simply too much to swallow. There was no secret alliance. The cartel didn't exist. Jessie had stopped them; she had to be satisfied with that. It had happened this way before and maybe it would happen again.

It was a lot like the army and DeLong, she decided. Get it done and out of sight. If you could pretend something hadn't ever happened, then maybe it would quickly be forgotten.

Lieutenant Banes and his troopers had found Lyman and his ranchers camped near Kiowa Creek and getting ready to raise hell on the reservations. No help had arrived from Fort Reno to back Banes up. The young lieutenant had stretched himself taller than he was, as other men had done that day, and faced more than a hundred mounted men. If they wanted to kill Indians, fine, Banes told them. First, they'd have to gun him down and the six troopers behind him.

The ranchers backed off. They didn't have the stomach for that. The attack at the Cheyenne camp didn't seem such a brave and noble act now that it was over. It didn't taste good at all. Most of the men were relieved that they wouldn't have to do a thing like that again.

The army, the federal marshals, and especially the newspapers were raking the ranchers over the coals. Yet nothing would come of it, Jessie knew. The Indians were dead; it was a most regrettable incident; it wouldn't happen again. That was it in a nutshell.

Until the next time, Jessie told herself. Things would go back to the way they were. In a few years, she was sure, the cattlemen and the steady stream of settlers would turn greedily to the Indian lands again. The Indians didn't really need all that much space, they'd contend. It was valuable and it was lying there doing nothing. Someone could put it to good use . . .

Ki left Jessie to go and see about arranging for horses and supplies. If possible, Jessie wanted to start back for Texas in the morning. The evening sky was clearing and it looked as if tomorrow would be a scorcher. Jessie thought about Charlie. His herd was likely in Dodge City now, sold and loaded on the railroad heading to market. Maybe this drive would cure him, Jessie thought to herself. Maybe he'd settle down to something else. She grinned, then, knowing such a thing would never happen.

Matt Bilder occupied a corner in the small room that served as Camp Supply's hospital. He smiled broadly as Jessie entered, stood, and showed her how well he could hobble on a crutch.

"Be back dancin' in no time," he bragged. "Hell, I shouldn't be taking up space here."

Jessie kissed him on the cheek. "What you ought to be is flat on your back," she said firmly. "If I were that leg of yours, I'd complain about the abuse."

"If you were this leg," Matt said wryly, "I wouldn't keep it hanging idly. What I'd do is—"

"All right," Jessie said, "never mind that. You are a sick man, Matt Bilder. I don't want you getting all excited."

"I got a good answer for that; you want to hear it?"

"Seems to me you've got the same answer for everything."

Matt smiled and then turned serious. "I don't reckon you've

heard, Jessie—I just found out myself a couple of minutes ago. They found Heywood Street. He's dead."

"My God!" Jessie stared. "How, Matt? What happened?"

"Like Enos said, he left the post right after Ki rode in from that ambush. We figure he got a message of some kind and went to the settlement." Matt paused and looked at his hands. "They found him by the river. Someone cut his throat from ear to ear."

"Why? I can think of a lot of people who didn't like Street, me included, but—" Jessie caught Matt's eyes and drew in a breath. "White Bull? Matt, is that what you're thinking?"

"I'm thinking no one is ever going to find out one way or the other. I do know there are Kiowas in the settlement and that it wouldn't be too much trouble to get some kind of message delivered to Street—something that would interest him enough to bring him out of the fort. Indians like to settle up their debts, Jessie."

She was silent a long moment. "Poor Sarah. I'll have to go see her. I shouldn't say it, I know, but I'm not real sorry that she's a widow."

"Maybe she won't be too sorry she is either," Matt said.

Jessie took his hand. "What are you going to do now, Matt? I've got an idea it isn't scouting for the army."

Matt looked pained. "You got that right enough. I don't know. Go to Montana, maybe."

"Montana?"

"Haven't seen it yet. And it hasn't got to see me."

Jessie grinned. "I don't know if Montana can handle Matt Bilder."

"I thought maybe you'd write me a letter I could carry," he said soberly. "Tell 'em how to treat me."

"Honestly, Matt!" Jessie hit him playfully on the arm. "You're leaving, aren't you?"

"Now, how'd you know that?"

"You got leavin' in your eyes. Same as me."

"In the morning, I think. Soon as we can get away."

"Uh-huh. And tonight?"

"What about tonight?"

"I found me a chicken," he said solemnly.

"What?" Jessie burst out laughing.

"I'm dead serious, lady. I told you I had a longing for fried chicken."

"And you figure I'll fry it for you, right?"

Matt looked alarmed. "Hell, no, I don't. I wouldn't trust you with a job as important as that. I'll do the frying."

Jessie grinned. "That's all you want, then? Someone to share your fried chicken?"

Matt shrugged. "I'm a man with a crippled leg. There's nothing more than chicken I can offer."

"Huh! I got taken in by that cripple story once before, remember?"

"Who got taken in?"

"Well—"

He laid a hand on her cheek and brushed back her hair. "You reckon you'd fall for the same story twice?"

"I might. It depends on the quality of that chicken."

"Lady," Matt said firmly, "don't count on gettin' started back south real early in the morning."

Watch for

LONE STAR AND THE OREGON RAIL
SABOTAGE

forty-fifth novel in the exciting
LONE STAR
series from Jove

coming in May!

The hottest trio in Western history is riding your way in these giant

LONGARM

adventures!

The Old West Will Never be the Same Again!!!